NO LiFe
12

THE
GAMER
SIBLINGS
BATTLE
THE DEVIL

YUU KAMIYA

"Now, as the hero—
let the Devil's
dungeon crawler
game begin."

"…That's…not *actually* him, is it—?"

"Mweh-heh-heh… Ah, my deepest apologies, but I'm rather preoccupied with relishing in the Devil being in such high spirits for the first time in many moons. If you would please listen quietly, then."

…*Uh, sure…*

"The legendary armor used by a powerful female Dwarf warrior—it protects its wearer from all attacks, it does!!"

"Protects what?! My dignity?! It's not even protecting what little of that I have left!!"

"Don't worry, Steph!! Protection and coverage have zero correlation when it comes to ladies' armor—it's common sense!!"

THE TEN COVENANTS

The absolute law of this world, created by the god Tet upon winning the throne of the One True God. Covenants that have forbidden all war among the intelligent Ixseeds—namely.

1. In this world, all bodily injury, war, and plunder is forbidden.
2. All conflicts shall be settled by victory and defeat in games.
3. Games shall be played for wagers that each agrees are of equal value.
4. Insofar as it does not conflict with "3," any game or wager is permitted.
5. The party challenged shall have the right to determine the game.
6. Wagers sworn by the Covenants are absolutely binding.
7. For conflicts between groups, an agent plenipotentiary shall be established.
8. If cheating is discovered in a game, it shall be counted as a loss.
9. The above shall be absolute and immutable rules, in the name of the God.
10. Let's all have fun together.

CONTENTS 12

No Game No Life

YUU KAMIYA

12

YEN ON

NEW YORK

NO GAME NO LIFE Volume 12
YUU KAMIYA

Translation by Richard Tobin
Cover art by Yuu Kamiya

NO GAME NO LIFE Volume 12
©Yuu Kamiya 2023
First published in Japan in 2023 by KADOKAWA CORPORATION, Tokyo.
English translation rights arranged with KADOKAWA CORPORATION, Tokyo through TUTTLE-MORI AGENCY, INC., Tokyo.

English translation © 2023 by Yen Press, LLC

Yen On
150 West 30th Street, 19th floor
New York, NY 10001

Visit us at yenpress.com
facebook.com/yenpress
twitter.com/yenpress
yenpress.tumblr.com
instagram.com/yenpress

First Yen On Edition: December 2023

Edited by Yen On Editorial: Rachel Mimms
Designed by Yen Press Design: Jane Sohn, Andy Swist

Library of Congress Cataloging-in-Publication Data
Names: Kamiya, Yu, 1984– author, illustrator. | Komen, Daniel, translator.
Title: No game no life / Yuu Kamiya, translation by Daniel Komen.
Other titles: No gemu no raifu. English
Description: First Yen On edition. | New York, NY : Yen ON, 2015–
Identifiers: LCCN 2015041321 |
   ISBN 9780316383110 (v. 1 : pbk.) |
   ISBN 9780316385176 (v. 2 : pbk.) |
   ISBN 9780316385190 (v. 3 : pbk.) |
   ISBN 9780316385213 (v. 4 : pbk.) |
   ISBN 9780316385237 (v. 5 : pbk.) |
   ISBN 9780316385268 (v. 6 : pbk.) |
   ISBN 9780316316439 (v. 7 : pbk.) |
   ISBN 9780316502665 (v. 8 : pbk.) |
   ISBN 9780316471343 (v. 9 : pbk.) |
   ISBN 9781975386788 (v. 10 : pbk.) |
   ISBN 9781975345495 (v. 11 : pbk.) |
   ISBN 9781975370350 (v. 12 : pbk.)
Subjects: | BISAC: FICTION / Fantasy / General. | GSAFD: Fantasy fiction.
Classification: LCC PL832.A58645 N6 2015 | DDC 895.63/6—dc23
LC record available at http://lccn.loc .gov/2015041321

ISBNs: 978-1-9753-7035-0 (paperback)
   978-1-9753-7036-7 (ebook)

10 9 8 7 6 5 4 3 2 1

LSC-C

Printed in the United States of America

⏻ PRELUDE

——"Do no harm unto others..."

It's safe to assume those who use a worn-out phrase like this have never played video games. They probably can't even wrap their minds around the fact that there are winners and losers in gaming.

...Let's say, for example, that you're a Good Samaritan. One day, you go to a food court, grab some lunch for yourself, then sit at one of the publicly available tables. As you eat your lunch, you notice the food court begins to fill up with customers, and eventually, you see a person who seems at a loss because there are no more seats.

From the simple act of you taking that seat...you've impacted someone else's life in a negative way.

Is this anyone's fault? You needn't worry, for it certainly isn't yours, being the Good Samaritan you are. You had the right to take the open seat, but through exercising that right, you caused someone else to lose out...

——I'm sure you enjoy winning games when you play them. Even if your win is at somebody else's expense.

How about getting into a good school? Pretty great, right? Even if your acceptance into the school means somebody else was rejected.

Fundamentally speaking…it's impossible to live your life without harming others. Society is just one big game of musical chairs—a zero-sum game.

By you gaining something, somebody else inevitably loses out on that same something. This concept isn't even limited to society. So long as we live our lives at the expense of others, the act of living is a burden in and of itself…

——There's really no denying it.

No matter how mindful you, the Good Samaritan, are of what's best for others, *there are those who will despise you for acting that very way, and this makes your existence alone a burden for them…*

So I must ask: When you go around saying *"Do no harm unto others,"* do you really believe you have indeed lived your life without bringing harm to anyone else…?

If you can answer *"Yes"* with confidence, then I'm sincerely jealous of you. You've probably had an easy life, since you've made it this far being oblivious of whose heads you've been stepping on.

——*Do no harm unto others.*

If there is one way to do this—and there surely is one—then it's: *Never to be born* in the first place…

■■■

The Kingdom of Elkia sat on the western part of the continent of Lucia, and this was its capital, Elkia.

A red moon sat high in the sky, but there were no stars that night. They were dimmed out by the countless lamps and torches that dotted the lively, celebratory capital.

* * *

On the central canal that connected to the bay, Dhampirs and Sirens were singing together in harmony.

On both sides of the same canal were large groups of Werebeasts, all bedecked in yukata as they shouldered large palanquins and marched down the promenade.

Behind them were the Dwarves, mounted happily on bipedal humanoid robots as they followed thereafter.

Numerous steel airships floated above the capital, shining lights of their own on the large crowd.

There were also Flügel present, floating leisurely among the Phantasma, Avant Heim, through the brightly illuminated, starless sky.

Finally, the Fairies followed, too, adorning the entire cityscape, including the few Ex Machinas present, as they went.

——It was a large parade, one that captured the eyes of all in attendance while simultaneously making them doubt what they saw.

With the parade tightly packing the streets below, the buildings that lined them were filled to the brim with spectators.

Those spectators, along with the large swaths of people following behind the parade, weren't limited to Immanities.

There were citizens of Oceand, the Eastern Union, Hardenfell, and Avant Heim who followed, as well as citizens from the newly independent Fairy nation, Spratulia.

Members of the various nations made themselves proudly apparent with flags, national colors, and insignia as they each chanted a celebratory song while they marched.

They were all headed for the same destination—the city square in front of Elkia Royal Castle, where a group of Immanities in traditional attire awaited their arrival.

The march culminated in the moment when the national flags were raised together by delegations gathered from across the world...

* * *

——The seven flags for each race were held up under a single flag for the Commonwealth.

It was a sight no one until only recently could've ever imagined. Especially in the city of Elkia, which had quickly manifested into the symbol of multicultural coexistence for Disboard.

Who would believe that only a year ago, this was a destitute nation on the verge of collapse? Nobody had even dreamed this possible since the establishment of the Ten Convenants—no, since the dawn of the Ixseeds.

A fortunate stroke of serendipity brought these nations together to turn a new, inconceivable page in history.

Each sentient being present there, on that day, that night, in that city had a hand in turning that page. They all looked to one spot as they arrived—the castle balcony.

There stood the seven representatives of each of the races. They were who made this unseen dream a sure reality—yes...

The leader of the Werebeasts, a golden-haired fox-woman with two tails—the Shrine Maiden.

The last male Dhampir, whose lovely youthful face melded with the night sky—Plum.

The Siren queen, who seductively swayed her scaly tail back and forth—Laila.

The firstborn Flügel, who gently touched down on the earth with unmoving wings—Azril.

The Ex Machina there on the Befehler Einzig's behalf, a cybernetic girl whose creation superseded all knowledge—Emir-Eins.

The Dwarf representative there on the chieftain's behalf, a young girl with mithril hair and bright orichalcum eyes—Til.

The Fairy representative, a tiny, traitorous maiden who showered flowers about as she danced—Foeniculum.

And finally, an Old Deus, small in stature, who swooped down miraculously out of thin air—Holou.

*　*　*

Each representative was either their race's agent plenipotentiary or its equivalent by proxy. However...none of them was the true star of this historic night. The roaring cheers and applause grew even louder when the final two figures made their appearance on the balcony——

The first was a young man who wore a dark blue tailcoat that glistened in the night sky and a crown meant for a queen around his arm like an armband.

The second was a small girl who wore an evening dress that sparkled like a starry sky and used a crown meant for a king as a hair clip.

That's right—the grandiose parade, the thunderous applause, and the cries of joy that shook the earth were all for these two.

The event was to mark the first-year anniversary of Elkia's royal siblings' coronation.

An event that for the older brother, Sora, simultaneously and inadvertently marked:

The crossing into his *nineteenth year as a virgin*...

■■■

——It had all started one week earlier.

"We're going to throw a memorial ceremony to mark the one-year anniversary of your coronation as Elkia's monarch—next week."

Sora and Shiro were preoccupied with a combination of reading Jibril's archives and playing video games in the royal library when their young redheaded friend, Stephanie Dola, hit them with this news.

"...Next...week...? Seems...sudden...," said Shiro.

"I get that I don't know how these things work, but you'd think it'd take a lot longer to prepare for an event like that, no?" said Sora.

"And even if I don't know how these things work, it's fair to assume that you probably need to ask for *our* approval beforehand…?"

Sora and Shiro shared their dissatisfaction with narrow glances, to which Steph responded with a serious look.

"Would you have approved it if I'd asked beforehand?"

"Nope. Not a fat chance in hell."

"That is why I went behind your back and have been diligently making preparations on my own! ♪"

It was no mystery, either, how she'd pulled it off. Sora and Shiro were rulers with zero interest in politics—setting up such a ceremony unbeknownst to them was laughably easy.

Sora and Shiro quietly clicked their tongues at Steph in unison, whose confident grin suggested implicitly she'd accomplished just that.

——*Steph's a tricky girl. She's really starting to figure us out.*

"The Commonwealth of Elkia is one of the world's two major alliances. As its leading power, we will invite the world's leaders to a grand celebration marking both of your coronations as Elkia royalty. It's a chance for us to show the fellowship between the multiple races that make up our member states both domestically and internationally—something that has substantial political and economic significance. I have already picked out outfits for the both of you and have authorized a strict schedule for the day of, which is—"

——*"You two ain't weaseling your way out of this one,"* yeah, yeah…

Without saying it explicitly, Steph prevented any way for them to back out of the event. However, her long, drawn-out speech was lost on the siblings, who were staring blankly into space.

"Man…it really has been a year since we were transported to Disboard…"

"…Hard…to tell…if time flies…or if it's…super slow…"

Looking back on it…a lot had happened since the two arrived here in Disboard, the world on a game board.

Though mostly through *going with the flow*, the siblings ended up the dual monarchs of Elkia—this world's Immanity nation that was an inch away from ruin.

They went on to form a Commonwealth with the Eastern Union, bringing Oceand, Avant Heim, and Hardenfell into their alliance, as well as finding new allies in Old Deus, Ex Machina, and Fairy. Just as Steph said, the Commonwealth was one of the world's two major alliances. This much had happened all in one year.

As Shiro had just mumbled, this past year had been both long and short at the same time......

——*Wait, what...?*
Hold the phone. A year—a whole friggin' year has gone by—?!

"——Um, hello? I'm explaining how the ceremony is going to play out... Are you listening?"

Sora and Shiro, who obviously would never pay attention to an explanation like this, were in no position to listen even if they'd wanted to.

The two of them scrambled to take out their cell phones, glaring at the screens as they lit up.

The screens, each individually maintaining the calendars of their original world, showed:

"WHAAAT?! I turned nineteen ages ago?! How the hell did I miss this?!"

"...No, no, no... My height...and bust...haven't budged...even a millimeter...?!"

What does this mean?

That Sora, who had long introduced himself as an *eighteen-year-old virgin*, had at some point—long ago, in fact—regressed into a nineteen-year-old virgin, and Shiro had turned twelve without growing physically by any tangible metric.

The two recoiled, lamenting over this unsavory news to the skies above:

But wait! It's not over yet! I refuse to accept this harsh reality!!

*   *   *

"Y'know what! Our birthdays were renewed the day we were reborn in Disboard!! Yeah, that's it!! I mean, surely that's what our documentation says, right?! *Steeeeeph?!*"

".......!! Yeah...! What Brother said! I-I-I'm still...an eleven-year-old!!"

——This world didn't share a calendar with their old world. The two siblings, born of a different world, didn't even have a birth certificate when they came to Elkia!

The only documentation they had was the official documents they had forged, er, *made* for their initial coronation, which had the day they arrived in Disboard marked down as their birthday!!

This means I'm still an eighteen-year-old virgin, and Shiro is still a flat-chested eleven-year-old!!

The two vehemently made this case to Steph, who quietly nodded along and said, "I suppose you're right, which means that four days before the ceremony, or two days from now, will be your birthday. Thus, the ceremony will double as a celebration of both the one-year anniversary of your coronation and birth—hey, are you two listening to me?!"

Sora and Shiro obviously weren't listening, and they were absolutely not in the right headspace to listen, either.

So—not only did we manage to completely miss our birthdays from our original world, but in two days, we will unequivocally and irrefutably be Sora, the nineteen-year-old-virgin, and Shiro, the flat-chested twelve-year-old...

Steph's voice sounded distant to the mortified Sora and the teary-eyed Shiro...

■■■

——And so came the fateful day, a memorial ceremony to mark the first anniversary of the siblings' coronation into Elkia royalty.

The event started with a magnificent parade and lasted for seven whole days of ceremonious grandeur.

The first major event to be held was a sharing of traditional performance art between each of the Commonwealth member nations. The leaders of each race and nation met individually, sharing their salutations and congratulations while partaking in big banquets.

This was topped off with each of the agent plenipotentiaries and their proxies coming together to give joint declarations, saying things like "Our nation maintains amicable relations with the Kingdom of Elkia and all other nation-states and races under the Commonwealth," and "We shall spare no effort in fostering mutual growth henceforth."

Through cooperation on the Dwarves' and Fairies' parts, each of these speeches was broadcast throughout the entirety of the Commonwealth.

——Everything moved perfectly according to Steph's thoroughly planned schedule, thanks to her meticulous coordination with the other nations.

It should be obvious that Sora and Shiro were not permitted to wear their usual attire for the length of the festivities.

Sora wore a tailcoat, and Shiro an evening dress—both utterly stifling garments.

Speaking of stifling, the two had to stifle their phobias against socializing and making eye contact while they desperately fought off a seemingly endless chain of boredom, trembling, and exhaustion.

Each of the agent plenipotentiaries—the Shrine Maiden and Plum in particular—had to stop themselves from laughing at this part of the show.

This continued until the hellacious seven-day period came to an end——......

On the seventh night of hellaciousness, Steph was walking Sora and Shiro—both with lifeless eyes and dragging their legs like zombies—through the halls of Elkia Royal Castle when she announced...

"Congratulations to the both of you! Up next is the final—or should I say—main event!!"

"...There's...more...? And wouldja mind tellin' me just where in the hell do you get all of that energy...?"

"...I need...sleep... Steph...when are you...sleeping...?"

Steph had spent the entire seven days at the siblings' sides.

In other words, she was on the same by-the-minute schedule that she prepared for them—in fact, she was managing the entire ceremony from behind the curtain on top of this. Naturally, she should've been leagues busier than the two *hosts* of the ceremony...??

The siblings looked at her with suspicion, and Steph, tapping into her unknown source of vitality, responded with a big smile.

"You two are forgetting about the biggest event of them all: *your birthday party*!!"

——*Right.*

The two were indeed told that this ceremony was a joint celebration of both the one-year anniversary of their coronation and their birthday.

Despite this, there hadn't been any *birthday festivities* yet—

"I truly am sorry for making you have to suffer through all those boring events, which is why I'd like to finish with a bang! I've arranged for a private birthday party between us and those who personally wish to celebrate your birthdays!!"

A private birthday party... Okay.

Steph surely was saving the best for last as a surprise for the two. It was probably her way of thanking them.

But:

"Right...our birthdays... Well, at least Shiro is probably excited for hers...I bet..."

"...I'm turning...twelve... Even though...I haven't grown an inch, I'll be...*twelve*..."

"Why are the two of you acting like being thrown a birthday party is the end of the world?!" Steph hollered.

Sora looked deathly ill while Shiro muttered to herself in delirium. What was supposed to be a big surprise ended up draining what little light was left in the siblings' empty eyes.

"I, um...perhaps packed the ceremony schedule too tightly for the two of you—yes, that must be it. I-if this is the case, then I'll explain it to everyone and we can hold it another—"

"Oh...no, Steph. It's not that, per se..."

Sora shook his head, stopping Steph from wincing from all the guilt she felt, and said:

"Birthdays are only fun *until you turn eighteen*..."

.............,

"...............Huh? Really, now...?"

Sora had spoken with such assurance that Steph was now doubting her own worldview on the matter.

"I'm surprised you didn't know this... Here, let me fill you in..."

He took a deep breath before continuing.

"To start off, what do you think are the *merits* of getting older?"

"...? Merits...? Well...there are plenty?"

"Yup. That's because getting older unlocks more rights."

More rights, specifically:

"Physical growth, mental development, and more autonomy over what you're allowed to do."

"...Although I...didn't grow...a smidgen...," Shiro mumbled resentfully, but her nodding suggested that she agreed with the latter half of her brother's assessment.

"Autonomy, or even more simply, freedom. Freedom to sign a contract, to get a driver's license, to move out of your parents' house, to work and save money—basically, the freedom to live your life as you see fit!"

"...! ...The freedom to...get *married*! Only...six, more years...!" Shiro added excitedly; it sounded as if she'd found a reason to live again.

That reason was lost on Sora, who just nodded, glad that his sister was now over her mental slump.

Marital freedom was another big one—it was, in other words, sexual freedom.

Or more aptly—*the freedom to interact with sexual media and content!*

"You see, Steph!! All I ever wanted to do when I was a child was to grow up fast!! This sentiment hit me like a truck during puberty when I began dreaming daily of turning eighteen!! For it was the momentous day I would be able to take into these hands pornographic games, *hentai*, *doujin*, and watch porn online all on my own—the ultimate form of freedom! I counted the months—nay, days—until the fateful moment I'd come of age!!"

"Everything you've said so far has to do with sex! Do you not have anything else to look forward to?!"

"Nope! Nothing!! A man's brain is composed of sixty percent horny thoughts!!"

"You're saying that's a fact?! No, wait—I'm pretty sure that only applies to you and you alone, Sora!"

The remaining 40 percent of male thoughts are taken up by wealth and social status—essentially, a man craves being attractive to hot women! And the sole reason is that on the other side of successfully finding an attractive mate, it is sex that awaits a man! So logically, in a broader sense, it's fair to say that a man's mind is 100 percent occupied with pursuing sex!

Sora then took a step back and, recognizing that there may be a slight variation on an individual basis, made the humble decision to refrain from speaking in hyperbolic terms.

"It should be clear by now that all birthdays until the age of eighteen are indeed without demerit!! Therefore, no person in their right mind would ever argue against throwing a party to celebrate a birthday with a party before that cutoff!! But dare I say—!!"

Sora had kept up this impassioned speech until this point, when his enthusiasm took a sharp nosedive.

* * *

"Dare you say what…?"

Steph gulped as she posed that question to Sora, whose expression was now devoid of all emotion despite having been so animated only seconds ago.

All that awaited beyond age nineteen were cigarettes and alcohol…minutiae that were of no interest to Sora, and even if they were, the unlocking of these new rights ended at the age of twenty.

And what awaited beyond twenty? Beyond thirty? Beyond forty?

"There's virtually nothing new—no freedom nor rights—to be gained beyond the age of twenty."

In fact, it was worse than that—!!

"You have to work and pay taxes—obligations! That's all you get from there! All while your body withers away and your mind loses its flexibility as each year creeps by!! What was once a life where every new day was a day you looked forward to becomes sullied by immense mental stress! The time you must spend at work takes away your freedom to do what you wish while you simply count the days until you perish!!"

"It's far too soon for you to be worrying about your age, Sora. I also implore you to refrain from making such scathing remarks about adulthood until *after you've fulfilled even one of your current obligations*—you've been king for a year without doing anything!"

"…There's one more benefit…waiting for you at…twenty-five, Brother…when I turn eighteen… Although, it's also more of…an obligation, at this point…"

Sora took Steph's apt retort and Shiro's ambiguous remark and tossed them to the wind.

He stood firm with his belief that *not a single birthday beyond eighteen was of any worth!!*

——Shiro may have had her reasons for getting one year older, but what reason was there for *Sora* to celebrate turning nineteen?

Once he'd finished making his case and despair threatened to overtake him:

"Soraaa! You're putting way too much thought into this! A birthday is just a celebration for living another year—it's really that simple!!"

Steph retaliated after realizing she was getting caught up in Sora's momentum, but:

"Okay. Then riddle me this, Steph: What does it mean to *live*?"

"———Ughhhh... What is it this time...?" Steph grumbled at this new philosophical question Sora had so abruptly posed.

———What does it mean to live...?

From the moment a person is born, it is determined that, at some point, they will die.

For a human being, assuming they lived a fortunate life and are blessed with good health into their old age—they live up to around one hundred and twenty years old, at the very most.

Conversely, a person could die tomorrow—or at any second, for that matter. There's no stopping an unforeseen, untimely death.

Therefore, is one's life not but a countdown to their death that starts from the moment they're born?

If this is the case, then what does it mean *to live*?

"———I'd argue that to live...is to *have hope*."

"............"

"It is what you do, or try to do, and what you continually strive for. I think *that's* what it means to live."

This *life* we live, or...more poignantly, the death we live for will come eventually, and once it does—after we rot away and turn into soil—we'll learn that it was all meaningless.

With this, an inevitable death, in mind...is to live not to strive for what you hope for?

A person who has no intention of doing anything, no desires to be fulfilled, who simply lives for the sake of living—

—surely can't be considered actually *living their life* but simply in the process of their *long-winded death*...

* * *

"On that note, let's take a moment to reflect on this past year that is supposedly worth celebrating…"

This year—when Sora became king surrounded by a diverse group of bona fide babes. Despite these optimal circumstances—it ended with Sora girlfriendless and still a virgin.

In other words, Sora surmised that, in all likelihood, he would spend the next ten, no, hundred years—*a pathetic virgin*.

This last year amounted to nothing more than a proof of concept for him— So! Where in the world was he to find…any hope…?

"So you want me to spend this day celebrating yet another year *lived*? By my definition, a year without hope is a year not lived, so there's nothing to celebrate at all… In fact, you could even argue that we may as well hold my funeral…"

Sora's level of resignation was almost endearing, but Steph wasn't convinced.

"…I'm starting to find it almost remarkable how fixated you are on finding a girlfriend to the point where it has caused you such despair…"

"…You know, Brother… You could have, a whole harem…if you weren't such a…wuss…"

Shiro had now joined Steph in wincing at Sora in astonishment.

It was around this time when the group made it to the banquet hall, at which point Steph, perhaps having grown tired of Sora's antics—

"Aaarghhh! Either way, you're coming with me!! We'll find out if it was worth celebrating after we go through these doors!!"

—tightly gripped Sora's hand and opened the doors.

——And what awaited the three was…

■■■

"Sora! Shiro! Happy Birthday, please!!"

The moment they entered the banquet hall, a single voice drowned out the rest of the room's idle chatter. It belonged to a tiny Werebeast girl with a big set of ears and a fluffy tail who leaped toward the trio—Izuna Hatsuse.

"......................."

Sora and Shiro were at a loss for words as they took in everything.

It was just as Steph told them: *Those who personally wished to celebrate the siblings' birthday were present.*

They saw Izuna, who was embracing them both, along with Emir-Eins, Til, and Holou.

Jibril was there, too, her halo aglow. They were all clapping at their arrival.

——Sora was surprised to see Izuna's grandfather, Ino Hatsuse, as well as Plum, too.

Ino's presence made sense; he was probably there to keep an eye on his granddaughter. Plum, on the other hand, was almost certainly there to accompany the oversized water jug he sat on.

"Oh! Foeniculum said she'll come, too," Steph added. "She left me this note about how she's 'a *teeeeensy* bit busy stirring up interracial love throughout the city!' and will join us later."

The siblings continued to stare blankly—

"But that's neither here nor there! Let's get the birthday boy and girl to their seats. ♪"

—until Steph tugged at Sora's hand, bringing him to a seat at the end of a long table.

Sora and Shiro took in their surroundings once more—the banquet hall was much livelier than usual.

It was filled with paper and ribbon decorations—most likely made by the guests present—along with bright tapestries and a generous assortment of colorful candles and flowers.

And on the table where they were sitting was something Steph must have made herself: a smorgasbord of food that managed to look far more delicious than anything they'd eaten in the past week—

"Master? My apologies; is there something that is not to your satisfaction?" Jibril asked.

"Huh—? Oh, no… It's not that. Not that at all…"

"…We're just…um…so surprised…or should I say…"

*Looking back on it, neither of us have ever had our birthdays cel-
ebrated like this before. We never even had this many people who
wanted to celebrate our birthdays on a personal level.*

The siblings didn't know how to react to all the applause and festivities, so they just sat there dumbfounded when—

—someone came forward and elegantly pinched the hem of her
skirt on either side.

"Celebration: Master and Little Sister, this unit wishes to com-
memorate the anniversary of your births on this day from the bottom of her 'heart.' Congratulations."

Offering a curtsy that went even deeper than usual, Emir-Eins
continued:

"Small gift: Einzig has prepared a present on behalf of the Ex
Machina for Master. Please accept it. Hee."

She spoke as if her expressionless face were blushing, but then:

"Hey—?! I thought I told you to wait until after dinner and the
cake to give your present!!"

"Affirmative: This unit did not consent to said request. Victory
goes to the one who makes the first move. This unit prioritizes gaining favor with her master above all else."

Steph stepped in to try to stop Emir-Eins but was easily shunted
away by the Ex Machina, who proclaimed her intent on taking the
initiative in the battle of love—when something else happened.

——*Ping.*

A high-pitched notification sound could be heard coming from
Sora's and Shiro's phones. On their screens read the words UNKNOWN
FILE RECEIVED.

The phones weren't asking if they *wanted to receive* the files but
were declaring their *reception* after the fact… This meant that the
devices the siblings brought from their own world were remotely

tampered with seamlessly to forcibly receive a third-party file… A glaring lack of security.

Sora tapped the notification, showing his Ex Machina companion a dry smile of resignation while wishing she wouldn't use her technological manipulation on him.

The moment he laid eyes on the contents of the folder that was sent to him, however—

—Sora felt *alive* again…

"Report: Analysis determined copulation between Master and this unit impossible due to Master's and Little Sister's wishes. However, Master's prior remarks and actions established that deeds of *self-pleasure* do not infringe on said wishes. Additionally, what Master assumably desires above all else is the replenishment of pleasurable images previously removed from Master's device by Ex Machina."

What the siblings saw on their screens was precisely that—a present producible only by hypercomputation. Emir-Eins had hyperanalyzed the ecology, conscious and subconscious thought processes, and behavioral patterns of Sora and Shiro, filling in the holes where she needed.

What was on his phone screen was perfection—sweet, dear perfection!

"Concern: Do *selfies* taken by this unit…qualify as fuel for Master's…*deeds of self-pleasure*…?"

The images sent to Sora were of the beautiful mecha-girl, which showed her…well, to put it in less direct terms…baring it all—and the collection took up copious amounts of data.

There were hundreds upon hundreds of images and high-quality videos that used up 10 percent of his phone's storage.

"Yes, Emir-Eins. Thank you. I'm almost certain I have lived my life for this very moment…"

Sora had made a great leap from the depths of his depression to show a newfound hopeful outlook on life.

* * *

He gave a thumbs-up with a smile as bright as the daytime sun and thought:

I can make it through another year with these!!

"You gave that long-winded speech about what it means to live only to find that meaning instantaneously...?"
Steph was clearly fed up, but her remark was—as expected—ignored.
Sora, whose will to live had heated up faster than a cup of instant noodles, stood tall and with great vigor—before it hit him.
"Hm?! Wait a tick... You didn't send these to Shiro, too, did you?!"
His brain finally processed the fact that his sister's phone had emitted the same *ping* as his own. He hurriedly turned his attention to Shiro, who was in his lap, staring silently at her device.

"Negative: Little Sister has no desire for selfies taken by this unit. Sending aforementioned data to Little Sister would be unethical. Concomitance: It is forbidden for these images to be seen by anyone but Master. Report: Einzig has prepared age-appropriate data for Little Sister. *Nicht zu wichtig.*"
Emir-Eins's answer made Sora feel ashamed of himself. His fully bionic companion had successfully prepared the perfect present for him. Why in the world did he expect her to ever overlook something simple enough for a mere human to worry over?
No longer concerned, Sora felt bad about ever doubting Emir-Eins, whose gifts left nothing more to be desired—but this still begged the question.

"...? Okay, but...what exactly did you give Shiro to have her so—?"
"Brother...could you...pipe down...? I need to...focus..."
Shiro cut Sora off, rapidly swiping her finger across her phone screen.
"Confirmation: Master's previous world—Japan—has no age restrictions on text-based media."

Emir-Eins stepped into the conversation once more to answer Sora's question.

"Disclosure: Little Sister received a twenty-thousand-word *novel*, carefully written by Einzig in Master's original language."

Let me get this straight… A mechanized race has finally tried its hand at literature…

It made sense: Ex Machinas were more humanlike than humans in many ways.

What piqued Sora's interest next was what exactly it was about the book that had Shiro so glued to her screen.

"Summary: An erotic novel about Einzig and his beloved Spieler. Einzig gave this unit strict orders to send novel to Master, but this unit rejected them based on her own judgment. Just to Confirm… would Master like to…read the novel?"

"Who'd even want to read something like that? You made the right decision, Emir-Eins—but why is Shiro so into it?!"

Is the book that interesting?! Enough to be that engrossed in it?! A book by that hunk of junk?! About me *and that hunk of junk—?!*

"…They got you down…to a tee… The Ex Machina are…seriously legit…"

——As difficult as it was to believe, Shiro was largely satisfied with her present…

The Ex Machina had come to understand a side of Shiro that not even her brother yet knew.

"Assertion: A present has meaning only if its recipient enjoys it."

Emir-Eins puffed out her modest bust with pride and gave a thin smile. Her words, however, were not for Sora's and Shiro's ears, but for the person standing behind them.

"…………"

With cross-shaped pupils set in amber-colored eyes, Jibril stood back and watched the exchange, seething. Emir-Eins's grin twisted into a sneer as she continued, all the while ignoring the Flügel.

"Query: Paraphernalia held by Irregular Number: skull of an unknown life-form that offers a ninety-six-point-seven percent chance of mentally disturbing Master; and an ancient Flügel text decipherable by neither Master nor Little Sister. Total: two items. Why would one offer such articles on a birthday? This unit is left perplexed."

"...Erm...?!"

"Hey, uh...Jibril? Presents are more about the thought that goes into them than the actual—"

Whatever present Jibril chose, there wasn't a doubt in the siblings' minds that they were important to her.

Jibril stood there trembling, unable to come up with a retort. Sora tried his best to defuse the tension, but—

"Affirmative: It is the thought that counts. Effort must be made to think about what the recipient of a gift will feel upon receiving it. Ergo, an issue of effort."

Emir-Eins agreed with Sora, but before he could get a word in edgewise—

"Inevitability: A gift without sufficient thought becomes an imposition. A burden. Foolish."

—she then turned to Jibril and flashed a perfect smile, like one would expect to see on a doll.

With an overtly well-calculated tilt of her head, Emir-Eins asked in a mechanical fashion:

"Query: Are the two aforementioned items meant to be gifts for Master and Little Sister?"

"_____"

"Correction/Self-Evident/Apology: Impossible. This unit was aware of the strikingly low IQ of the Flügel race, but Master's self-proclaimed number one servant has spent a year with Master. Ergo, this unit never expected Irregular Number to offer a gift so lacking in proper thought and effort. Allow this unit to express humble regret for the remarkable error in judgment: My deepest apologies. ♥"

———......,

A brief moment of silence passed. What was likely only a few seconds felt like an eternity due to Emir-Eins augmenting her own voice to sound exactly like Jibril when she gave her apology, which successfully enticed a rise out of the Flügel, bringing her homicidal urges to never-before-seen levels.

"Master...Lord Shiro...it pains me to have to ask for permission to do this at the celebration of your births, but may I borrow your tablet and excuse myself from the festivities for a moment? I will be back in ten...no, five minutes. My deepest apologies."

Jibril weighed her urge to dismember Emir-Eins against her desire to properly celebrate her masters' birthdays, and apparently, the latter won out. She took the tablet into her hands before giving a bow and vanishing into thin air.

And then:

"Report: Sequence for collecting selfies for Master's enjoyment from Irregular Number now complete. Master: Requesting a reward for the hard work that went into making this possible. Pet me...?"

——Evidently, goading Jibril into taking her own set of selfies was a part of Emir-Eins's present.

Sora was patting Emir-Eins's head as gently as he could for her outstanding plan when he had a thought:

——Jibril and Emir-Eins sure have gotten closer lately...

"You're taking forever, please!! I have a present, too, please!!"

Izuna had been waiting diligently when the two cut in line to give their gifts, and she'd finally run out of patience.

She pushed Emir-Eins out of the way and stood before the two siblings.

"Sora! Shiro! Here's a present from me! Take it, please!!" she shouted while holding out a folded strip of long, thin paper.

What appeared to be a chain of handmade tickets had the following spelled out in poorly written Immanity:

"A ticket to do whatever you want for a day...? Huh...? You'll do whatever we want?"

"...Izzy...you mean...*whatever*...we want...?"

"Izuna, you—WHAAAAAT?!"

Ino Hatsuse let out a shriek when he heard Sora and Shiro read the contents of the tickets aloud.

Izuna, however, paid no attention to her grandfather's outburst:

"I thought long and hard about what would make you guys happy... I thought about it a whole lot...but I couldn't come up with anything... Sorry, please..."

Her ears and tail drooped in sorrow when she said this, but they sprang back up as she continued:

"Which is why you'll decide for me, please! Sora, Shiro! What'll make you two happy, please?!"

There was a spark of pride in Izuna's tone as she told them of her compromise.

This brought about a second shout—no, a loud howl, while also being a yelp, that shook the banquet hall.

"I-Izuna?! You've never given your granddaddy a coupon for so much as a back rub!"

"? Why the hell would I give you a back rub, Grampy? You're so freakin' strong, you don't even need one, please. Go to a damn masseuse if you wanna get rubbed that bad, please."

"That's not the problem here!! A granddad wants his granddaughter's cute little hands to bop away at his shoulders is all—no, that isn't the issue here, either!!"

Ino stifled a heartfelt scream and wiped his tears before pointing at Sora and Shiro and sternly howling—!

"Tickets to do *whatever they want*?! What were you thinking, Izuna?! Who knows what atrocities these two glorified apes will come up with for you to do—? Guh?!"

——The old man must've tried to take the tickets out of Sora's and Shiro's hands, because he was shunted backward.

However, the tickets had been *given* to the siblings by Izuna and were now their property.

The Ten Covenants prevented Ino from *plundering* them, but they didn't stop him from baring his fangs and growling.

——*Return the tickets to Izuna, now. Or else I'll challenge you to a game and make you give them back, even if it kills me—!!*

The way he menaced the two made his intent clear, but—

"Grampy...you're pissing me off, please..."

Rage contorted his cute granddaughter's amiable expression.

"Do you seriously think Sora and Shiro would do any nasty shit to me, please?"

"...Argh..."

You're probably right, Ino thought.

Sora and Shiro held themselves to a strangely high moral standard— Ino never really thought they would do anything indecent to Izuna. He was actually surprised by how much trust he placed in the two Immanity deep down.

However—that didn't change anything. While he knew they wouldn't do something fishy to Izuna, he was certain they would think of some cockamamie way to abuse the tickets.

"Also, stop calling them apes, Grampy! It's goddamn rude, please!!"

"——Ugh... Aaaargh?!"

Izuna was asking her granddad to stop berating her friends... No—in fact, she was asking more than that. With his nation being a part of the Commonwealth, a multiracial republic, he needed to respect the other races.

Once his beloved granddaughter pointed out his poor manners, the old man hung his head low in shame. He may have not been entirely off the mark, however——

——*Ha...Mwa-ha-ha-ha...*

"Thank you, Izuna. We'll take our time to think of a good way to put these tickets to use, okay?"

"...Thanks...Izzy... ♪"

"Sounds great, please! Just tell me what to do whenever the hell you want it, please!!"

Her pure eyes glistened as she said this. It was clear how much she trusted the siblings. They answered her gaze with a big smile—one that was deceptively wicked.

Mwa-ha-ha-ha... Izuna Hatsuse. Such a clever little girl—yet so naive! It's a shame to have to pull one over on you like this, but them's the laws of nature in this world! It's trick or be tricked!

For once in his life, Ino Hatsuse was unequivocally right about something—!!

——People betray one another. No bonds, memories, or shared history can keep you safe!!

That's right! Now's a good chance to teach you not to trust others so easily.

——Remember how I said I needed time to think about how to use these? Psh! Gimme a break!

I knew I'd use four of the five tickets for torture *the moment you handed them to me—!!*

You heard me: torture! The first ticket will involve: water...!

I know—we can have Steph help us give Izuna a bath and make sure to wash every inch of her!!

For ticket number two—how about some bondage...?!

Once she's nice and dry after her bath, we'll hold Izuna down and give her a thorough brushing!!

Just think of the fluff! She's already so fluffy as it is!! We'll make her even fluffier, whether she likes it or not—heh, but we're not finished with our torture yet!

You guessed it—the third ticket will be used to imprison *her...!*

She'll be forced to play games with Shiro and me until she can barely keep herself awake, all while we enjoy her amply fluffed fur...!

And for our finisher, ticket number four—abuse!

We'll share her fluffy tail as a pillow for the night—!!

Mwa-ha-ha-haaa... We'll save what we'll do with the last ticket until we see how she's reacted to the first four...

Ino had no way of knowing what atrocities the two had planned for his granddaughter, but it was written all over their faces that they would do *something*.

The three shared a stare-down, Ino with a death glare and the siblings with wicked smiles, when from the side—

"Are you finished yet?! It's my turn, it is!!"

—with a big *plop*, Nýi Tilvilg placed a giant, nicely wrapped gift onto the birthday table, causing it to creak under the present's weight.

The tension in the air was lost on Til, a Dwarf with tanned skin, orichalcum eyes, mithril hair, and two horns protruding from her forehead.

"There's only one gift suitable for a birthday, just one!! A special selection of craft ale, brewed by Hardenfell's finest brewery, the house of Valgrave—!!"

Til ignored the fact that the entire room was largely caught off guard by this abrupt presentation. With the biggest of smiles, she unwrapped the box and unpackaged a number of bottles, each roughly the same size as she was.

By the time she was finished, there were twenty giant bottles up on the banquet table. The bottles were so massive that it was doubtful the entire room could work together to finish a single one, let alone an entire table full—

"Oh, right! I know the drinking age in Elkia is twenty, so the bottles for King Sora and Queen Shiro are nonalcoholic, they are! Ale made by the Valgraves is always delicious, it is! You have my word!!"

Til's plan was to make Sora and Shiro happy by finding the best-tasting drink there was, and for there to be enough for the other guests to enjoy to make the party even better...!

The way she puffed out her flat chest made it clear that she was very confident she'd picked the perfect present.

However:

"…Oh, wow. Uh…thanks?"

"…Yeah… Thank…you?"

…………,

"Wh-what the?! Could it be that my present didn't make you happy at all?!"

Til was absolutely astonished by the lack of enthusiasm in Sora's and Shiro's responses.

"Er, no… It's just…we're not too interested in alcohol…"

"…It smells, gross…and nobody likes…a drunk…"

"And nonalcoholic beer is pretty much, like…bitter-tasting juice? Never really saw the point of the stuff."

"Wha-whaaaat?! A-are there truly Ixseeds who don't drink?!"

——The idea of there being a living thing with no interest in ale was beyond the realm of Til's wildest imagination.

She stood there, trembling, until Steph put a hand to her cheek in thought.

"I've never drunk alcohol before, either, but it doesn't exactly have the best reputation…"

"Nor have I—though us Werebeasts don't drink much in the first place," said Ino. "With the exception of Milady Shrine Maiden, who is quite the drinker, alcohol tends to be too strong for our palates…"

"Consideration: Ingestion of alcohol results in intoxication. Finding leisure in delusion is a meaningless pursuit."

Sora, Shiro, and Steph weren't of legal drinking age, so setting their opinions aside…

Alcohol was rejected on the premise of race by the older Ino and even written off completely by Emir-Eins as meaningless.

——*These people can't be serious, they can't!!*

Her orichalcum eyes as wide as saucers, Til was at a loss for words at their shocking response. Sora, observing this, felt inclined to ask:

"I'm confused. Didn't you always tell Veig that he reeked of liquor? I assumed you didn't drink, either—"

"The chieftain smells bad because he never takes a bath!! There's nothing wrong with drinking regularly, there isn't!! No, really, you gotta listen to me. This ale tastes incredible, trust me!"

An impassioned Til tried to persuade Sora, who was clearly reluctant to change his mind.

"I can tell you've never had any liquor before, I can!! H-here! Big Sis'll show you how it's done! Now, Sir, Ma'am! You too, Lady Steph! Take a swig of this nonalcoholic ale!"

Unable to accept her gift's less-than-stellar reception, Til busted open one of the bottles and began pouring glasses.

She had an intensity about her as she approached Sora, Shiro, and Steph with what would be their first-ever drinks, causing them to fold to the pressure and each take a glass.

Sora mumbled to himself as he took a sip:

"Fine...but they call this peer pressure back in my world. Also, Til, we get that you're technically older than us, but just how serious are you about the whole big sis thing—? WT actual F?!! This tastes friggin' amazing!!"

Everything changed as soon as his lips hit the glass.

"Oh? Is this alcohol?" said Steph. "Well, I suppose it isn't if it is nonalcoholic..."

"...This...tastes awesome... What the...?"

"Heh-heh-hehhh! See what I mean?! Even if it is Valgrave-brand ale, it'll never taste as good as the real thing, it won't. You have a lot to look forward to next year, King Sora!!"

Sora, Steph, and even Shiro all found the drink quite delicious. Til puffed out her chest in pride once more.

——Whoa. And to think the real thing tastes even better...?

If that was the case, then there was indeed a lot to look forward to on his next birthday.

"Report: Alcohol ingestion causes temporary decrease in frontal lobe function among living organisms. Confirmed long-term side effects include brain shrinkage and decreased liver function.

Master, this unit recommends against the habitual consumption of alcohol—"

"Shut your trap!! No one asked for your stupid bullshit robot opinion!! Thbbft!!"

Til interrupted Emir-Eins's objective evaluation with uncharacteristic ferocity.

"Water'll kill you, too, if you drink too much of it! Is life worth living if you don't have the time or money to have some booze every now and then?! Thbbbbbbbfft—!!"

Somehow...there was a powerful persuasion to Til's argument.

"Well well... Though it does have a strong taste to it, it has amazing depth and richness... Lady Nýi, the Werebeasts would enjoy this ale of yours. Might you be interested in exporting it to us? You'd make a lot of money."

"——Reception: This unit recognizes her lack of knowledge. Taste bud receptors now evaluating surprising new data... This stuff's good."

"Heh-heh-heh... See? See?!"

Not only Ino, but Emir-Eins, too, praised the amazing taste of the Dwarf ale.

Its taste was enough to have them do a complete one-eighty on their initial opinions, which prodded Sora to inquire:

"...Hey...think I could get a little sip of theirs, too...?"

"Of course you can't," said Steph. "It would be highly inappropriate for a king to break his own laws."

"You know what? You're right; I'm the king—which makes me the law! Starting from now, I declare Elkia's drinking age to be nineteen!!"

"That's not how that—!"

Sora was willing to go full despot if it meant he could get a taste of that sweet Dwarven ale—but Shiro had her sights set on a separate set of morals:

"...Mm... And I'm, the queen... So the legal age, for viewing pornographic material...and getting married...will be lowered, to twelve years—"

"Welp!! I guess it'd be outrageously selfish to allow such heinous bending of the rule of law!! A monarch is subject to his own law, the same as his people—an important part of a society founded on law and order! I'll have to wait until next year, Til!"

Sora, who spontaneously made a transition into the wise ruler of his nation, finished his declaration by chugging down a cup of the exceedingly delicious nonalcoholic ale.

■■■

Perhaps thanks to the booze Til provided, the party guests began digging into the food while the presents continued to roll out.

...Starting with a special gift...

"Myyy, I didn't think biffles like us had to prepare presents like thiiis."

The Dhampir boy, Plum, showed an alluring feminine smile from the top of the wooden lid of the massive water jug he sat on, only for a voice to be heard coming from inside it:

"Hey?! Why isn't this darn thing opening?! *I'm* the present, my dear. ♥ I'm all ready for you inside here. Will somebody let me out already?! Or could it be that my precious Sora is sitting on top of my jug?! Playing hard to get, are we?! Oooh, I like it!!"

The jug rattled back and forth while the muffled voice of Laila, the Siren Queen, could be heard shouting from inside it.

"Hark! Sora and Shiro! Dost thou truly find thyself content with a gift such as this?! Holou danceth as she always doth! Hypothesis— art thou tricking Holou yet again?!"

——*What is a present? What be it that bringeth Sora and Shiro joy?*

The Old Deus, Holou, placed great thought into this question, but was unable to come up with an answer of her own.

When she decided to ask the siblings point-blank, they answered without hesitation: a special birthday live show.

* * *

It wasn't long after she left before Jibril returned to the party with goods of her own to contend with Emir-Eins's. These were: a tablet filled to the brim with highly stimulating selfies and the rarest, most valuable book she could find written in a language Shiro could understand—both of which were accepted graciously.

"Wow... I heard that the cuisine in Hardenfell was too flavorful for our palates, but...this is very good."

"I thought you Werebeasts were crazy when I heard you ate fish raw, but I could eat this stuff all day, I could!"

"This seafood is goddamn tasty, please! What do you call this shit, please?!"

"It is an Oceand dish. It seems it's been flavored using Eastern Union spices."

"...Doubt: Oceand is an underwater city. How does one cook underwater?"

"Ah-ha-haaaa! You're riiight about that. Sirens—who get their seafood by opening their mouths and letting fiiish swim in—have no concept of gourmet. We Dhampir, howeverrr, appreciate the luxuries of life, such as fine diiining. I'm quite fond of how this dish came out."

"Hey! Why am I the only one not getting any food or drink?! Will you hop off already?! I'm fine and dandy with my beloved darling playing hard to get, but the rest of you best not try me!"

——The banquet table was surrounded by members of different races, all enjoying a meal together.

Watching the sight unfold before him, Sora took the time to do some soul-searching about his stance on birthdays.

The food was good. The (albeit nonalcoholic) ale tasted great.

He was looking forward to using Izuna's present, and what wasn't there to like about his favorite god/idol superstar, Holou, giving him a private show?

To top it all off, he had pictures of Emir-Eins and Jibril to enjoy—these were going to be saved for later.

Maybe birthdays were better than he was writing them off to be…

"Wait a minute…we haven't gotten a present from Steph yet."

——Obviously, Sora was well aware that the entire banquet, including most of the food and drink from each member nation, had been arranged by Steph. That she was the one who'd tested out all the recipes, found all the ingredients, and prepared them in a way that each partygoer could enjoy. The party itself was a present not only for Sora and Shiro, but for the participants as well.

With this in mind, Sora, who was too embarrassed to thank Steph for everything in a more straightforward manner, tried to flush it out of her with a small jab, as she wasn't the type to gloat about doing this all on her own, but—

"Ah, yes. I was going to save my gift for after dinner like I had planned, but…," she said with a wry chuckle. "I guess there's no point in doing that now."

To Sora's surprise, Steph excused herself to go get their gifts.

A short moment passed before she returned with two small, neatly wrapped packages.

"These are for you, Sora and Shiro. Happy Birthday."

Steph held out the packages, which the siblings took and opened.

——Inside, they found something they hadn't seen for seven days. It was an "I ♥ PPL" T-shirt and a pair of jeans, along with a black sailor outfit. The same old—actually, no—brand-new versions of their usual outfits. Clothes that should've been very dirty after a year of being worn continuously.

"I thought that these outfits must mean a lot to the two of you, so I had our seamstresses work on repairing them."

"_____"

Steph said this like it was nothing, but it was cause for the siblings' eyes to widen. Polyester didn't exist in this world—or as far as Sora and Shiro knew, at least. They shouldn't have even had the right fabric to test any dye or sewing methods on. As such, it would've been faster to re-create the clothes from scratch. This was likely what the seamstresses insisted, but Steph convinced them to try nevertheless, before eventually, perhaps with the help of Eastern Union textile expertise, successfully repairing the clothes.

In fact, an image flashed in the backs of Sora's and Shiro's minds of Steph joining the seamstresses to try to repair the clothes herself.

Steph, not the type to draw attention to any effort she made behind the scenes, however tremendous it might be, bashfully cleared her throat before speaking up.

"A birthday is when you say things you are normally too embarrassed to say."

Steph shared another reason to celebrate a birthday with Sora, who only just earlier had rejected the concept wholeheartedly.

What's worth celebrating is behind these doors—that's what Steph said earlier, and she was about to explain what exactly that was.

"This past week, and everyone and everything in this room, are the fruits of your year spent here."

Steph smiled gently and motioned throughout the banquet hall: This was the Commonwealth of Elkia, the nation the two siblings had started.

"_____"

Elkia, a kingdom where food was once scare, now was the host nation for a multiracial, multicultural banquet. Foods from each nation lined the table that the racially diverse guests happily shared together. This was all made possible by Sora and Shiro.

In other words:

In a world where everyone put their own priorities first—a world of war and deception—these two showed the world a glimpse of a dream, where people could share each other's losses. Where they could accept each other, and compromise, and come out better for it in the end.

The siblings showed the world a glimpse of this dream, and that it could be a reality.

Sure, they weren't finished yet. They had only just begun, and many problems stood in their way.

What mattered was that the journey had begun, and Sora and Shiro were the ones who made the world take that once-thought-to-be-impossible first step—

"There's something I want to tell you. Something I will tell because it's your birthday. Something I have to say."

Her sincere words were for Sora and Shiro alone...

"Sora. Shiro. Thank you for being born, and thank you for being alive."

She smiled. Overwhelmed, Sora and Shiro quickly scanned the room.

Jibril, Emir-Eins, Til, Izuna, and Holou were all looking at them. Even Ino and Plum—sure, they probably had their own opinions on the matter—seemed to be largely in agreement with Steph.

The people at this party were here to cross racial lines and celebrate their birthday, together.

"........................."

Still taken aback, the siblings came to the same conclusion:

——*We were never as ambitious as you make it sound.*
We just got summoned here by Tet, who challenged us to his game—and we aren't the type to back down from a challenge. Then we went around challenging anything we didn't like. We've only ever lived how we wanted to live in this world—and had fun playing games, that's all.

If that was as ambitious as their companions were making it out to be, then it was only thanks to Steph and the rest of the partygoers, who seemed to agree with her—not something the siblings did deliberately.

This world had been full of gamers before the two ever got here. If it hadn't been either of them, then somebody, somewhere out there, would've eventually accomplished what they had so far.

That said, it was Steph who spent the most time accompanying the two on their antics.

If she and the rest of the elite gamers at the party that night felt this way, then…

"…Oh, yeah…uh…I dunno what to say…?"

"…You're, uh…welcome…?"

——"*Thank you for being born, and thank you for being alive*"…

Sora and Shiro never thought the day would come when they could ever be thankful for anybody but each other.

Which was why their response to Steph's words came out bashfully. They sounded like they were asking a question:

"But, erm—! How should I put this? Was that entire seven-day ceremony really necessary? We almost kicked the can from exhaustion before making it to our birthday."

——Sora and Shiro were pretty embarrassed by everything. Everyone at the party was grinning—it was rare to see the siblings acting like this—and Sora tried to wave away all the eyes that were on him and his sister.

Asserting that this party alone should've been enough was simply a semantic trick Sora used to hide his bashfulness—but.

"Well…you see…," Steph began, averting her gaze in hesitation before Ino answered for her:

"It was necessary, indeed…as unfortunate as that may be…"

While there was no doubt in Sora's and Shiro's minds that Steph's…appreciation for them was sincere—

"We needed to let the world know in a big way that we, the Commonwealth of Elkia, are a powerful entity with unbreakable bonds and a force to be reckoned with. Some propaganda, if you will."

——The member nations needed to use their assembly, even if the main goal was to celebrate the siblings' birthday.

Ino continued to speak for Steph, who was gnashing her teeth from the overwhelming guilt.

The room, once filled with joyous celebration, took on a more solemn overtone as Ino continued...

"You see, the Commonwealth is at a clear disadvantage in the war being waged against us."

Sora and Shiro had already begun revolutionizing the world in the same way that Ino's master, the Shrine Maiden, once dreamed of doing before eventually abandoning that dream. The two rekindled her hope in that dream—however.

——By Ino's estimation, it wasn't long before the Commonwealth would be brought to its knees...

............,

"Sorry for the wait! ♣ Foeniculum, cute as ever and at your service!! ★ And have I got a present for you!! Something perfect for all the love that's in the air in Elkia tonight— Er, hey? What gives? Why the long faces, people? Did one of yous get caught cheatin'? Let's hear the sweet deets. Who was it? What races were they? Deh-heh-hehhh!"

A small girl *poofed* out of nowhere in Fairy fashion—it was Foeniculum.

The entire banquet was glaring at Ino Hatsuse for committing the cardinal sin of ruining the party. A sucker punch from his granddaughter—"Stupid Grampy! Read the damn room, please!"—spurred Ino to drown his sorrows in a glass of ale. Foeniculum quickly took that as a sign to engage in some alcohol-fueled shenanigans of her own......

■■■

——With that, the celebration was in full swing, and it was soon dark outside. The birthday party eventually disbanded once Shiro and Izuna began nodding off in the dead of night.

Sora carried Shiro on his back, taking her from the castle garden to the room they shared. Shiro, tuckered out after a long night of fun, changed into her old school uniform that she received from Steph, only to conk out soon after. Sora, on the other hand, made extra sure that his little sister was sleeping like a log before similarly changing into his favorite "I ♥ PPL" T-shirt but only to forgo donning his newly repaired jeans. Pantsless, he cautiously double-, then triple-checked his surroundings.

"Nothing to my left or right... Back and front, up and down are clear... I don't hear anyone nearby, either——————all right!"

He checked everything and everywhere he could, especially the depth of his younger sister's sleep—something he spent a good thirty seconds on—to make sure he was finally and fully alone.

In the darkness of the room, two sources of square light shone faintly. One from his phone and the other from his tablet.

——What was he about to do in the sanctity of his bedroom? This should be fairly obvious.

He had two devices loaded with hot-off-the-press pictures of Emir-Eins and Jibril to work over—!! And it would be entirely out of line to neglect at least taking a look at his birthday presents on the night of his birthday! Wouldn't it?!

But Sora was a gentleman and a scholar. He held out his phone and tablet with the sincerest of looks. He was in a bit of a bind, for he had to make a choice! Which device would he peruse first?!

His two close female companions had poured their hearts and souls into preparing these two collections, and prioritizing one over the other presented an unavoidable conundrum—Sora was absolutely torn by this.

As fate would have it...his right hand had business elsewhere, leaving him just one open hand—but two devices!

Forced to make the bitter decision over which device to start with, Sora held out the smartphone and tablet, when—!!

"Um, King Sora...? You should really wear some pants. You'll catch a cold, you will."

"..............................."

Sora was neither shocked nor surprised by the sudden sound of a Peeping Tom's voice coming from behind him.

Instead, he was calm and collected as he lazily turned around to discover that Little Miss Til had found her way not only into his room but to a spot right behind him.

"Nýi Tilvilg..."

"Yes! What is it, Sir?"

"Here's the deal. I'm pretty tired after such a long week, but I have this one last thing I gotta work out before I hit the hay. I'm really sorry, but unless this is super important, do you think you can save it for another day? Hm?"

——*FML, I can never get to the good part, as usual. I knew this would happen—it's why I kept my boxers on!*

Sora, unsurprised by Til's appearance, made an implicit request for her to leave his room, yet...

"Uh, I can't tell if what I have is more important than whatever it is you need to do—"

...Til, the self-proclaimed *grubby mole*, the sensibility-less Dwarf, was unable to pick up on the situational cues at hand.

"—but what did they mean by the Commonwealth being at a disadvantage? The way I see it, we'd clobber the Front in a battle, we would. How are they even a threat?"

————...........

"Ah... Right... So that's what you wanna talk about..."

——Til's concern was indeed far more significant than whatever lingering task Sora was about to whack away at.

With a deep sigh, the nineteen-year-old reluctantly pulled on his newly repaired jeans, and...

"...Honestly, you moles really need to learn to read the room..."

"Objection: Interruption of Master's important task as well as this unit's observation of it. Now demonstrating extreme disappointment."

"...Til? There's...a little something, called *timing* that...you really ought to learn about... 'Kay...?"

Jibril and Emir-Eins both materialized out of nowhere. They were joined by Shiro, who sluggishly propped herself up from what was—despite Sora's meticulous multifold checks—evidently her feigning being asleep.

The end of Sora's long first year in Disboard culminated in this moment. He stared at the ceiling with a single question on his mind: *Does privacy even exist in this world?*

He lamented over the trampling of his right to himself, though the concept was relatively modern even in his original world.

"D-did I do something bad?! I—I don't wanna die, I don't!!"

"No, Til. It's the exact opposite. Tonight, you've saved me. D-d-don't worry, now it's my turn to save you...!"

There was palpable hostility emanating abundantly from the Flügel, Ex Machina, and twelve-year-old Immanity.

Sora was thankful for Til, who was shrieking in fear. She managed to inadvertently protect what little dignity he had. With quivering knees, he placed himself between her and the three girls menacing her...

"Now that that's over with...I guess we'll start from the top with the current state of Disboard..."

Once Jibril, Emir-Eins, and Shiro were calm, Sora sat Shiro on his crossed legs and began to explain.

"I—I see, I do...," said Til. "But, um, do you think it's really okay for me to be here...?"

The three angry ladies still looked murderous where they were seated next to Til, who was sitting up straight as if on needles. To keep the attention off Til, Sora purposefully ignored her remark and continued:

"First... As was mentioned earlier, the world has been split into two factions: the Commonwealth of Elkia, and—well, quite frankly...the rest of the world that isn't in the Commonwealth: the *Anti-Elkia Commonwealth War Front.*"

——The Anti-Elkia Commonwealth War Front, or what was known colloquially as *the Front.*

The Front was spearheaded by the Elves in Elven Gard and included Dragonia, Gigant, Demonia, and Lunamana, in addition to multiple Phantasmas. It was a massive wealth of power brought together by one goal: the dissolution of the Commonwealth and dominion over its nation-states—which would amount to their individual destruction.

On the other hand:

"There's also us Immanity. Our only nation, Elkia, has split into two factions: those who believe in the Commonwealth—the Kingdom of Elkia—and those who side with the Front—the Republic of Elkia."

While Sora and Shiro were still the rulers of Elkia, and thus, the kingdom's agent plenipotentiary...*they were no longer the agent plenipotentiary for the Immanity race.*

Immanity was divided, and those who marched under the flag of the Front sought one goal: the end of the Commonwealth—which meant *absolute war.* A war that wouldn't end until one of the sides perished—the world was headed for all-out, total war.

Well, it would be, were this Sora's original world. Things worked a bit differently in Disboard, which meant:

"You're right, Til. The Front is barely a threat at all. And that's because they aren't united."

——While the world had been divided into two factions, so long as the Front's primary goal was destruction of its enemy...it was more of an angry mob than anything else.

In the event that they succeeded in their goal—disbanding the Commonwealth and gaining dominion over its nations, and thus, the Commonwealth's destruction—what would become of half of the world's resources, territories, and Race Pieces? What, would they split everything down the middle? Even stephen? That would be ridiculous, and the entire world knew it. As such, a clever name for their so-called alliance wouldn't change the fact that each race individually sought to claim as big a piece of the Commonwealth as they could.

In other words, there was deep-seated inner conflict within the Front. Not only that, but in the event the Commonwealth did fall, the only remaining threats for the races that made up the Front would be each other.

There was virtually no chance of there being any semblance of unity within the enemy forces. To make things even more difficult, they needed to fight in a way that concealed their strongest powers from each other, too.

All this, in addition to the fact that the lead nation of the alliance, Elven Gard, was on the brink of collapse…

"So yeah. There's pretty much no way in hell we'd lose to them in a head-to-head battle."

Four times. That's the number of times Hardenfell and the Eastern Union had challenged the Commonwealth to large-scale war games after war was declared on the Commonwealth, and the number of times Sora and Shiro, with the help of Flügel, Ex Machina, and occasionally Fairy—to use Til's phrasing—*clobbered* their challengers.

As per the Ten Covenants, the challenged reserved the right to decide the game. Should the Front have to fight on the Commonwealth's terms, it would put it at a tremendous disadvantage.

Could what amounted to an angry mob work together, share their secrets, and overcome this…? It was clear that their chances were nonexistent. Which was why four times was enough to know that—

"Inevitability: The Front's battle will not be waged against our alliance but our civilians."

Emir-Eins hit the nail on the head. Since the Front didn't have a shot at winning a war game, the only attack it could make was economical: by hitting the Commonwealth's individual corporations and private citizens.

With that said...

"...Doesn't that make them even less of a threat, though...?" Til offered.

The Commonwealth was by no means inferior to the Front in terms of trade and economy, which made it increasingly difficult to persuade any Commonwealth businesses to defect. Or at least that should've been the case.

"Here, Til. Lemme ask you a question."

Clapping his hands once, Sora said this with a big smile before continuing.

"Imagine a game where two teams are against each other. Team A is strong, but they die if they lose the game. Team B, on the other hand, is weak, but they probably won't die if they lose. Now, which team would you want to play on?"

"B! B! B! Definitely B! 'Cause I don't wanna die, no I do not!"

Til sat up in attention as she replied. Sora's smile never wavered; he nodded and agreed with her.

"Right? That's what most people would do. So in this scenario, Team A is the Commonwealth and Team B is the Front."

"Huh?"

With the stress of everything beginning to appear in Sora's smile, Emir-Eins and Jibril took his place to continue.

"Explanation: The Front's declaration of the Commonwealth's destruction created a situation where its member races could not fight at full capacity. Conversely, it created an environment where it is easy for members of the Commonwealth to betray it. On a civilian level, this environment poses a critically severe problem."

"...It comes back to how we were forced to neglect the republic's rebellion."

＊   ＊   ＊

The Elkian parliament—what was once the Commercial Confederation laden with spies for the other races—was the first group to betray the kingdom by declaring independence and forming the Republic of Elkia. It was a watershed moment where the kingdom, namely Sora and Shiro, needed to come down on the movement with an iron fist.

——Swift and sure punishments and rewards were the foundation of ruling over a kingdom. Letting treason slide would shake a nation at its foundation.

Sora and Shiro, however, were unable to come up with a way to punish the rebels without anyone dying, which forced them to look the other way.

Conversely, the Front was heralding the destruction of the Commonwealth, where the worst-case scenario was forced servitude in its member nations.

This contrast was out in the open for all to see, making the stakes clear for all. Namely:

"…Siding with the Commonwealth…means destruction… If we lose…"

"It stands to reason that siding with the Front, however, isn't as life-or-death, whether they win or lose—"

This was the point.

"From a risk management perspective, it's far too dangerous for anyone to want to stay on our side."

This meant that the Commonwealth was forced into a position where it couldn't take the initiative.

Making no effort to hide their agitation, Sora and Shiro muttered their next lines.

"Basically, the longer we wait, the more people we bleed…until it's *kaput.*"

"…How…annoying…"

This reality was all too clear in Steph's reports. Thanks to Steph's overwhelming competency and rapid execution of political tactics— the most recent coronation ceremony being a good example—the

Kingdom of Elkia was able to appeal its national security to the public, narrowly preventing any further loss of civilians even if it failed to win over the landowners.

Things were even worse for the Eastern Union, though.

Until only half a century ago, the Eastern Union was entrenched in a series of tribal civil wars that spanned over 6,000 years. With the treason committed by the republic going unpunished, it called into question the Shrine Maiden's power to keep those tribes bound together. Though there had been no public disaffections thus far, there was suspicion that many groups had connections with the Front.

When it came to Oceand, the presence of the Dhampir made it possible for them to switch sides at any time.

Even in Avant Heim, support for the Commonwealth within the Council of Eighteen Wings was beginning to sway due to the stagnation of the conflict.

Perhaps surprised by what she'd learned about the inner workings of the member nations of the Commonwealth, Til responded:

"...Wow, I never figured everyone had so much baggage to deal with, I didn't..."

Sora offered the astonished Dwarf a nod of solidarity. "Yeah, that's why I can't stand politics. But just so you know, you guys are the weird ones..."

The Fairies and Foeniculum knew exactly what they were getting into when they joined the Commonwealth, and it was safe to assume Einzig and the Ex Machina wouldn't go back on their promise.

But the Dwarves? There wasn't the slightest hint of a rebellion among them, and the reason for that was:

"*Anything to 'fock' the Elves* isn't a healthy worldview to live by... Just how much do you hate them anyway...?"

The Dwarves' collective insanity aside, the point was that the Commonwealth was slowly falling apart.

Til didn't seem persuaded, though. With her head cocked to the side, she returned to her original question.

"That doesn't change the fact that the Front is still weaker than us, it doesn't. Why not go on the offensive and show 'em who's boss? Especially those talking plants. What better way to teach them a lesson than knocking them down a few pegs?"

——Though a member of the Commonwealth herself, Til appeared to despise the Elves enough to occasionally suggest their destruction.

"I think it would be easier to get the world on our side by showing them the Commonwealth is undefeatable, I do…"

Sora showed a strained grin as he nodded in agreement…

——She was right, after all. While the Ten Covenants made it so that whichever side was the challenger was put at a tremendous disadvantage, this had always been the case for every victory Sora and the group had racked up until this point.

As the Front's inability to cooperate made them weak, then why not take them on individually, just as they had up until then?

Sora needed to answer Til's highly pertinent question.

"You're right. We need to go on the offensive to change the situation. I can see the holes in our enemies' defenses, too. Shiro and I have already thought out a couple of ways to approach this, and we have some of the groundwork set in motion, too."

"So then why…?"

This had Til hopeful—but both Sora and Shiro, and even Jibril and Emir-Eins, were either averting their eyes from her or looking visibly pained.

"…It's just not that easy."

"What? Why's that…?"

Instead of answering the question, the siblings gritted their teeth in frustration.

It was true the Front had neither strategy nor unity on its side. Normally, destroying it would be easy, but—and this was a big but—it made one devastating move that was in full effect.

——Its *declaration to destroy the Commonwealth*... This was made knowing that Sora and Shiro would let it go unpunished. It was also behind the establishment of the republic, the sole purpose of which was to absorb citizens who sought to hedge their risk in the conflict by defecting.

Sora and Shiro were wary of the person behind this, and that kept them from acting. It was the perfect first move, and it was entirely deliberate.

——This was the reality of the situation. One man had snatched the initiative right from Sora and Shiro and kept a tight grip on it.

The siblings were thinking this over...but then:

——*Ka-booooom!!*

Their train of thought was derailed by a massive explosion that rang throughout Elkia.

■■■

The explosion could be heard coming from far outside the castle walls. The residential area, to be exact. Ten seconds before it happened, Jibril and Emir-Eins—likely having sensed something was wrong—averted their gazes to far off in the distance for a moment before taking flight.

Everything was happening all at once, which had Sora and Shiro bewildered. The sound of the blast finally reached the castle—

"Wh-what the frick was that?! What's happening?!"

"...Was that...a meteor crash...?"

"Oh...OH?! I'd, uh, better run... Er, no, there's no time, there isn't. Here, Ma'am, let me borrow the inside of your skirt real qui———ACK!!"

While the siblings were concerned with the blast itself, Til appeared to have an inkling of what had caused it. She jumped to her feet and scurried toward Shiro in a panic.

A screaming Til tried to take refuge in Shiro's skirt, but an arm jutted out of the shadows and grabbed her by the nape of her neck before she could.

Everything was moving far too fast for Sora and Shiro to follow with their meager human eyes, leaving them to have to put the pieces together based on what they saw after the fact, necessitating a few more seconds.

Apparently, someone else had made their way into the room, likely through the window. They could tell it was a man wielding a dagger in his left hand with a greatsword sheathed on his back.

The man—who had rust-colored mithril hair and crimson eyes—lifted Til by the base of her neck with his right hand. He must've demi-shifted here, and with such incredible power making him look much larger than he actually was...

"'Hello, hello, if it ain't my fockin' niece... It's been, what, three months?"

His voice gave it away—the man was...

"Found myself a nice little asteroid, declared it *Planet Big Boobs*, planted myself a fat flag, and came back, ya hear? Are ya happy now?!"

"Oh nooo, that's it for my peaceful life, it is! Sir, Ma'am, I need your help———......... Er, uh, whoa! Uncle...! This is the absolute *worst* you've ever smelled, it is!!"

Til welcomed her uncle with a shriek.

"Aaah, shut yer fockin' trap! I dunno what you expected; there ain't no water in space. Heck, there's no spirits! I didn't have the luxury of using what little drinking water I had to wash myself, thank ya very much."

"Wait, so that makes it...three months since your last bath?! I can't believe this, I can't! Your face was filthy enough, it was! Go take a bath before coming to see me again! Thbbft, thbbft, thbbft!!"

"_____"

Here's what had happened: The Dwarf man, whose genius was lauded as reaching heights that would never emerge again, had made a heartfelt proposal to Til a mere three months earlier—only to be rejected outright, leaving him a broken man.

He was let down hard and told to *go to the planet of big boobs* before ever talking to Til again.

Something he evidently did by becoming the first Ixseed to achieve space flight, finding a small asteroid, planting a flag, and naming it appropriately. Which made the explosion from only moments earlier the sound of his ship landing.

But that was neither here nor there—the man had just returned from space!

Whatever unprecedented genius he had etched into history before was just outdone by a long shot. The world's most powerful Dwarf. A monster of sensibility. A god-level spirit arms smith and a living prodigy.

The agent plenipotentiary of Hardenfell: Veig Drauvnir!!

Back from space, his first attempt to woo his beloved Til was shot down faster than the speed of light. Veig assumed the fetal position, doing everything in his power to keep himself from tearing up... It was a sorry sight to behold.

"Hey...ya best bud's back from space... I wanted to make it in time for yer birthdays..."

After a brief moment, Veig turned to the siblings. He was talking in between sniffles.

"I'm real sorry... I didn't have enough time to getcha any presents... Here're a couple o' rocks I picked up on Planet Big Boobs and some moon I made a pit stop at..."

Veig chucked two pebbles toward Sora and Shiro.

——A rock from an unknown asteroid and a rock from a moon...

Sora and Shiro accepted the small gifts that likely had quite literal astronomical, historical, and scholarly significance.

"R-right. Thanks, I guess. Um, welcome back...?"

"...Be strong...Veig..."

Til was behind them, still dry heaving from whatever she smelled.

Her lack of sympathy for Veig made Sora and Shiro do their best to smile and thank him...

"Right... I'mma go wash up. I'll be back real quick... Sorry, but mind if I borrow your pond? Dammit... I even gave up drinking and smoking while I was in space..."

After his triumphant return from the cosmos, he'd come to see his beloved niece, Til, only to be rejected... He looked down and slumped his shoulders, which carried the weight of his immense talent, sniffling as he made his way to the door, when—

"Yeah, sure thing. But wow, your timing is as impeccable as ever."

It really was superb. This man's senses always led him to the best move.

Sora stopped Veig before he could leave. The Dwarf couldn't have come at a better time.

"There's something I want to talk to you about. If you're willing to keep your shorts on, let's go over it while you wash up."

"Oh...?"

It had to do with the question Til posed only moments earlier.

Sora wanted to know about the mysterious person who seized the conflict's initiative from Sora and Shiro, leaving them unable to act.

He asked Veig:

"What do you know about Auri-El Violhart?"

The Elf agent plenipotentiary and leader of Elven Gard:
Auri-El Violhart...

This man not only saw right through the poison Sora and Shiro had laced the well with, but was trying to use it against them.

He was also the first person to unequivocally defeat Sora and Shiro...to make Blank lose.

"I've researched everything I could about him, and even though I should have enough intel for what I want to know, something about the guy just doesn't make sense."

Sora had information on Auri-El Violhart. It wasn't even difficult to find. Information on his family, his history, and his upbringing was all there.

No matter where Sora looked or whom he asked, he only ever received one answer:

——*For better or worse, the man is perfect.*
Sora's instincts, however, rejected this. His gut told him this couldn't be the case.

Until he and Shiro could learn who Auri-El really was, the war with the Front would be fought in the palm of the Elf's hand.

Should Sora ignore his instincts and go on the offensive, he knew whatever he did would be used against him again, and this time, for good.

Sora was sure of this and, therefore, couldn't act on a whim.

"Veig, I've read that you've fought the guy directly three times before. Not only that, but you've won two of those three battles."

What better person to ask than Veig, someone who'd engaged with Auri-El before?

He had fought Auri-El Violhart in close combat—close enough to likely contest his own soul against his.

So what did the man whose sensibilities and instincts were on an entirely different level think about him?

"Hm...? Oh...that guy...?"

Veig removed his shirt and approached the castle pond, unperturbed by the question.

"Let's see. Settin' aside the fact that he's another blade of that useless long-eared grass..."

Veig muttered his response under his breath:

"...If I had to say it, I suppose he's the world's most annoying man, by a big fat margin."

He shared his instincts—the truth—with a fatigue that came from the pit of his stomach————............

■■■

——At the same time, just outside Elkia Royal Castle's main gates.

Jibril and Emir-Eins sensed a large quantity of mass plummeting toward the ground from a high altitude—Veig's space shuttle.

They knew this almost immediately, but it was no longer significant to them.

Their initial scan of the area led them to a *new spirit response*, which they shifted directly to.

And then—

"My, my. I surely hope a pathetic little Demonia didn't expect to infiltrate Master's castle. ♥"

Jibril's piercing hostility was aimed toward an empty space. However:

"Analysis: Unknown specimen determined to be the final of Demonia's Nine Nightmares—Schira Ha the Wise. Demand: Quickly reveal your intentions. Fail to comply and this unit will prepare to attack."

The living scanner that was Emir-Eins joined her Flügel counterpart in making it clear that crude concealment magic would have little effect in their presence.

"Mweh-heh… It wasn't quite my intention to hide…"

——A young, enchanting woman wearing a dark dress emerged from the emptiness. Her hair was darker and gloomier than the deepest ocean and long enough to touch the floor. Two horns crowned her head—one of which was broken—and from behind her hips sprouted four snakes, each with slitted crimson eyes, just like her own. Her beauty and hideousness were in perfect harmony.

The Demonia woman elegantly clasped her hands together in front of her stomach and used two of the four snakes to hold the hem of her dress for a slow curtsy.

"I arrived a bit too early to pay you a visit, so I decided to quietly wait for morning to come, but… Mweh-heh… It seems my appearance alone was enough to draw you out, and for that, I do apologize."

There was a grace to her. She spoke politely, and with a soft smile. But the tone of her voice sounded as if she was mocking them, and with a belittling gaze, she said:

"It appears you two are members of the *hero's party*. Do you mind if I introduce myself?"

"«« .... »»"

The Demonia asked permission in a way that was both polite and wicked. A confused—but still cautious—Jibril and Emir-Eins silently maintained their diligent watch.

"I would like to give a curse to celebrate this wonderful meeting of ours. My name is Schira Ha—I was created by the Devil and served as one of his Nine Nightmares. Only just recently I was appointed the head of the Devil's Army Joint Chiefs of Staff... Mweh-heh..."

——She was effectively the head of Demonia.

"In the days of yore, I was once recognized for my unparalleled wisdom that surpassed the Devil: me, the wisest of them all! Nonetheless, I am but a humble servant to His Majesty. I am pleased to meet your acquaintance... Mwehhh-heh-heh-heh."

——And she was Demonia's greatest mastermind.

The woman introduced herself with an intelligent, alluring voice that also had a playfully evil edge to it.

Jibril and Emir-Eins remained vigilant—

"Mweh-heh... Now, I must apologize for coming at such a busy time, but I— Oh? My apologies... Where did I put it...?"

Schira Ha was in the middle of bowing politely when she cut herself off and rummaged around in a hidden pocket in her dress until she seemed to find what she was looking for.

"Ah, there it is."

It was a small piece of folded paper: a note. She unfolded it before the two women, who were starting to look just as confused as they were wary.

Schira Ha moved at her own pace, gently clearing her throat before announcing:

"Let's see... **Listen all, far and wide! We have come to announce**

your despair, *cough!* **...Tremble with fear—the time has come for the Devil's Army to finally destroy the world!!** ...That's all, *cough!*"

Her throat must have hurt from reading the note, for her eyes were tearing up.

Nevertheless, she finished by thanking Jibril and Emir-Eins for listening to her declaration and curtsied once more.

"Mweh-heh... As such, the two of you will be obliterated. I hope you're ready!!"

The four sets of snake-tail eyes narrowed with aggression— however.

"" .... """

Jibril and Emir-Eins—both of races that were once irreconcilable enemies—looked at each other and, curiously enough, found they shared the same dubious expression.

——*Demonia's so-called mastermind isn't challenging us both to a game at the same time, is she...?*

"Mweh-heh...! Now, challenge me to whatever sort of game you may!!"

——Evidently, she was.

The pair just shrugged. The Demonia, meanwhile, awaited their response to her wicked challenge with an oddly elegant stance.

...*Okay? Then, uh, let the game begin...?*

The two obliged—

—only to clobber this Schira Ha the Wise character in a grand total of three minutes.

⏻ CHAPTER 1
PHANTASMA
THE DEVIL APPEARS!

Four days passed after the final day of the coronation ceremony. The VIPs and special envoys from each nation were on their way home, and the cleanup had just finished.

Elkia Grand National Library—Jibril's archives.

Sora and Shiro were now on the fourth of Izuna's do-whatever-you-want-for-a-day tickets—sharing her thoroughly fluffed tail as a pillow while they read a book, thus in the midst of experiencing supreme bliss—when:

"…Sooo, uh…shouldn't you be on your way back to Hardenfell?"

"…Why are…you…still here…?"

——The siblings addressed a loud noise that came from the corner of the library. It was a person hammering away at something.

"Huh? What do you mean by 'why'? My current home is with you, it is. No?"

——*Wait… I'm not misunderstanding something, am I? Are you two trying to abandon me?*

Til stopped hammering and immediately began shivering like a young puppy. Her rusty-blue orichalcum eyes filled with tears.

"I guess it's fine," said Sora, "but if you're gonna stick around, maybe we should figure out the whole older-sister bit—?"

True, Til was there due to a series of misunderstandings, but Sora and Shiro didn't really have any reason to chase her out.

That said, Sora did take this opportunity to address Til's three-month-long insistence that she was the *older-sister* type, though it fell flat because anything he said after *I guess it's fine* was entirely lost on Til.

"But wow!! Can you believe these Flügel archives? It's a veritable treasure chest filled with texts on magic theory, it is!! I'm making so much progress on my spirit arms here, I am!! And I also get to be with my two favorite people: That's you, Sir and Ma'am! Not to mention, I can have materials brought here from Hardenfell—ah…it's like a dream workshop here, it is!!"

This room has everything I want and everyone I want to be with in it… I've found my paradise, I have!

The gleam in Til's eyes conveyed this sentiment, but she wasn't finished:

"And my stupid uncle is already home, he is! He and the goons who made me the chieftain by proxy while he was away won't impact my life any further, they won't! I hated those asshats enough already, I did! I'm never gonna go back now that my uncle's there! Thbbft!"

This place was Til's own Shangri-la, and she made it clear that Veig's absence was a big part of that. Sora watched her, and his "best bud," wherever he may have been, surfaced in his mind…

…You're gonna be okay, Veig—never give up.

Til is working on her spirit arms—she still wants to surpass you! That means you should still have a shot! Or…I think so, kinda sorta maybe…?

Anywho—better fireproof the library ASAP for when Til's spirit arms inevitably explode.

He took out his smartphone and added emergency planning for such an event to his long list of tasks. Once finished, he found himself staring aimlessly at the screen, lost in deep thought, before eventually muttering to himself.

"...I think I see a way out of this, but...the Front has yet to make any real moves..."

Just as Sora had assured Til a few days earlier, he already had a few plans set in motion. All of these, however, required the enemy to make their move and show an opening before ideally kicking into gear.

On the other hand, if the Commonwealth continued to do nothing, it would slowly bleed supporters. It didn't look like the ideal opportunity to attack was going to show itself anytime soon.

Sora was beginning to find the resolve to make that first move, even if it meant swallowing the risk involved, when...

".....Memory lapse: ——. Ah."

"I—I am so very sorry, Master!! I-it appears that I have completely forgotten—"

——For the past four days these two had kept themselves hidden.

Jibril and Emir-Eins were waiting for Sora to use their selfies— or perhaps more aptly, they were waiting to see whose selfies Sora would view first. But Sora had yet to view either—and the pair reappeared, each lowering their head in sorrow as they shared new information.

Information that broke both Sora's and Shiro's brains.

"The ex-head of the Devil's Army, Schira Ha, has come to see you on behalf of Demonia..."

......

............?

"——————————They're here?! When, exactly, did they come?! There's a representative from Demonia in Elkia?!" Sora hollered at the two, who lowered their heads even farther.

"...W-well, not quite... She is..."

"Disclosure: The representative arrived eighty-nine hours prior. Apology/Penitence: Her arrival was eliminated from this unit's memory banks. I'm sorry."

The pair were clearly sorry about this newly divulged information. Not only Sora and Shiro, but Til, and even Izuna, who'd been sleeping up until that point, all eyed Jibril and Emir-Eins questioningly...

■ ■ ■

"Mweh-heh-heh... I've been waiting to meet you for quite some time."

Once they remembered their guest—Jibril and Emir-Eins brought everyone to where they were keeping Schira Ha. They were joined by Steph, who arrived in a panic.

"By Demonia's greatest wisdom vested in me by the all-powerful Devil, I, Schira Ha the Wise—ex-head of the Joint Chiefs of Staff for the Devil's Army—was able to foretell your...eventual...appearance before me... Mweh-heh-heh!"

Schira Ha was a captivatingly beautiful, though somewhat dim-witted-looking woman, who showed a wicked smile from behind the bars.

She looked at her seven visitors with rainbow-colored eyes that were split down the middle by long, thin pupils.

"I was beginning to think you may have forgotten about me, which made me feel so sad and lonely...but it seems my suspicions were unwarranted, O party of Heroes. I applaud you, for you have managed to effectively torture me without breaking the Covenants. Mweh-heh-heh-heh-heh...*sniffle*."

Given her so-called wisdom, it should've been abundantly clear that they had indeed forgotten about her. Or maybe she didn't want to accept the truth. Though Schira Ha seemed somewhat gaunt—she must've been in the jail for four days and four nights without food and water—her eyes still had a lively brightness to them, even if they were slowly tearing up.

* * *

"Okay, Jibril and Emir-Eins. Let's start off with an explanation of...... Actually, scratch that. First—"

...*Gurrrgllle...*

From the belly of she who called herself Schira Ha the Wise came a loud rumbling.

"Let's get this lady something to eat—er, you know what, Steph? Why don't we take this to the banquet hall..."

"Y-yes... But of course... I'll have some food prepared for her, on the double!"

Sora and Steph got to work making their poor—no, elegant—guest feel right at home.

■■■

"Right... So how 'bout we start with a review of Demonia?"

Sora sat down at the table in the banquet hall with the group and their almost forgotten guest. He put his elbow on the table and rested his cheek on his knuckles before turning to his friends with his question.

——After a year in this world, a good portion of which Sora and Shiro had spent researching its races, they had significant information on the Demonia from both Elkia's and Jibril's archives. Nevertheless, Sora wanted to brush up on the topic, and it was Jibril who came forward with a bow.

"——Ixseed Rank Eleven, Demonia."

The name "Demonia" encompassed all of the various subspecies that originated from their single territory: Garad Golm.

Emphasis on *various*—evidently, there were many types of Demonias who shared little to no qualities with one another. There were orcs, goblins, slimes, skeletons, chimeras, and so on and so forth. From an earthly perspective, they were what people would typically call *monsters*. The race even contained humanoids, like Schira Ha. She was considered a *demon*.

The explanation went on:

"Demonias range from beings barely capable of communication to highly intelligent. A truly diverse race—"

It wasn't only their appearance, but their temperaments as well—even their intelligence varied greatly. Just as it said in Jibril's archives, Demonia's vast diversity made it almost difficult to consider them a single race.

"The race was originally created by a mutant Phantasma known as the Devil. This is thought to be the reason that, despite the diversity, all Demonias share the same greater goal, which is the world's destruction."

"Uh-huh..."

Sora nodded along, aware of everything Jibril had said so far.

——*A race created by the Devil...who wants to destroy the world...*

It was a tale as old as time, and though it raised a glaring contradiction, the siblings kept this to themselves for now.

"So...what's a Demonia doing here...?"

Sora motioned to the woman who was eating up Steph's home-cooked meal, her first in four days. Schira Ha did make it a point to be mindful of her manners as she quietly continued to cut the food on her plate and eat it.

The group watched dubiously before one member turned to Sora and replied...

"Report: Spirit response sensed from the castle gates ninety hours ago."

"Right..."

"When we confronted our visitor, she stated she wished to declare our destruction," Jibril added. "Specifically, she challenged us both to a game which wagered ownership of the loser's everything, including their life..."

"...Go on...?"

"Result: This unit selected speed chess. Victory was claimed within one hundred seventy-three point six seconds, gaining us ownership of this specimen and her rights."

"...I-is that so...?"

Jibril and Emir-Eins finished their matter-of-fact relay of what happened, to which Sora responded somewhat confusedly. He then spoke for the room in addressing Schira Ha directly.

"So...you mean to tell me you challenged Jibril, a Flügel, and Emir-Eins, an Ex Machina, to a 2v1...? You gotta be pretty dumb to do that..."

——As per the Ten Covenants, the challenger was always at an incredible disadvantage. On top of this, Schira Ha had challenged this world's two most OP races at the same time...

...Huh? Am I misremembering it? I'm pretty sure this lady intro-duced herself as Demonia's wisest earlier, didn't she...?

——If her self-introduction was indeed true, then it could mean something bad for Demonia...

"Affirmative: This unit produced the same conclusion. This unit also took the treatment of this specimen into consideration."

Sora listened in utter shock as Emir-Eins made her agreement with his assessment clear and continued her report.

"Course of events: Irregular Number insisted 'Just kill your-self. ♥ One more body count for me! ♥' This unit denied suggestion. Specimen was detained pending Master's directive—until the mat-ter was temporarily lost from this unit's memory banks. I'm sorry."

...Uh...okay...

"I guess it was good that you stopped Jibril's idea. GG. And you were right to wait for my decision."

Sora commended Emir-Eins for avoiding a plan that would result in a dead body, but...

"...Isn't it...weird that...Emir-Eins...forgot something...?"

While Emir-Eins was at times—well, most of the times—a bit fallible despite being an infallible machine, was it possible for a machine to *accidentally* forget something...?

Shiro had mumbled her suspicions out loud, but it was Jibril who answered:

"Well, you see...Demonia, as they stand now, are neither an enemy nor an ally of the Commonwealth—they are a completely meaningless race..."

"Conclusion: The Devil vanished four hundred and eight years ago. Demonia's threat level without him determined to be minuscule. Schira Ha the Wise's capture not deemed a priority significant enough to interrupt Master's morning routine. Accrual of active tasks resulted in loss of data... I'm sorry. Now transferring this specimen's rights to Master."

The two were deeply apologetic about the mistake.

Ownership of Schira Ha was so unceremoniously passed to Sora and Shiro, who stood there confused.

——*Demonias are a completely meaningless race that can't take sides?*

——*Not only that, but the Devil has been absent for four hundred and eight years...?*

Sora wanted to learn more about these two statements, but before he could ask...

"Mweh-heh-heh... My purpose in coming here is to correct those very misconceptions—"

Having finished her meal, Schira Ha politely wiped her mouth with a napkin and gave an evil, albeit airheaded, laugh.

She then stopped and let out a small "Oops" to herself before bowing her head to Steph.

"That was very delicious. I thank you for your kindness... Mweh-heh."

"Oh? Um, yes… It was nothing, really…?"

Schira Ha then clasped her hands together. There was a refinement to her mannerisms, such as her speech and gestures. She finished showing her appreciation for Steph's kindness with a forced, out-of-place evil cackle that had everyone confused.

As soon as Schira Ha lifted her head, she flashed an even wickeder grin and raised her right hand.

"""_____?!"""

Her gently clenched fist must have signaled something; Jibril, Emir-Eins, Izuna, and even Til—everyone who wasn't an Immanity—instinctively struck a battle stance.

One of Schira Ha's snake tails took out what looked like a cue card——

"Um, let's see… 'Behold, mortals! Abandon all hope! The Devil cometh once again!'——*cough!*"

Schira Ha read the card in a loud voice, coughing as she opened her raised hand.

The sky was immediately engulfed in darkness. Thunder roared, and the wind began whirling heavily around the group.

"_____?!"

Sora was the only one to notice that Til had turned pale as she let out an audible *gulp…*

The world began melting around them.

They watched as everything swirled into a twisted mess centered around the open palm Schira Ha held high above her head.

Before they knew it, the group was no longer in the banquet hall but in an empty field… The sky was bloodred, and the thunder was even louder. It felt like the world could fall apart at any second. There were jet-black clouds swirling directly above them, from which black tendrils began oozing downward…

* * *

"——What the frick…?"

Sora managed to say something, although he very clearly sounded afraid.

But wait—this world was protected by the Ten Covenants: No harm could be done to anyone here. Whatever they were watching wasn't reality. Sora knew it must've been an illusion. This knowledge, however, provided little comfort for the overwhelming anxiety and frustration welling up inside him and his companions.

Something's coming… Something that none of us can control…

And sure enough, something did come. The threads of darkness that melted from the clouds fell into one spot, culminating in a cluster of inconceivable darkness.

The words spoken next sucked all hope from any life nearby.

"I am the Hope-Consuming Beast—"

It was the incarnation of fear and despair…

"I am the destroyer of all, an immortal illusion—"

An evil that consumed all life.

"Poor, hapless souls fated only to die, I beckon you! Have you mere mortals enjoyed your four centuries of fleeting tranquility?"

Upon hearing this new voice, their minds were blank, but they knew. The sheer impact of the spectacle made it very clear what was happening and who the owner of the voice was.

"Foolish mortals! It appears you've forgotten my name! Then I shall speak it—!"

As these words were heard, two black wings unfurled, causing the sky above to clear up. The swirling clouds of darkness above shattered into a million pieces, which fell to the open field under the bloodred sky that shone above. The broken pieces of darkness condensed into a single point, where *he* appeared, and exclaimed:

"'I—am—*the Devil*…!!"

* * *

..............,

........................,

Everyone stood there, staring in silence at what the darkness had become: the Devil himself. His body was covered in beastly hair, and he sprouted a pair of black wings. His golden eyes scowled at the group.

"...Ah. It appears my imposing figure has left you speechless... This is inevitable, I suppose, for not even the most *valiant of heroes* could gaze upon this visage of utter despair unperturbed. I shall grant you the time you need to find your courage once more, O heroes."

The Devil flashed a delighted, wicked smile.

"——I see what's happening. Your despair, your fear... They are but symbols of your reverence for me. Then it is with the utmost generosity that I shall forgive you weaklings for your insolent silence. Ha... Mwa-ha-ha... GAAAAAH-HA-HA-HA-HA-HA-HA-HAAA!!"

The self-proclaimed Devil proceeded to laugh loudly for a good while.

But you see, his audience's silence was...not quite out of reverence—

"...That's...not *actually* him, is it—?"

Sora was the first to say something, but Schira Ha cut him off, speaking quickly while maintaining her usual politeness.

"Mweh-heh-heh... Ah, my deepest apologies, but I'm rather preoccupied with relishing in the Devil being in such high spirits for the first time in many moons. If you would please listen quietly, then."

...Uh, sure...

Sora, dumbfounded by it all, zipped his trap. He looked away from Schira Ha and back at...*him.*

The Devil wasn't wrong: Everyone was indeed speechless at his form...or maybe his "character design" would be a more fitting description.

* * *

All that darkness had condensed in one spot to form: a puny, black furball…

With soft-looking paws and fluffy-looking fur, he was a cute little…*something.*

His wings were actually big, long ears that…well, did seem to flap to keep him aloft.

To put it frankly, he was small and round…like a cute Pok*mon…

The terror everyone felt during the buildup to his appearance—that was real. The voice gave it away pretty early, though… The over-the-top lines and loud laughter were…well, here's an example: It was like listening to a voice actress famous for loli-girls branching out to *shota* characters… He had a cutesy, high-pitched voice that was easy on the ears—and super adorable.

The Devil's attempts to be imposing only enhanced how cute he sounded.

"Fear me! Hail me! Weep before me!! The time has cometh for the Devil's Army to conquer this divided world!!"

Yeah…anything he said just sounded cute.

The Furball King was using his aggressively cutesy voice to declare something.

"And to the fools who will fight until the very end: You, O Heroes—you have my pity! How you persevere despite your inescapable terror! How you so courageously fight the despair by clinging to whatever little hope remains! That foolhardiness is precisely what makes you worthy of my favor!! Ha-ha-ha… MWAAA-HA-HA-HA-HA!!"

With that, the Furball King cackled adorably, spread his wings—or, uh, ears?—and…

…once more, the surrounding space warped. The open field under the bloodred sky turned into a massive forest. They could see the creepily dark silhouette of a tall tower appear within the depths of the forest.

...It was difficult to tell whether the Devil was controlling their vision or if he was manipulating the world itself. What they saw, however, was a cinematic aerial shot of the ground moving underneath them.

As the tower approached, the group soon realized that what they'd initially thought was a forest was actually a great army that covered the entirety of the land they stood on. It was composed of goblins and orcs and many other monsters with names none of them knew. Upon closer inspection, there were even what looked to be Elves and Dragonias in the mix.

——It was a sight to behold. The army really did look capable of destroying the world. There was even ominous background music playing. But in one corner of the shot were the following words written in Immanity:

THE DEVIL'S ARMY (VISUAL RENDERING)

The group remained speechless. The Furball King continued to flap about, cackling, while the scene moved away from the tip of the tower, until their vision went dark. The first thing that came into view was a new set of Immanity words, which the Devil read aloud with his cute voice...

COMING SOON: THE END OF THE WORLD

—————————,

In the next few moments, the group found themselves back in Elkia Royal Castle's banquet hall. They were no longer in an open field, or gazing down at an ominous tower. Whatever movie they'd just watched had come to an end; it was indeed an illusion.

Which left them with the reality——

"Mwa-ha-ha!! What do you think, Schira Ha?! How was I?! Charismatic, yes?!"

"Indeed, you were, Your Evilness!! You were so, so cute—I mean awe- and fear-inspiring! I was moved to tears by the show!! Mweh-heh..."

"Gahhh-ha-ha!! Then see to it that the Film Division is rewarded heavily for their fine work!!"

"Ah, you must forgive me, Your Evilness! For your Schira Ha is currently a prisoner—"

"Mm?! Ah, yes! Yes, of course. Then it will be from my own personal allowance that I shall bestow upon thee a snack!!"

"Oh! Your Evilness! Your kindness moves me so. I think I may just cry!"

With the illusion now over, all that remained were the tiny, black furball—the Devil—and Schira Ha, who tearfully praised his every word.

Sora, who had cringed through the entire show and was still cringing, eventually broke the ice.

"Um... So, uh, did you want us to call you Schira Ha...?"

"——Pardon? Ah...yes. You heroes have captured me, so you are free to call me whatever you please... Uh, mweh-heh-heh..."

"Okay... Also, you don't gotta force yourself to laugh at the end of every sentence."

——*It's pretty obvious that laugh's out of character for you anyway...*

Schira Ha responded by lowering her head with an ever-so-elegant smile.

"Mweh-heh... I appreciate your offer, but it is my duty as head of the Joint Chiefs of Staff to use this laugh... I may have relinquished my position, but it seems fitting to still use it."

So the laugh is a part of the job...

The elegant Schira Ha continued to use her evil laugh, which only added to the raging storm of questions in Sora's mind. He was trying to figure out where he should start, when...

"...Argh...I'm...I'm sorry, please... I can't take this shit anymore, please!!"

"Ack! H-hey, Schira Ha! What is this blasted puppy?!"

——Ever since the Devil appeared, Izuna had been on all fours, ready to pounce. She'd been wagging her tail relentlessly but must've run out of patience because she leaped right at him.

"Have you lost your mind, foul cur?! A hero you may be, but does your pluck know no bounds?!! Do you not realize that this is THE DEVIL you are attacking?!"

The furball gave a cute little shriek, but that didn't stop the young Werebeast from latching onto him. Evidently...something about his form excited Izuna's inner beast.

She then proceeded to bat him around like a cat toy.

".......Okay, let's start with a few questions. First—"

Having taken some time to figure everything out, Sora began by asking what he'd initially tried to ask earlier.

Namely:

"It's just...uh, you're basically a walking, talking stuffed animal... So you're really the actual, genuine Devil, in the flesh...?"

"Unhand meee! I told you I would go easy on you weaklings, but I have my limits, too, don'cha know?!"

The furball, eyes tearing up as he spoke, could not escape Izuna's clutches.

——Surely, he was the Devil's familiar...or something... Or perhaps his form had been manipulated.

In any case, Sora wondered if he was actually the true-blue Devil.

"Mweh-heh-heh... Verily, we are in the magnificent presence of the Devil!"

Schira Ha lowered her head with respect for her furball ruler, who was squirming to escape, before adding:

"More specifically, *the Tower and the Domain located in our nation are the Devil's body.* The form you see before you is but a small fragment of His Evilness's *core.* While this may be only the smallest glimpse of his great power, you are indeed feasting your eyes on the Devil himself. Mweh-heh..."

* * *

"……Okey-dokey…"

"…The Devil…is fluffy…"

"Listen, pooch! I am the DEVIL!! This is BLASPHEMY!! You dare GNAW upon the DEVIL'S hide?!"

For whatever reason, Izuna started nipping the furball—which evidently was the Devil, even if it wasn't his entire body.

Which meant that the words they heard spoken during the video before had been his own.

"Mweh-heh… Incidentally, we do make to-scale stuffed animals of the Devil in this form, and they sell like hotcakes. Demonia's finest artisans place great emphasis on the texture of His Evilness's fur and fluffiness. Would you like one? Mweh-heh-heh…"

Schira Ha produced said stuffed animal as she spoke.

——*I kinda do…*

Izuna was already using the actual Devil as a toy, but Shiro, Steph, and even Sora found themselves vaguely wanting a plushie of their own.

"Uh…let's save that for later," said Sora. "Mind if I ask my next question…?"

"…Mweh-heh… How unfortunate… Just look how absolutely cute—I mean *terrifying* he is…"

Schira Ha, with her wicked smile, quickly put the stuffed animal away, looking somewhat upset as she did.

Having confirmed the premise of the current circumstances, Sora moved on to a series of bigger questions, which he barked out in order, one after another.

Those being——

"Why're you gonna destroy the world *now* of all times?! Can't it wait?! Could'ja read the frickin' room?!"

* * *

——The Elkia Commonwealth and the Anti-Elkia Commonwealth War Front...

The world was split into two factions that were deadlocked in a war of attrition!! It didn't get much more finicky than this, and now a *third party* was getting involved?!

"Stop trying to make things more complicated! Wouldn't you guys be on the Front's side anyway?!"

The stress of it all made Sora claw at his head, but...

"...Mweh-heh-heh? I'm not quite sure how to respond to the question."

Schira Ha merely offered her trademark evil laugh along with some confusion of her own.

"With half the world's population marching under Demonia's flag, the Devil has risen again. Is this not a better time than ever to destroy the world? Mweh-heh-heh."

Schira Ha sincerely tried to answer his question—*I may require more time to come up with a proper answer*—when Sora realized:

She has a point...

He nodded firmly, recognizing his mistake, but then discovered he was overlooking one teeny-tiny detail...

"Could you not destroy the world *ever*?! And you keep calling the Devil's Army half the world—are you including *the Front* in your little head count?!"

Sora also had thought this during the video earlier. The Devil referred to himself as if he *was* the Front.

Did the Devil—and all Demonia, for that matter—fancy themselves as spearheading the Front's offensive?!

Is the entire race, including its creator, a bunch of idiots?!

Sora was beginning to get an actual headache as he ran through all this when:

"Mweh-heh... My deepest apologies, but I'm not quite sure what you mean by that question," Schira Ha replied as she politely cocked her head to one side. "The Front's victory means destruction, and beyond their initial victory awaits further war. That certainly would not be a prosperous future for the world. Perhaps it is the wisdom vested in me that makes it clear that their true and final desire is for the world's destruction. Mweh-heh-heh..."

——*Any sentient being should understand this much.*

Schira Ha had shown that she truly was puzzled by Sora's premise, in a way that was almost arrogant. Sora, Shiro, and Steph fell silent, which Schira Ha must've taken as them agreeing with her, because she continued...

"As such, it is our best interpretation that the Front has succumbed to the Devil and his army's ultimate objective of global annihilation and joined his forces. This ambitious objective, which would have been impossible to accomplish alone, has now become feasible with the assistance of half the world. Truly remarkable, isn't it? Mweh-heh!"

Schira Ha the Wise was trembling with excitement. Her haphazard use of her evil laugh actually felt wicked this time.

——*This lady might legit be as wise as she says. Or at least...wiser than anyone in the Front...*

Sora set aside these new doubts—ones he wished he could object to—and moved on:

"Fine—one more thing. I want you to answer this question you keep dancing around..."

Sora took a deep breath to ask his final question: the one on everyone's mind, the premise to everything...

"Why do you wanna destroy the friggin' world in the first place?!"

This was Disboard—a fantasy world.

Sora had heard about the Devil before, and the idea of the Devil wanting to destroy, or maybe take over, the world was a tale as old as time itself, so he'd never given it a second thought. But now that the threat was staring him in the face, it seemed absurd. He needed an answer to this basic question, one that was only occasionally asked in the fantasy works of his own world.

And that was:

"Won't you guys die if you destroy the world?! Why, tho?! What's the friggin' point?!"

——*If you wanna commit suicide, go ahead, but keep the rest of the world out of it!!*

There were a lot of stories in Sora's mind as he asked this honest question. However—

"Mweh-heh... The reason for that is............. Hmm...? What was it again?"

————,

"I suppose when push comes to shove, it is purely because the Devil desires it... It is a bit strange, though, upon further reflection. Pardon me, Your Evilness, but have you ever considered why you wish to destroy the world? Mweh-heh..."

Schira Ha tossed the question to the Devil, as if the thought had never crossed her mind.

"Oh?! Why, you ask? That's because I am the DEVIL!!"

"Of course! Oh, Your Evilness, I beg your forgiveness for asking such a glaringly obvious question."

"You are forgiven! Now, do something about this pooch!"

She seemed satisfied enough with the Devil's answer even as Izuna kicked him around like a ball. Sora, on the other hand...

"Jiiibriiiill! These idiots haven't fleshed out their backstory! The hell is this world's 'Devil' anyway?!"

...wanted a proper explanation for the insanity.

■■■

The group relocated once more, this time to the throne room. But a change of scenery didn't bring an end to the adorable cries for help…

"Somebody, release me from this canine's clutches this instant, or face my wrath! I am THE DEVIL, don't you know?!"

"Nuh-uh…please. This shit's mine now. I'm not coughing it up to anyone, please."

It seemed Izuna had taken a strong liking to her new Devil plaything. With cute, bleary eyes, she pleaded with Sora not to give up her new favorite toy.

He nodded with a gentle smile, then turned to the Devil and said:

"No… You're *not* the Devil."

"What say you?! I *am* the Devil! Gaze upon me!!"

"The more I look at you, the more I know that's a lie, but anyway: The fact of the matter is, you're not the Devil," Sora insisted.

Izuna was infringing on the Devil's will by using him as a toy; the fact that she could *make the Devil a toy* was all the evidence Sora needed:

"You're *a piece of the Devil*—a piece that Schira Ha possessed when she came here—not the actual thing. In other words, you're Schira Ha's possession. And we own Schira Ha's everything, and ipso facto, her possessions."

"_____"

——Therefore, this fuzzy little Devil was not protected by the Ten Covenants.

"Which means, there's nothing you or anyone can do to stop Izuna from using you as a toy… Sorry, but you're NGMI."

"But there is! If Schira Ha owns this piece of me, then either you or she can make this pooch stop!!"

"That's where you're wrong, though."

"…'Cause…we don't, feel like…stopping her…"

"I am so deeply sorry, Your Evilness! Now that I've fallen into the clutches of the heroes, there is little I can do… Ah, the way this young girl is treating you is so adora—I mean terrible!"

"Schira Ha!! I can see that you, too, have no desire to help— Hey— stop spinning me around!!"

With it established that no one present had any second thoughts about the Devil becoming a toy, Izuna started playing with the ball of fur much more vigorously. As Schira Ha enjoyed the show, the group reconvened:

"Explanation: Specimen known as the Devil is a mutant Phantasma, Ixseed Rank Two."

"To put it simply, Phantasmas are defined as *living phenomena*."

Emir-Eins and Jibril obeyed their master's orders for information about the Devil by starting with an explanation of Phantasma.

"Phantasmas are based on phenomena that happened in the past or historic realities still unfolding now. The mass awe and fear derived from these phenomena manifest in a physical form and take on an existence of their own."

——*Yeah, that makes no sense...*

Sora and Shiro rolled their eyes. Phantasma were second only to literal gods... Their existence didn't have to make sense.

"Some examples include: a floating landmass, a fog that causes everything it touches to decay, and a continent-sized storm—all of which are based on past calamities that gained sentience resulting in Phantasmal forms."

"Logical: No new Phantasma specimens observed following establishment of the One True God. Phantasma is a race of individual specimens that survived the Great War."

"...Oooh..."

"...Riiight. I get it...?"

The siblings seemed to at least get the gist of things.

——There were earthquakes and tidal waves in their own world, and stories of mythical monsters that resembled these calamities throughout its history.

Bahamut and earthquakes, Typhon and typhoons, Vritra and droughts, Orochi and floods—in any culture, there were natural calamities personified as monsters.

...Honestly, it was impressive that Immanity had managed to survive the Great War at all...

"That being said, the mutant known as the Devil is quite unique in many ways."

Jibril and Emir-Eins continued their explanations now that Sora and Shiro had grasped the concept of a Phantasma.

"The Devil was born from a phenomenon that has yet to happen: the world's destruction. Therefore, its form is not a set re-creation of a specific calamity but more fluid in nature in order to bring about said destruction—or so it is thought."

"Specification: The Devil is an indiscriminate attack to end all life. Methods: Creation of Demonia and expansion of the Devil's domain."

"The Devil is also a Phantasma shrouded in mystery, particularly in his behavior patterns—he calls those who seek to destroy him 'heroes' and invites them to his core: the Tower."

"Supplement: So long as a Phantasma's core remains intact, it will revive with time. Paradox: Destruction of Phantasma core results in Phantasma host's destruction... The Devil's core is located in the Tower. Objective behind inviting enemies inside remains unclear."

Right...

Sora and Shiro were at a loss with this information.

So the Devil was the potential for the world's destruction, which was why he sought to destroy the world without having any real reason to do so?

But at the same time, he invited what he called "heroes" to try and stop him...

Mulling over what he learned from Jibril's and Emir-Eins's explanations, Sora looked to the ball of fur Izuna was batting around.

——I see. That explains why he calls us "heroes." In which case...

"Well, since we have the head honcho here, let's see what he has to say... Hey, Furball: Why're you contradicting yourself?"

The Devil welcomed those who sought to destroy him.

Sora didn't expect to get a real answer out of him, and he was right:
"Mwa-ha-ha-ha, AHHH-HA-HA!! Foolish hero!! I do so because
I—AM THE DEVIL!!"

"Yeah, this is getting us nowhere. Izuna, be a little rougher with
him for me, will ya?"

"Whoa?! Wait—why?! Was that not the perfect answer, Schira Ha?!"

"Indeed, Your Evilness. You answered perfectly and with unri-
valed cuteness. Mweh-heh…"

Sora left the Devil and his yes-woman, who only gave nonanswers,
for Izuna to deal with.

Considering the inanity of this evil furball, there was a new question on his mind…

"…With this li'l nugget calling the shots, I'm surprised Demonia
survived the Great War in the first place…"

Flügel, Ex Machina, and Old Deus had spent the war massacring
each other indiscriminately…

With the world having come to the brink of complete destruction,
this little guy must've been all over the place challenging everyone.

Not only that, but he most likely rolled out the red carpet to his
Tower—and core—each time…

*Forget about the world… Maybe he's on a mission to speed-run his
own self-destruction?* Sora wondered dubiously, but he didn't need to
wait long to receive an answer.

"Indeed. Regretfully, it was physically impossible to defeat the
Devil."

"Record: During the Great War, Ex Machina invaded the Devil's
Tower sixteen times. All dispatched units were lost in each attempt."

——Spelled out in plain terms by Emir-Eins: Not even the god-
slaying cyborg race could defeat the Devil.

She and Jibril continued calmly explaining things while the others listened in shock.

"The Phantasma known as the Devil is called by many a name due
to his peculiar nature."

"Examples: The Phantom of Destruction. The Black Nightmare. The Hope-Consuming Beast. The Apparatus of Ruin, and..."

——*The Domain of Despair...*

"As his name suggests—the Devil harbors within him *a domain that consumes all hope.*"
"_____"

"Explanation: Upon infiltrating the Domain of Despair, living beings—organic, inorganic, tangible, intangible—lose any and all hope, which is then unconditionally consumed by the Devil. Observed results include suicide or cessation of essential functions. No known methods to bypass this effect exist."

"Those who challenge the Devil lose their will not only to fight, but to live, resulting in their death."

Everyone listening was at a loss for words, but the two weren't finished yet.

"Furthermore, no one has ever returned from entering the Devil's Tower."

"Inevitability: All available information is based on what occurs outside the Tower. Data unconfirmed."

This meant:

"The Devil is the area he controls, centered around the giant Tower. The world inside his Tower grows as time passes, until it spills over and encroaches into the real world."
"_____"

"With this being the case, there were many who tried to defeat the Devil during the Great War."

"Established: Recorded attempts by Ex Machina, Flügel, Dwarf, Elf, and two weaker Old Dei. Report: Zero records of success."

Not even a god could overcome the despair.

It spread across the land, leaving all those it consumed void of hope.

So what would become of the world if this domain ever fully engulfed it?

* * *

"Disclosure: Largest expansion of the Demon Lord's territory on Ex Machina record is of the entire continent of Galarm. This included up to forty-seven percent of the two neighboring continents as well. All signs of life in the encroached areas were confirmed to cease."

After Jibril and Emir-Eins finished...

"_____........."

...Sora, Shiro, and Steph were speechless. All of this was outrageous beyond comprehension. They now understood why the phenomenon was referred to as despair.

What's more:

"Hold up—this goddamn F*rby is responsible for these horrors?! You're breaking my brain right now!!"

"Gahhhh-ha-ha!! You fools! Do you now understand the DEVIL'S WRATH?!"

The Devil—a furball capable of unimaginable destruction— laughed maniacally, only to...

"Now that you understand, how about you GET THIS POOCH OFF ME?! I'm getting drenched in drool over here!!"

...continue pleading for help to make Izuna release him. Apparently, the little Werebeast had been too focused on using the Devil as her personal plaything to pay attention to his explanation.

But Sora and the others were in no place to pay him any mind, either. They left him to Izuna while they groaned among themselves.

"So if the Devil expands the territory he controls—this *Domain of Despair*—to the entire world, then it'll actually cease to exist?"

This was a force of nature that not even a god could defeat, one that would end all life on Disboard on a whim.

To think that very force of nature was a cute stuffed animal with the voice of a toddler ...

Sora, Shiro, and Steph were amending their initial impression of the little guy as a threat—a change that took considerable effort—when...

*   *   *

"Negative: Ah, Master. You needn't worry about that."

"Indeed. For while the Devil may be undefeatable, incapacitating him was very simple. ♪"

...Jibril and Emir-Eins made it clear that there was no need for such measures.

Despite all the talk of despair, they were pretty relaxed about the entire thing.

"Explanation: By attacking the entire area that contains the Tower housing the Devil's core, his territory could be literally *vaporized*. This created a minimum of eight years until his next revival."

"His core remained unscathed, so he will always revive, of course, but burning the Tower to the ground was as easy as one, two, three. ♥"

As the two discussed the methodology of dealing with the Devil during the Great War, a certain someone interjected:

"That!! I've been meaning to ask about that!! Have you no honor?! The hero is supposed to challenge me to heroic combat, not blow up my Tower out of nowhere!! Though, hmmm, I guess since I, the Devil, always return, your lashing out was never more than a meaningless struggle!!"

Sora and Shiro were left dumbfounded by the little furball's impassioned accusation for the eternity's worth of pain he'd been put through...

...So lemme get this straight: This plushie-ass Devil comes back to life like "Mwa-ha-ha... Gahhh-ha-ha-ha! The world is mine to destroy, mortals! Come, O Heroes! See if you can stop me————wait, what?" and then gets carpet-bombed into silence every few years.

Hmmm... He's the Phantom of Destruction, the Hope-Consuming Beast...and he controls this Domain of Despair... The Devil is undoubtedly a monster and an avatar of ruin... But y'know...I can't help feeling sorry for the poor little guy.

The Devil had brought the world to the very brink of destruction, only to experience even greater despair at the hands of those more OP than he was.

——So, relatively speaking, he wasn't much of a threat. And to further add to his sob story:

"Oh, Master—I should mention that with the dawn of the Ten Covenants, we can no longer destroy his territory as we used to. Furthermore, the Domain of Despair has lost its life-ending effect."

——,

"...Well, yeah... That's, what...I figured..."

"I mean, ending all life is kinda..."

"It goes against everything the Covenants stand for..."

In other words, the Devil was never a threat during the Great War, with how easy it was to wipe out him and his forces, and even now, he was basically powerless. Sora, Shiro, and Steph stared blankly.

In other words:

"The Devil's Domain of Despair is confined to his Tower, which would require mutual agreement to enter as a game."

"Incidentally: The Devil cannot move his Tower or his territory. Conclusion: This furball cannot do anything."

——The Devil went from "cute furball" to "terrifying furball" to "poor little furball"...

The trio's evaluation of him went up and down like a roller coaster. Just when they were beginning to pity the Devil...

"Right... So now that we've established that he is indeed the furball he presents himself as—"

"——No! I *am* the DEVIL!!"

"Yeah, sure. Anyway, you guys said something interesting: You insinuated that Demonia was worthless without the Devil."

A furball though he may have been, nothing changed the fact that he'd risen once more, which begged the question for Sora: Where did Demonia stand now?

* * *

"Yes. Now that the Devil has returned, my evaluation of Demonia is due for a slight adjustment."

"Affirmative/Reevaluation: Demonia's worth has changed from Worthless to Effectively Worthless. Updating data."

The race's collective worth went from zero to basically zero, and the logic behind this was:

"There are two reasons for this: First, Demonia is fundamentally both weak and stupid."

"_____"

Jibril smiled as she held up the first of two fingers. She'd stated all this as if it was an obvious fact.

"Details: Extreme variance among individual specimens' intelligence and capabilities. However, the maximum of either value is very low. No threat posed in any games. Irregular Number's assessment is highly accurate. Demonia is weak and stupid."

Emir-Eins added her ruthless input, which forced Sora to retort with a bit of a wince, "Uh, b-but wait... Schira Ha introduced herself as *the Wise* earlier, right...?"

——*Surely her moniker is some kinda title for, like, SS-rare characters...y'know...? She even said she was the wisest of them all...*

A befuddled Sora pondered this as he waited for an answer.

"During the Great War, whenever the Devil revived, he created particularly powerful groups of minions to be his elite guards: the Eight Eradicators, the Seven Slayers, the Four Guardians, et cetera..."

Jibril explained more of this world's history, which never disappointed in how clichéd it sounded.

"But every time he did, we Flügel more than anyone else enjoyed hunting these powerful minions as if it were a little game. Weak as they may have been, there was nevertheless a rarity to be enjoyed in beheading the occasional strongest of the weak and stupid. ♥"

"............"

Flügel gruesomeness never disappointed, either. Jibril kept smiling as she continued her explanation.

"Schira Ha the Wise is among the first rare Demonias created over forty thousand years ago, and the only survivor of her brethren, the Nine Nightmares. It is true that she was the sole Demonia elusive enough to escape us Flügel."

Schira Ha was grinning placidly the entire time.

"So...she's gotta be pretty strong, right...?" Sora asked.

Eluding the Flügel for over forty thousand years must've required unimaginable power.

Sora and Shiro could tell why Jibril wanted to kill her so much after they caught her, but:

"Negative: This specimen has no combat capabilities. Intelligence is below average. However, during the twelve times Ex Machina firebombed the Devil's territory—this specimen retreated from the battlefield before the hostilities began. This specimen went AWOL."

"In other words, the only wisdom she has is the wisdom to abandon her king before utter annihilation. ♪"

Schira Ha didn't have any real power or wisdom, other than to run away and hide.

Jibril and Emir-Eins made this known to all present, and one individual was caught completely off guard:

"...Wait. I was wondering why she always survived... Did you really leave me behind, Schira Ha?!"

The shock in the furball's tone was as palpable as the tears welling up in his eyes.

However:

"Your wish is my command, Your Evilness! Your orders were for me to use the wisdom bestowed upon me. Mweh-heh..."

While it wasn't entirely clear what "wish" she was responding to, Schira Ha quickly turned to Jibril and Emir-Eins and launched into a wicked speech...

"Mweh-heh-heh... It is as you say. I, Schira Ha the Wise, am the weakest of the Nine Nightmares— Nay! I can say with confidence that I am the weakest of *all* the Devil's elite guards!!"

She spoke as if this was a point of great pride—but she wasn't finished!

"The great wisdom vested in me by His Evilness made it very clear that if I ever attempted to place myself between him and the relentless volley of explosives deployed by Flügel and Ex Machina hands, I would have offered less protection than a single sheet of paper!!"

She exclaimed, "However!!" and her wicked grin grew even more twisted.

"The Devil—as cute as a button though he may be—is immortal! His Evilness would survive any onslaught and rise again—whereas I, Schira Ha the Wise, would perish. And should that ever happen, upon whose shoulders would the duty of leading Demonia, supporting them, and laying the groundwork for world destruction during the Devil's slumber fall, if not on his wisest servant's?!"

She continued with her voice on high!

"Mweh-heh-heh… It was none other than the omnipotent Devil himself who bestowed me with this knowledge—"

Thus!

"In the name of His Evilness! For the future of his people! And above all, for the world's annihilation—I must use the wisdom gifted to me to *survive*!! It should be plain as day that the all-knowing, all-powerful Devil used his cunning foresight to concoct this master-stroke of genius——is it not, Your Evilness?!"

———,

…After a very pregnant pause:

"…Ah… Y-yes… Gah-ha-ha!! You've done well to interpret my edict, Schira Ha! Your title befits you!"

"But of course, Your Evilness! It was a simple task, thanks entirely to the knowledge you've bestowed upon me!!"

Tears streamed down the furball's fuzzy cheeks as he nodded to his servant, who got on one knee and bowed her head in blind faith to him.

* * *

"...I believe the interactions between Demonia's most intelligent servant and her creator speak for the race itself. ♥"

——Just as a fictional character cannot be smarter than its author: If the creator is an idiot, then so, too, is their creation.

Jibril smiled as she belittled the intelligence of the Demonia race. However...

——*I dunno about this...*

Sora had a hard time taking this claim at face value, but he kept that to himself and squinted while he asked his next question.

"'Kay... Let's say you're right. It doesn't quite make their race worthless, though, yeah?"

Even if Jibril and Emir-Eins's evaluation was 100 percent accurate, and Demonia really was a race of bumbling idiots, then Demonia could easily be taken advantage of—and perhaps even become a priority for the Commonwealth.

Jibril bowed politely before replying, "Yes, this was but the first reason why Demonia should not be considered a threat. Now, the second, more significant reason—"

Namely: why Demonia could be neither friend nor foe.

"—is that Demonia's Race Piece is always in the Devil's possession." Jibril held up a second finger as she said this.

——.........

——...........

"——As such, whether the Devil has returned or not is irrelevant; Demonia is harmless and powerless."

"Supplement: Thus, worthless. Recommendation: Ignore. Leave them be. Forget about them."

Emir-Eins agreed with Jibril's summation.

"..........."

Sora remained silent, lost in deep thought as he processed this information.

* * *

——*Okay, I get it. If what these two are saying is true, then Demonia and the Devil are harmless, but they're also undefeatable...*

Maybe Emir-Eins was right, and they should just ignore them, leave them be, forget about them...

But I'm not in any place to do that now, am I...?

Defeating Demonia was essential to the Commonwealth's overarching goal as well as to dealing with the Front.

Not only that, but Sora's mind was still plagued by the initial reason for Schira Ha's visit. He was mulling over this when:

"...I, uh...don't think that's such a good idea, I don't..."

Til had been there the entire time, listening quietly until she muttered these words. As a Dwarf, she knew something no one else did, and that triggered her sense of impending danger.

Sora looked up at her slowly.

"Mweh-heh-heh... Yes. I, Schira Ha, would likewise advise against such measures..."

Something about the elegant way she talked sparked fear in him.

"That is precisely why I, Schira Ha, stand here before you... Mweh-heh-heh...?"

Despite having so foolishly challenged Jibril and Emir-Eins to a game only to invariably lose, and even though she was in Sora and Shiro's possession—her gaze and voice were dripping with confidence.

There was a wicked intelligence in her eyes, not unlike that of a snake staring down its prey.

——"You heroes have *no choice* in this."

Schira Ha said this with a hungry, serpentine grin, sending chills down everyone's spines......

■■■

Meanwhile, on the continent of Valar in the Republic of Elkia—what used to be Tírnóg—the fledgling nation's impromptu capital was bustling with people working busily under the moonlight. And there was no end in sight of new refugees flooding the capital, which was still dealing with the chaos of establishing itself as a new nation. At the very center of the capital was a white building made of chalk stone—the republic's government office. There sat the parliament president—a young raven-haired girl dressed in all black: Chlammy Zell. She grabbed a single sheet of paper from the top of a large stack on her desk and scowled at it beneath the lamplight.

"I wanna hurl..."

These words were something of a mantra for her at that point as she angrily began putting pen to paper.

Oh look, another form from people expressing their desire to leave the Commonwealth to join the Front... What a load of crap. This is all I've been getting the past few months. It's always the same blah, blah, blah. Let me guess, another excuse as to why they're gonna betray their country and people, and what they have to offer us—

...This was her job.

From a conservationist standpoint, siding with the Front was the obvious thing to do, and the very point of the establishment of the republic: a risk-hedge apparatus. At the same time, choosing to do so also meant the end of the Commonwealth, as well as its domination and possible demise.

In other words, these people were a bunch of traitorous bastards who didn't mind sacrificing their own people, and also a bunch of lousy hypocrites needed to justify their own acts of betrayal.

Of course. That is the rational option. I know it must be difficult for you.

It was the same thing every time, and every time, she said it with a smile while doing her best to fulfill their interest.

From the political and business officials back in Elven Gard to those they colluded with, as well as the republic forces, it was never-ending pandering to those above and below her, and from all sides.

If I ever get used to this nauseating work…it'll be the end of me…
I'm sure there's only one reason that I've managed to keep my sanity despite this mind-numbing work, and that's…

"Chlaaammyyy, don't you think it's about time for bed? ♥"
With a smile bright enough to light up the dim office, an Elf with pale-gold hair and four diamonds for pupils—Chlammy's best friend, Fiel Nirvalen, was there for her.
"Yeah… Thanks, Fi. I'll head to bed once I'm done with this."
The cup of tea Fi made for me will get me through this last batch.
Chlammy took a deep breath. She didn't need Fi to tell her to go to bed; she wanted to be done with this work as much as Fi wanted her to be.
What started as a mountain eventually dwindled down to its last paper, and Chlammy let out a big sigh of relief as she finished filling it out, only for…

"Good work. But there's one more I'd like you to take a look at…"
The sorrow in Fiel's voice was evident as she came forward with another sheet of paper.
Chlammy took it from her with a puzzled look and began reading through it.

"…The Devil's revival has been confirmed, and is to be closely monitored by our allies…? What's this supposed to mean?"
Chlammy raised her brow as she read the directive. It came straight from the council of elders back in Elven Gard.

——Demonia was never a threat in the first place.
As far as Chlammy knew, the higher-ups saw potential use in them for their sheer numbers—as throwaways for the Front. Besides, the newly revived Devil's powers were inhibited by the Ten Covenants

anyway. It was strange to receive orders about his revival, as there was nothing they could really do other than ignore it entirely... Chlammy was visibly puzzled. Fiel spoke up while holding her pointer finger to her cheek:

"*According to undisclosed information from central intelligence...*"
They began a telepathic conversation that was masked through multifold magic. The sudden feeling of words pouring directly into Chlammy's mind foreshadowed the gravity of the information to come. She didn't have time to be surprised by the voice that rang out in her mind, as what she was about to hear was far more shocking:

"*...The Devil's Domain of Despair is* still in effect."
————,

————,

"*That's...impossible...*"
The Domain of Despair—an illusionary field that caused all life within it to lose the hope and desire to live. It just wasn't possible for something as monstrous as that to function under the Ten Covenants.

Chlammy was sure of this, but Fiel shook her head.
"*I shall explain the premise for you...*"
Fiel implied that this may not have been the case. She began leisurely...

"*You understand that the Demonia agent plenipotentiary is the Devil, yes?*"
"*Of course. I'm pretty sure you explained that to me before.*"

————During the Great War, the Devil was in a never-ending loop of revival and immediate destruction at the hands of Flügel and Ex Machina.

The war came to an end while he was still in his dormant phase.

This meant that the Devil was not present for the establishment of the Ten Covenants.

However, Demonia, which remained loyal to him even in his slumber, offered their Race Piece to him.

The result:

"Demonia's agent plenipotentiary has been, for all intents and purposes, absent. Well...until now, I guess."

"That's riiight. ♪ You're so smart, Chlammyyy! ♪"

Fiel patted her on the head for her gold-star answer, but Chlammy brushed it away while she sorted out the facts she knew.

——The Devil was a Phantasma, so as long as his core remained intact, he would come back to life over and over again. He still existed during the downtime until his next revival.

Therefore, Demonia's submission of their Race Piece to the Devil was valid even during his dormancy, creating an environment where the Race Piece could not be stolen, while also removing the presence of anyone capable of making agent-plenipotentiary-level decisions.

This was why Demonia was, for the longest time, viewed as worthless. Or so Chlammy thought, but Fiel was about to tell her something new.

"The Devil's first post-Great War revival was confirmed four hundred and fifteen years ago."

——Why hadn't the Devil risen during the five thousand years before then?

But conversely, why did he revive after those five thousand years? This remained a mystery.

"Just like he did during the Great War, the Devil challenged heroes from around the globe to defeat him. He essentially challenged the entire world to a game."

...Oh?

"What was the game, and what did he wager?"

Never mind the Great War; the world now operated under the Ten Covenants.

Chlammy wanted to know what the rules for the engagement were, as well as the reward, which Fiel told her with a nod.

"As we understand it: The challengers were allowed to form a seven-member party of heroes to enter the Domain of Despair and climb the Devil's Tower. With hope as their sole weapon, they needed to make it to the top floor of the Tower and defeat the Devil himself, winning everything he owned. If their hope was consumed on the way, they would lose."

......Oh-ho...? thought Clammy before asking:

"And I'm guessing everyone dumb enough to try it ended up getting their butts kicked, right?"

"That's riiight. ♪ Many races attempted the climb, but all of them ended the same way."

After all, winning against the long-absent Devil earned the victor everything he owned, including Demonia's Race Piece. The Devil would become the victor's possession, along with Demonia, who pledged absolute loyalty to their creator. It was only natural for the entire world to try and claim this for their own before someone else did.

——And just thinking about it made Chlammy sick.

Nevertheless, the fact that Demonia's Race Piece remained in the Devil's possession pointed to one natural conclusion:

Whoever had challenged him was defeated, and there was not a single survivor.

——If the heroes entered the Tower based on mutual agreement, it made sense that the Domain of Despair would retain its notorious effect.

It was the same Domain of Despair that kept Flügel, Ex Machina, and Old Deus from defeating the Devil during the Great War.

Even if it were a game, it should've been clear that entering the Devil's Tower could've only spelled utter defeat—

"Once it was clear that the game was unwinnable, the world

collectively stopped its attempts at climbing the Tower—that is, except for the moles."

"*The Dwarves?*"

"*Yes. The moles over in Hardenfell were the only ones to keep trying. And they did for seven years, over one hundred times.*"

Why, though…? Why would someone try winning an unbeatable game more than one hundred times—?

Fiel affirmed Chlammy's confusion with a nod before continuing by showing her two images that appeared in her mind.

"*First, here is the population change of Hardenfell in Dagahn between four hundred and fifteen years ago and four hundred and eight years ago.*"

The population of over five hundred thousand began a sudden and rapid decline exactly four hundred and nine years ago.

The image showed that it fell all the way to zero within the span of a year.

"*And this is the Domain of Despair's spread during the Great War, placed over a world map from four hundred and seven years ago…*"

The second image was of a large circle spreading from Garad Golm before consuming all of Hardenfell and Dagahn.

The data suggested an answer to the initial question: Why had the Dwarves challenged the Devil over one hundred times?

——Because they *had to*…

And if that was the case, then the Domain of Despair still maintained its devastating effects even under the Ten Covenants.

The loss of hope in five hundred thousand individuals four hundred and nine years ago was clear evidence of this.

"*No—that can't be! The Ten Covenants are absolute!!*"

Chlammy shook her head. She wasn't so willing to take the information at face value.

The One True God had laid down the laws of nature, laws that not even fellow gods could break!!

* * *

"Yes, this is only a possibility. Something Elf intelligence is still unsure of."

While Fiel agreed with Chlammy's assertion, she continued:

"Nevertheless, the top believes there is a high chance this possibility is a real threat..."

The Ten Covenants canceled out any intent to cause harm to others, but...what if there was no intent?

Or what if the damage caused by the Domain of Despair was an indirect result?

Chlammy knew she couldn't write off the possibilities, so...

"Fine! Let's forget everything about how the world works and pretend they might be right."

Then!! Chlammy was shouting inside her mind.

"If the Devil's Domain of Despair engulfs the entire world, we're all good as dead!! And they want us to monitor the situation?! What the hell are those geezers thinking?!"

——If this really was true, then it superseded the Front and the Commonwealth's conflict.

It called for the world to join forces to figure out the problem, Chlammy thought.

With wide, alert eyes, she groaned on the inside, but...

"If the Devil's Domain of Despair does spread, it will only affect the Commonwealth's territories for the time being... It plays into the Front's favor—"

"Who gives a shit about that?! Those idiots!!"

Chlammy couldn't hold it in any longer. She ended up shouting out her reaction to Fiel's response.

Leaving it be would result in the deaths of hundreds of thousands of Ixseeds, and this played into their favor? Whose favor?!

It played into no one's favor: There was zero proof they could stop the spread of the domain, which meant leaving it to grow could spell not only the Commonwealth's or Elven Gard's own destruction, but the end of the entire world?!

——*They're so stupid!! Just how rotten to the core are these people?!*

"I know, Chlammy… I know…!!"

"——Ngh!"

Fiel gently grasped Chlammy's trembling hands, which allowed Chlammy to feel that her friend, too, was shaking with rage. She gasped.

Oh… There's no way Fi thinks this is okay, too… But there's nothing we can do to go against the top's will… Fi could've kept this information to herself, if she'd wanted to. That way, I would've remained oblivious to it… But she didn't. She shared it with me.

"I'm sorry…Fi… I didn't mean to yell…"

"It's fiiine. I know you're tired."

——Fiel trusted Chlammy. They were equals, they were partners, and they were in this together.

Chlammy was beginning to calm down as she felt her friend's hand gently caressing her, when a thought crossed her mind that was connected by telepathy.

"…Do you think they can win…?"

Sora and the Commonwealth had Hardenfell on their side, so they must have had further intel on the situation.

And if they did, they would never allow anyone to fall victim to the despair. Chlammy knew that, at the very least, they wouldn't give up.

Sora was going to accept the Devil's challenge—she knew it. But…

"…No one has ever defeated the Devil…not during or after the Great War…," Fiel said once more.

Chlammy tried to calm herself.

She then shared the next question that popped up in her mind:

* * *

"...But the Devil only just revived... Doesn't that mean he was defeated four hundred and eight years ago?"

Seeing as the Devil was in a dormant state for four hundred and eight years, didn't that mean that someone—probably the Dwarves—defeated him once?

Chlammy posed this to Fiel, who cocked her head to the side in slight confusion.

"That's what I thought, too, buuut...it doesn't explain why Demonia still exists."

Oh, this is true...

It was just as Chlammy had imagined before:

"Had the moles won, they would have either erased the Devil from existence or made him their puppet. At the very least, Demonia's Race Piece would have been in Dwarf's possession this entire time."

——But this wasn't the case.

Which meant that the Dwarves had somehow forced the Devil back into a dormant state, perhaps maybe by a tie... Regardless, it didn't change the fact that victory was still unachievable.

"But they'll try. And when they do, they'll try for a perfect victory."

Chlammy was sure of this, and Fiel agreed wholeheartedly.

——So what did it mean to challenge the Devil?

First, there would be a party of up to seven heroes.

Sora and Shiro are a given...

Chlammy and Fiel together imagined who would fill the remaining five spots.

"They won't go in without Jibril and Emir-Eins for their firepower, intellect, and analytical skiiills."

"...And with the experience on the Dwarves' side, they'll most definitely bring either Veig or Til. Perhaps even both?"

"The rule about hope being their sole weapon is a bit strange. That could mean they may not be able to use magic. In which case, they will need a Werebeast—Izuna Hatsuse, I assume. Which would make seven."

This was more than likely the optimal party Sora and Shiro would go with. But if any of these individuals had their hope consumed and lost their life during the game, it would amount to the Commonwealth of Elkia losing one of its core members, and almost definitely lead to its collapse.

Yeah...I know.

We're the Front...and they're the Commonwealth...our enemies.

Chlammy understood that it wasn't her place to worry about the group, but...

"You needn't fret over it, Chlammyyy. Sora and his friends will pull through. ♪"

"...? That's odd of you, Fi, to trust Sora's group..."

Even if Fiel merely said that to cheer up Chlammy, who was visibly concerned, it was still so unlike her that Chlammy couldn't help but be surprised.

"Trust them? Heh-heh. Surely you must be joking, yeees?"

Fiel flashed a very telling grin as she continued.

"They're the ones who got us in this mess in the first place. They sent us here with the impossible task of destroying Elven Gard from the inside without even giving us a saaay in the matter. ♪"

......*Yeah, I guess that's true, huh?* Chlammy gave a strained smile.

Well, hopefully they figure something out.

Chlammy sent off her words of encouragement to the faraway Kingdom of Elkia as something of an afterthought before leaving with Fiel for their bedroom, to get a well-deserved good night's sleep.

⏻ CHAPTER 2
PHANTOMA
THE HERO FLEES!

——Garad Golm……

The home of Demonia located on Galarm, Disboard's smallest continent. Evidently, Demonia's territory spanned the entire continent, and the land they laid claim to had never been under the control of another race.

There was one reason for this: The Devil—the Tower and its domain had stood in Galarm for as long as history could remember.

But as it would turn out, that long history might come to an end, for seven brave souls sought to challenge the immortal Devil anew. It was a party of heroes, who set foot on the continent after arriving via long-distance shifting.

Well, at least they believed they set foot there… It was where they were told they were going before they teleported…

"It's fr-fr-fr-freezing here!! Wh-wh-wh-where the hell are we?! The South Pole?!"

"——Br-Br-Brother! I-i-it's...so c-c-cold—e-e-everything, hurts..."

Of the seven heroes, Sora and Shiro stood out in their usual outfits with nothing but a backpack each. Their favorite outfits, however, offered minimal protection against the loud, blistering wind, which drowned out any shouts for dear life in complete darkness. Thankfully, they received an answer from a friend, who must have been right next to them.

"Explanation: Galarm, closest continent to Disboard's southern pole. Current season in the Devil's capital is winter. Complex geographical features and sea currents bring cold wind from the southern pole. Blizzards are frequent. Current temperature is minus thirty-one degrees Celsius."

Apparently, they had arrived at the capital of the Devil's territory. They only barely managed to hear the report provided by the party's third hero—Emir-Eins—over the relentless wind.

——*You could've told us that before we left Elkia...*

Though Sora couldn't actually voice this—his teeth were too busy chattering while he and his sister clung to one another—his sentiment was evident.

"Report: This unit's surface temperature has been adjusted to fifty-four degrees Celsius. Hold me, Master?"

As it turned out——keeping the siblings in the literal dark was all part of Emir-Eins's plan...but Sora and Shiro were in no position to express their discontent. They immediately took the opportunity to latch on to their mechanical companion—

"My apologies for the wait, Master. It took me a moment to appropriately calibrate my magic. ♪"

The fourth hero, Jibril, could be heard from the darkness as she cast her magic. A small orb appeared above the trio, putting a quick end to Emir-Eins's devious plan.

"...Tch/Request: Irregular Number, disclose your reason for casting magic at a speed far faster than normal."

"I'm always willing to push the limit for Master. ♪ You needn't worry about this, though. I doubt a false servant who causes Master harm for its own gain would understand in the first place. ♥"

By the bead of light above them, they could see the two women glaring at each other.

Plus, the fierce wind had been blocked off and the harshness of the cold had been softened to a slight briskness.

W-wow...that was too close for comfort...

Sora and Shiro were at ease knowing they wouldn't freeze to death.

"...It's still goddamn freezing, please. I hate the cold, please..."

"Hey, pooch! I'm not your toy, and I'm not your hot water bottle, either! I am the DEV—"

The fifth and littlest hero was Izuna Hatsuse. She must've instinctively dug her own foxhole upon arriving in the new frozen world, because she was sharing her hate for the climate from the tiniest opening in the ground.

Which left the sixth and seventh heroes. They, too, like Sora and Shiro, were initially relieved to have found a lifeline in the dark frozen hellscape, but they quickly switched gears and hollered in confusion.

"Uh, uh, uhhh?! Why did you bring me and not the chieftain, Sir?!"

"That goes double for me!! My presence here is the biggest mystery!"

And these members were: Til and Steph. Their questions both asked well before departure, but thoroughly ignored by the group...

"I—I mean, it's common knowledge how inept I am at games. Forget about games—we're going into combat, where we have to defeat any Demonias that try to kill us!! What are you expecting from me?!"

——According to both Schira Ha's explanation of the game and Til's understanding of past records, the game was essentially—

—a dungeon crawler.

The seven-member party—five active combatants and two substitutes—were to enter the dungeon and defeat any Demonia mobs that aggroed them until they reached the hundredth floor, where they would need to defeat the Devil, who awaited them. The dungeon itself was the Devil's Tower, and since it was a part of the Devil, it was affected by his Domain of Despair—an area of effect that consumed all hope of those who entered it.

In addition, the only weapon the party could use to fight the enemies in the game was *their hope*, or so Schira Ha had said.

——These two aspects notwithstanding, the game itself was fairly simple.

In a game such as this, it made sense why a Flügel, an Ex Machina, and a bloodbreaker Werebeast were present. Til's presence made some sense, too, as the Dwarves had *probably* reached a tie game with the Devil once before. That being said, the question remained why the party would bring Dwarf's weakest member, Til, over its strongest, her uncle Veig. Steph's presence there was an even bigger puzzle, and she and Til wanted answers.

Sora looked at the two and took a deep breath before nodding confidently and sharing his long-awaited answer—which was!

"It *just felt right*! My gamer senses tell me that this is the best makeup for our party!!"

"You're starting to sound like the chieftain, you are!!"

"And here I always pegged you as more of the logical, strategic type..."

Heh... Of course, this is a logical party build. My logic just needed some help from my gut to fill in the gaps, is all.

Sora, flashing a bold grin, kept this to himself. Suddenly:

"Erm...Sora? I thought you were worried about us making the first move?"

——*Yes, while it's true we mustn't allow the Domain of Despair to run rampant and are thus left without much of a choice...if we make a move that ends in failure at this stage, it could spell the end for the Commonwealth, which has kept us from doing anything so far. We*

*don't even know if we can beat the Devil, nor do we have an inkling of
what's in store for us if we do manage to defeat him...*

Steph had discernable worry on her face as she whispered to Sora,
who responded...

"Yeah, it's fine. We were actually waiting for something exactly
like this, and it's the ideal time to *get started*," Sora answered confidently, leaving Steph slightly confused, yet nonetheless ignored.

"So...Schira Ha. Where to next?" he asked.

Thanks to Jibril's magic, the party had access to the bare minimal light and warmth, but what awaited on the other side of their
magical refuge was a blistering blizzard in the dead of night—they
couldn't even see anything.

——This was a problem when they needed to rely on shifting,
which could take them only as far as Jibril's or Emir-Eins's eyes
could see. While they were in Garad Golm, they were going to have
to walk the rest of the way.

There was a good chance they could get lost before they ever
reached the Tower...

Sora winced at Schira Ha.

"Mweh-heh-heh... Fret not, O Heroes... For it appears our escort
has arrived."

Schira Ha, who did seem to be quietly waiting for something up until
this point, finally spoke up. She gazed into the darkness, and from
within its harsh winds emerged a single source of flickering light.

"His Evilness has already prepared a guide for us, mweh-heh-
heh..."

"Gah-ha-HAAA! But of course! We wouldn't want our heroes
dying of frostbite before they even got to the Tower, now would we?"

Evidently, the furball, still in Izuna's clutches, had called for someone to come and escort the party to his Tower.

*It's not every day you get a Devil who saves the heroes who are sup-
posed to slay him...*

The group kept this shared sense of irony to themselves as they watched what the source of light was emerge from the darkness.

——It was a large carriage pulled not by horses but by...centaurs? There were two of them...each with the lower body of a horse and the upper body of a human. Either way, the centaur-like creatures pulling the wagon must've been Demonias.
Its doors soon opened, revealing a humanlike figure.

He was smiling evilly—or so one could only assume. It was difficult to tell what kind of face he was making, because his expression wasn't so easily readable—or perhaps more aptly, he didn't have an expression.
The escort was wearing an expensive-looking tailored suit, and with one hand pressed to his chest, he gave an elegant bow.
"Kah-kah... It is truly a pleasure to meet your acquaintances, heroes. I am——"
"——YEEEEEEEEEEEEEEEEK?!"
Steph interrupted the skeleton's self-introduction with a loud scream......

——It turned out centaurs really were pulling the carriage.
It looked like it was made of human bones, but it had quite a lavish, inviting interior. Save for Jibril and Emir-Eins, who had a natural resistance to the frigid weather, the rest of the party sat comfortably within the roomy carriage.

"Kah-kah... Let's try that again, shall we? I am Genau Ih, leader of the Skeleton Lords and Schira Ha's successor as the head of the Joint Chiefs of Staff."
His jaw rattled as he spoke with what the party imagined was a wicked grin.
——Following Schira Ha's retirement, Genau Ih was Demonia's second-in-command under the Devil.

The polite Demonia finished his self-introduction with a deep bow.

"Nice to meet you... So, uh, where's your voice coming from—?"

——What piqued Sora's interest most of all was the physicality of how the skeleton projected his voice without...a voice box, among other things. Sora's intrusive question for the overly polite gentleman, however, was cut off abruptly by Steph:

"I am so, *so* sorry!! You surprised me, and it was dark, and I just—!!"

Steph was more embarrassed by her initial reaction to his appearance than anything.

"Kah-kah...kah-kah-kah— It's quite all right! On the contrary, it was truly an honor for me to receive such a reaction!"

Her shame was wasted on the Demonia, however, for he seemed to take her fear as a compliment.

"That's not fair, Genau Ih! These heroes aren't even the slightest bit afraid of me!!"

"Oh, Your Evilness! Their fear stems from the terrifying way you created me!"

"Mweh-heh... Which means that any fear they have for us is fear for Your Evilness...!"

"——Why, yes!! Gah-ha-ha! Perhaps the heroes have finally come to realize how terrifyingly evil I truly am!!"

The little furball must have liked the flattery his underlings showered him with. They seemed sincere, too, or as far as the group could tell, at least.

"So...you guys *want* people to be afraid of you?" Sora asked.

"It isn't necessarily that we *want* you to be afraid of us, but that your fear is inevitable! For I am the Devil!!" the furball insisted yet again, trying to release himself from Izuna's unforgiving clutches.

"Kah-kah... Demonia will lead the world to its destruction. So it only makes sense that we are feared! It may come as a surprise that you, ma'am, were the first to have ever shown your fear, for which I thank you from the bottom of my heart. And I find you quite the wonderful Immanity damsel for it!"

Genau Ih finished by taking Steph's hand and kissing it. Seeing this, Sora and Shiro thought...

——*Okay, so this is the race that wants destroy the world more than anything else...but they were shrugged off and ignored during the Great War, only to be considered worthless once the Covenants were established...*

The idea that a Demonia would feel gratitude after being feared made a bit more sense considering how rare it must've been until then...

"Kah-kah... But I must say, Schira Ha. It is a delight to see you in such good health and vigor."

Meanwhile, the polite skeleton touched upon something that the siblings were curious about.

——Namely...

"I feared for your fate when the Devil ordered your death."

"————————Huh? I ordered no such thing."

"But of course, Your Evilness! However, upon your most recent revival—"

"Mwa-ha-ha... GAH-HA-HA-HA!! The material world feels incredible after my four-hundred-and-eight-year slumber!! Let us make haste and destroy it! SCHIRA HA! I command you to go forth, find the hero candidates, and bring them to me!!"

"——that is how your humble servant remembers you wording your orders."

"Oh, well...I suppose I did say that, but..."

You actually said that...?

The Devil was oblivious to the carriage full of people squinting at him in disbelief. The polite skeleton used his tone and gestures to skillfully convey his concern.

"With the Front being under the Devil's Army's flag, the hero candidates would have to be selected from the Commonwealth..."

"Y-yes… This much should be obvious."

"My lesser intellect perceived these orders—sending Schira Ha the Wise against the Elkian monarch who has defeated and now commands the Flügel and Ex Machina—as a death sentence…"

…………?

————.…………?

"————————I, wait… Hmmm?"

————Thirty seconds of silence passed before the Devil eventually processed the chain of logic, and it was all the rest of the group needed to finally understand why he'd sent Schira Ha against Jibril and Emir-Eins without a plan.

————He gave his orders *without really putting too much thought into them…*

"Mweh-heh… It seems the likes of you, Genau Ih, cannot fathom the depths of the Devil's Greater Plan… It is inevitable, I suppose… Please, feel at ease—but do be mindful of your place."

"————!"

However…Schira Ha had a different view of the matter. She maintained her wicked smile and elegant mannerisms while firmly reprimanding her successor.

"Do you truly believe the Devil lacked the far-reaching foresight to comprehend your own measly concerns?"

Her sharp snake eyes homed in on the skeleton, who shuddered as if he'd been zapped by lightning.

Foresight…? What foresight…?

Even Mr. Evilness himself let an awkward "wait" slip out from Izuna's arms just now…

The entire group stared in disbelief at Schira Ha, who ignored their gazes and proceeded to lay out the facts for them!

"For after I relinquished myself of my position as head of the Joint Chiefs of Staff, I forfeited myself to the party of heroes!! And as would be proven true through the power of the Covenants, I was able to make it known to them that they had no choice to but accept this journey! This—*this* was surely the Devil's Greater Plan!"

"I-is it true...?! Y-Your Evilness!!"

"Mweh-heh... The Devil also foresaw the party of heroes' disposition to opt for the path of least sacrifice, even when it went against their interest. Thus, he knew his humble servant would remain unscathed while in their custody!"

"It's all so clear to me now!! Oooh! Your Evilness!! Please forgive this brainless pile of bones's disparagement unto you!!"

.........,

"Ah... V-verily... You are forgiven... For I am a magnanimous ruler... Heh, heh-ha-ha..."

Though he maintained his arrogant persona, it was fairly evident that the Devil knew what he was doing, because he averted his gaze as he said this. Nevertheless, the skeleton's bones were literally shaking with gratitude at the Devil's supposed generosity.

"Only you, Schira Ha, have the incredible perception required to read into the Devil's words with such profound depth...!"

"Mweh-heh... It was His Evilness who blessed me with my wisdom. Wisdom only second to His—it would be blasphemy unto Him for me to miss such details despite this gifted wisdom!"

Watching Schira Ha gloat over her boundless wisdom and loyalty once more, Sora realized:

——*I'm starting to think Demonias are smarter than people give them credit for...*

Even if they let their imaginations run wild when it came to hidden meanings behind their leader's words...

"Well...with that issue cleared up, I would now like to guide you to the accommodations the Devil has prepared for you, O Heroes."

The skeleton bowed after being granted amnesty for his blasphemous obliviousness, but as it would turn out:

"——Or at least I had come here with that very intention, but if you would, please allow me to guide you straight to the Devil's Tower instead..."

...........?

"Er... That's where we were planning on going anyway, but what's all this talk about accommodations...?" Sora asked.

Evidently, the skeleton's bow was out of sorrow, which left the group confused.

"Hey!! You're not trying to pit a party of tired heroes against me, are you?! I order you to give them a full night's rest at our finest inn!!"

——Apparently, the Devil wanted the party in their best condition for the game.

The furball was livid that his servant had rejected his orders, however:

"Oh! I beg your forgiveness, Your Evilness!! Given the sudden nature of the decree—all inns are currently closed for the day!!"

"Ack! Hmm... Mmm... Th-then so be it..."

——"Closed for the day" was a good enough reason to put an end to the exchange.

The Devil's decree was shut down by...business hours...

"...Y-you don't think that the Devil...isn't all that respected around here, do you...?" Til couldn't help but whisper into Sora's ear, but...

"Mweh-heh?! Wh-wh-what are you trying to say?!"

"Kah-kah-kah!! The Devil's authority is a shining beacon of darkness that dims the lands far and wide!!"

"Eeep?! I-I'm sorry, I am! But what does shining darkness even mean?!"

Schira Ha and the rattling skeleton must have caught Til's off-the-cuff remark; they ran straight toward her, and she immediately took refuge under Shiro's skirt, though not without pointing out the irony in the statement just made.

Schira Ha cleared her throat before addressing their confusion:

"Mweh-heh… Garad Golm follows a strict eight-hour workday and four-day workweek."

She bowed her head politely for her sudden show of dishevelment.

"Mweh-heh… Work outside of these hours is paid threefold and requires the worker's consent, and its application must be submitted to our Labor Department at least two days in advance. This merely means that it isn't so easy for us to bend these rules on such short notice."

Though spoken in the wickedest of tones, Schira Ha described what sounded like a very hospitable work environment.

Unable to suppress his surprise at the seemingly paradoxical presentation, Sora asked, "Even if it's the Devil's orders…?"

"Mweh-heh… Nonsense! Should the Devil order it, not only the inns but all of Demonia would awaken and go straight to work with tears of joy streaming down their faces! However—"

"That would be abusing my power!! But enough of this!! You shall take the heroes directly to my Tower!!"

——The Devil seemed as magnanimous as he touted himself to be, at least in terms of workers' rights.

The Devil… The so-called *Phantom of Destruction* who was trying to end the world…

——In any case…setting aside the surprisingly lenient working environment…

The centaur-drawn carriage appeared to have finally reached the capital.

The snow was weaker than it was in the wilderness, and from the window, the group could see the flickering lights of a town dotting the townscape.

"Y'know, when I heard we'd be going to Garad Golm—basically a nation of monsters—I just…"

"…You'd think…it'd be, in a cave…or something…"

"This town seems to be on the same level of Elkia in terms of civilization…"

Sora, Shiro, and Steph were shocked by the sight as they advanced into the city.

While everything was made of stone, the many tall structures clearly marked it as a city. Perhaps due to the diversity of their people, from its buildings to its doors, everything was massive. At the same time, it took only a glance to recognize that the placement and the structure of these giant buildings were meticulously planned.

"...Also, I've been wondering this entire time, but are these seats made of *silk*...?"

"Mweh-heh... Indeed, the silk spun by the arachne tribe is among the world's top quality, which was dyed by the slime tribe, who is known for their dyeing techniques. The body of the carriage was fashioned out of wood provided by the orc tribe, which was then built by the goblin tribe, known for their woodwork. Have you taken a liking to it?"

Schira Ha flashed yet another wicked smirk. She took great pride in her nation's industry, but this left Sora groaning with yet another question.

"Sooo you mind tellin' me why...the race trying to end the world is this civilized...?"

One would expect a more rough-and-tough, barbarian feel from the people who wanted to destroy the world.

Not to mention that, if there was such a difference in the intellect and ability between species of Demonia, it wouldn't be shocking if it were a more starkly disparate nation.

Sora and the others had pictured something more rustic, but Schira Ha and the skeleton addressed their doubts.

"Mweh-heh-heh...? Why else would they be this civilized if not for the sole purpose of bringing about the world's destruction?"

"Kah-kah... Yes, it is all Schira Ha the Wise's—and transitively, the Devil's—will!"

Really now...?

The group turned to the Devil, who was still trapped in Izuna's hands, but...he exercised his right to remain silent and let Schira Ha do the talking.

"All wisdom exercised by me, Schira Ha the Wise, is a mere by-product of the Devil's own will."

——*So Schira Ha is responsible for Demonia's level of civilization.*

This was Sora and Shiro's interpretation, and Schira Ha was quick to ask a question of her own.

"Mweh-heh… What do you think is necessary for destroying the world, if you don't mind me asking…?"

——*Hmmm……*

It was Sora's first time thinking about world destruction, as opposed to world peace.

It didn't require much deep thought in his original world. In fact, it was more likely the world would find a way to destroy itself.

"Maybe, like…immense military might…?" Sora replied.

Schira Ha nodded wickedly in agreement, but not without specifying one detail.

"Mweh-heh… It is as you say. Though, to be more precise, it is *immense national might.*"

She continued with her usual wicked smile and evil tone.

"Mweh-heh… Then, what makes a nation mighty if not its own people?"

She spoke plainly with words that made Sora, a ruler himself, want to run for the hills…

"The great and powerful Devil created a diverse people, each of them receiving their own unique characteristics. Though we may be different, there is no higher or lower social standing in our society, and we've sculpted our nation into a place where all beings can excel—this is what makes us powerful."

"…………"

Sora and Shiro were struck dumb by what seemed like a perfect answer, but Schira Ha wasn't finished yet.

"For example, we could not have cultivated the frozen earth of this frigid environment without the help of the wyrm tribe. The slime tribe excretes a liquid that can be made into medicine, and the orc tribe's strong bodies allow them to handle a wide variety of labor-intensive jobs, while the goblin tribe focuses more on fine-tuned craftsmanship. Each of these tribes was a necessary piece of the puzzle that went into creating the city you see before you, mweh-heh."

"............"

"In the same vein, without their help, I, too, would starve. As it is my duty to keep my people alive and thriving, I used the wisdom bestowed unto me by the Devil to do so. This much should be a given, should it not?"

——*Yeah, it definitely should. Everything she said is highly logical... but such logic is usually written off as pie-in-the-sky ideals.* When it comes to actualization of such ideals, there are many problems that arise, namely...

"Does this mean Garad Golm follows a feudal system? What do you do about your people's career choice in relation to the fluidity of your economy when—?" Steph began to ask before a wickedly grinning Schira Ha interrupted.

"Mweh-heh... Allow me to stop you there, for Demonia boasts a diverse population. Let's take some of the larger species, for example—they receive a tax break on their food as they require more sustenance than most. When it comes to career choice, we impose no path on any individual—in some cases, even extra-tribal careers have proven highly fruitful—we do intend on eventually creating a support system for such individuals, and—"

———————————She went on to list example after example of intricate political systems implemented to balance out the minutiae that made the so-called ideal perceived as difficult. Somewhere along the way, Steph had taken out a pencil and paper and listened as if it were a lecture, when—

"Mweh-heh-heh... My apologies. It was not my intention to allow myself to get too caught up in the many details. What I mean to say is—"
Schira Ha brought a quick end to her lecture:
"Our diverse people require a society where they retain the ability and will to be able to use their diverse talents. In other words, each

and every Demonia is a member of the Devil's Army—and a special treasure made by the Devil himself! He takes firm responsibility for his people, and immense pride in each and every one of them!! We are a powerful nation all moving toward one shared goal! That is, in my best estimation, the bare minimum required for us to eventually realize the world's destruction."

Schira Ha's conclusion, based on the wisdom given to her by the Devil, was cause for Sora to let out an audible *gulp.*

"Wow… Who would've imagined that this world already had a country where diverse people lived together, hand in hand…"

If only they didn't have the whole world annihilation part…, he mused, clutching his head.

Ah, so this is the society Elkia is working toward. A society I thought didn't exist in this world…

——But here it exists…to destroy the world. They're so close to perfect, and yet so far away. Why does it have to be like this? If only it was just a little more, you know…

"Sora… Why not use your dominion over Schira Ha to make her work with us?" Steph asked. "We could definitely use her as an adviser… Honestly, I wouldn't mind working under her myself."

——Demonia, a race of idiots? It couldn't be.

At the very least, Schira Ha the Wise was as intelligent as her name suggested. She was, without a doubt, among this world's wisest individuals. The problem was…what she was trying to use her knowledge for…and that was a *big* problem……

■■■

——They continued riding the carriage through the capital for another hour before finally reaching their destination. The group—with the exception of Jibril and Emir-Eins—all gazed in awe at the sight.

"Mweh-heh... *Ahem*, if you would, please."

"Kah-kah... Welcome, party of heroes. You stand before the Devil."

The Devil—Schira Ha and Genau Ih's creator and leader. The two bowed pridefully, and behind them, Sora, Shiro, Steph, Til, and Izuna got their first glimpse of their opponent, which elicited an audible *gulp* from the entire group.

So this *is the Devil...*
It had finally sunk in, making them tremble.

——This was the tallest structure any of them had ever seen, and though strange in nature, it was indeed a tower.

It was less of a physical structure and more of an illusionary nightmare.

The Tower was uncannily similar to the sort of non-Euclidean geometric structure people imagine from the well-known Cthulhu Mythos—unlike any physical structure one would expect in a three-dimensional-space world that twisted and turned randomly and jutted toward the sky in a difficult-to-describe way. It filled all who gazed upon it with dread and made several things very clear:

Were it not for the Covenants, whoever laid their eyes on this Tower would certainly lose their sanity.

This Tower would sap the hope from all who entered it.

This was the Hope-Consuming Beast. The Phantom of Destruction. The Domain of Despair... The Devil...

"Ga-ha-ha-HAAA!! How's THAT for a tower?! Pretty frightening, eh?! Has it finally set in? The TERROR of the DEVIL?! SCHIRA HA!! Begin the game now before the heroes succumb to their fear and attempt to flee!!"

"Mweh-heh... Ah, I'm afraid I cannot assist, Your Evilness. Your humble servant is currently in the possession of the heroes..."

"Sir! Then with Your Evilness's permission, I shall head the Joint Chiefs of Staff and oversee the game."

"Oh...you're stuck with them...and now you're the...? ...Right! GENAU IH! LET THE GAME BEGIN!!"

What should've been a moment for the party to feel some real fear was ruined by the furball forgetting who did what, and the intensity of it all just kind of...fizzled out.

Once everyone had returned to their senses, the suited skeleton made an announcement:

"With that, O party of Heroes, I believe you've been informed as to your task, but allow me to..."

He bowed and proceeded to rehash the outline of the game they would be participating in:

The seven-member heroes' party was to clear the Tower dungeon.

Of the seven members, five could be active, with the other two waiting inside their inventory.

The heroes could use only *hope* to fight whatever Demonias appeared within the dungeon until they made it to its top floor, where they would have to destroy the Devil's core. Should they emerge victorious, they would become the owners of the Devil and everything in his possession.

If the entire party's hope was consumed before doing so, they would lose, and the game would come to an end.

There was one last thing for the skeleton to add:

"Should anyone in the party abandon the game, that will be considered a loss, and their hope will be promptly consumed."

And:

"Please note that you may not leave the Tower during the game."

He made it clear that quitting halfway through and leaving the Tower was against the rules.

"That is all. If you have no further questions, then we shall begin the game by the Covenants."

Are you ready...? The skeleton awaited their answer.

"Hm... 'Kay, mind if I ask three questions?"

With the rules fresh in his mind, Sora presented a few issues that were eating away at him.

"First: What's to keep you from jumping us the moment we enter the Tower?"

"Mweh-heh... At ease, heroes. There is a preparation room where you will acquire your weapons of hope. It is a safe zone where we cannot attack each other."

——*Weapons of hope...*

Sora watched as the skeleton nodded at Schira Ha's mention of the hope-derived armaments. The idea of using hope as a weapon was something he'd been thinking about since Schira Ha had first mentioned it back in Elkia.

Which brought him to his next question:

"Okay, question number two: What exactly do you guys mean by *hope*?"

——That was going to be their only weapon for the duration of the game.

Should their hope be consumed, they would lose. Hope was a key aspect of the game, but the concept itself was still way too nebulous. Sora took this chance to ask the same question he'd asked Schira Ha before they left Elkia.

But it was neither the skeleton nor Schira Ha who answered him:

"Review: A spiritual activity that makes up the 'soul.' Defined as part of the 'heart.' A feeling."

"It is primarily a mechanism of the soul's desire to exist—a concept shared by all living beings."

"...Yeeeaaah... That's what I thought you two would say..."

"...We can't...get a straight answer...around here..."

It was exactly as Schira Ha had said before, but this time, Jibril and Emir-Eins were the ones who broke Sora's and Shiro's brains.

Evidently, just as *souls* seemed to exist in definite terms in this world, the idea of *hope* stemmed from the "soul" and was clearly defined.

The siblings were forced to accept the definitions being given to them as fact, it looked like...

"My last question might sound kinda random, but it could be the most important one of all."

Since figuring out what "hope" really meant was not in the cards, Sora had one more query:

"This country runs on a strict four-day workweek with eight-hour workdays, right...? What happens if the schedule runs awry...?"

——Once they entered the Tower, they would not be able to leave.

Would the staff inside the Tower have to go home at a certain time? Say there was a boss enemy that the party couldn't beat; would they have to wait for it to come to work the next day?

"Kah-kah... You needn't worry about that... I shall see to it personally that the game operates twenty-four seven."

The skeleton politely answered Sora's question, to which he responded with, "Oh, so you guys bend the rules there a bit, eh...?"

A country could only be so lenient with these sorts of things. There were always exceptions. Ideals were, in the end, ideals. Sora was almost disappointed upon hearing this, but there was more to the game's operation than just that...

"Yes... Four overseers are set to manage the game on six-hour shifts each. The boss monsters are being kept on standby with bonus pay, and they will be dispatched when the heroes close in on their posts... On the whole, this game has required tremendous coordination between all of Demonia and the Labor Department... My bones ache thinking what I would have done if not for the schedule produced by Schira Ha the Wise before she relinquished her position..."

"Mweh-heh... Yes, the planning that went into that did quite the number on me as well."

Sora's disappointment was wasted, for the response was superb. The country ran like a well-oiled machine, one where the pressure fell not on the workers but on the higher-ups. Sora and the others were impressed.

"But of course!! What kind of Devil would I be if I forced my heroes to fight on a four-day workweek?!"

——And yet the leader of all this was apparently oblivious to his subordinates' efforts.

Ideals will always be ideals..., Sora thought as he stared off into the distance.

And then came the time——

"If there are no further questions, then let us make our pledge to the Covenants."

With that, the skeleton raised his hand, and all eyes fell on Sora.

During the Great War and since its end—not a single soul had beaten the Devil. Not even an Old Deus.

Should they really be challenging him to a game...?

Everyone waited for Sora's answer.

"Yeah, let's do this. ——*Aschente!*"

If Sora was this confident in his decision, then his friends were with him. Shiro, Steph, Til, Izuna, Jibril, and Emir-Eins: All seven party members joined the skeleton—and the Demonia staff that awaited inside the Tower—in making the mass pledge:

Aschente.

"Mweh-heh... Oh, Your Evilness? If you wouldn't mind...you, too, must *Aschente...*"

"Hm? Oh...right, you're all waiting for my consent to begin! Yes, of course! Then so be it! The Devil, too, agrees to your challenge, O Heroes!! Face mine wrath—*Aschente!!*"

With Schira Ha's reminder, the furball agreed to the game from within Izuna's embrace.

The door to the dark, evil Tower ominously opened.

*   *   *

"Kah-kah... I will be excusing myself to the staff office. Ta-ta for now, O Heroes..."

The skeleton offered one last deep bow before departing.

"Mweh-heh... Come, heroes. I shall take you to where you will begin."

With Schira Ha leading them, Sora and the party entered the Tower——

■■■

Through the massive door and into the Tower they went, where they found an expansive room void of life. It was not unlike Elkia Royal Castle's throne room in terms of size and scale, but taking into consideration the massive size of the door they'd just passed through, it felt unusually small. When they turned to look back, the door they'd originally passed through had turned into a size that matched the room's.

Just as its outward appearance suggested, the Tower didn't follow the conventional concept of physics.

Either way, this must've been the safe zone that Schira Ha had described to them before. There was a small window through which the night sky peered into the massive room, and in its center was a large magic circle made of strange patterns and symbols.

At the very center of said magic circle were seven balls of light, each swaying ever so slightly, and a small floating bag.

"Mweh-heh... Now, heroes... Each of you must touch one of the lights."

Though cautious, the party followed Schira Ha's directions and held their hands out to the light nearest them.

The next instant...

"I see what's going on here... These must be our weapons of hope."

——It was one of the rules of the game: Their hope was their only weapon. The rules made more sense now that they were physically holding those weapons.

A dimly glowing weapon materialized into each party member's hands. Sora looked around at them all before nodding to himself.

"So basically—our hope takes on the form of an actual weapon?"
"...Mm-hmm... I can...work with...this..."
Sora and Shiro each examined their armaments, which seemed to fit perfectly in their hands. Schira Ha affirmed their suppositions with a nod of her own, only to cock her head to the side with a bit of confusion.

"Mweh-heh... Impressive of you to understand, heroes...but I must ask: What race ever used weapons such as those, and in what time period...?"
Seeing as each person's weapon took on a shape of its own, the only sort of weapons that could materialize were weapons that actually existed within the beholder's mind.

It must've been strange for Schira Ha, who'd been alive for tens of thousands of years, to see any given weapon for the first time.

The siblings shared a wry chuckle; it was no wonder she'd never seen their weapons before.

Sora had what looked like a high-caliber Anti-Matter Rifle, and Shiro held two fully automatic Machine Pistols, one in each hand. Both weapons were not of this world.

As for the rest of the heroes——

"...Hey, is this thing supposed to be some kinda...weapon, please?"
"Gahhh-ha-ha! One befitting a Werebeast, whose greatest weapon is their body! Speaking of which, how about you let me go now?! Are you listening, pooch?!"
Izuna held the rowdy furball tight in two large paw-shaped Kitty Gloves that glowed faintly like the siblings' guns.

"Does this look right...? Setting aside the fact that it's all glowy and stuff, this looks like my spirit arm, it does..."

Til appeared concerned, seeing as this Great Hammer was much like her usual weapon, just shinier.

"Oh? I've never understood the novelty of a weapon before...but I quite like this."
Jibril took a liking to the weapon her own hope had chosen for her: an evil-looking Scythe.

"Analysis/Estimation: Remote-control-operated miniature aerial attack aircraft. An ideal weapon. This unit is not a *Kämpfer* battle unit."
Floating around Emir-Eins and similarly glowing was a group of Drones that looked like they could shoot laser beams.

——*So this is what they meant by* hope. *Doesn't seem like we have to worry about the game operators tampering with our weapons.*
Sora felt much better now that this ambiguity had been cleared up.
"Um...," Steph began. "I've only ever heard about weapons in stories, but—"
All forms of violence and weapons had been eliminated six thousand years ago. For a modern person, the idea of a weapon was nothing more than a long-lost artifact of history. Steph was aware of this going into the Tower, but even then, what manifested in her hands didn't quite fit what she had in mind...

"—I'm fairly sure this isn't even categorized as a weapon!!"
She cried out in confusion as she held up a giant shield, eliciting wide-eyed stares from Sora, Shiro, and Izuna.
——It was...a Great Shield... The perfect weapon for someone who wished no harm to others and sought only to protect them... Someone like Steph.
Not only that, but despite strict definitions, it was nevertheless a valid weapon.
What had everyone wide-eyed was not the shield, but—

"…Steph…what's with…your stats…?"

"…S-Stuch… A-are you a monster, please…?!"

—the bar—or bars—that hovered above her head…

Two bars appeared above each party member's head when their weapons materialized. Based on the rule that loss of all hope meant losing the game:

"These must be our status bars. Lemme guess: The red bar on top is our HP, which goes down when we get hit, and the blue bar on the bottom is our MP, which we use to attack, right?"

"Mweh-heh… Indeed, hero…… But that's quite the pinpoint guess you've made."

Schira Ha was caught entirely off guard by Sora's remark, which was less of a guess and more of an inference from his own world's tried-and-true game mechanics. Now that the rest of the party was caught up on the status bars, Til yelled out a new question:

"…D-does that mean Lady Steph is immortal?!"

"Stuch has three goddamn HP bars… I think you broke her, please…?"

"What's everyone talking about…? Is there something wrong with me…?"

Steph soon realized she was the odd one out with how everyone was looking at the space above her in shock. The group stared at Steph's HP bars with a strange, almost anxious curiosity, when…

"Huh. Looks like Steph will be the key to this game after all," mumbled Sora, the only one who appeared to grasp the situation.

"The key—?! What's that supposed to mean?! …Oh!!" Steph's eyes glimmered with excitement. "So you *did* have something in mind for me when you brought me along! Let's face it: No one would expect me to be useful for this sort of game, but you must have insight on how to win! Don't you, Sora—?!"

——I knew it! There's no way Sora would so flippantly include me in the party!

Steph looked to Sora, eager to hear about his well-thought-out plan, but...

"I mean...since we're gonna use hope as our weapons, I figured that, out of all of us, you have your head in the clouds—er, uh, want to protect your friends the most."

"Right! I'm not quite sure if you're complimenting or disparaging me, but I'll take it!!"

Steph rolled her head back, her expression rife with equal parts hope and despair.

Sora and Shiro, meanwhile, had a very different problem. They stared at each other's status bars and muttered among themselves.

"I'm a bit concerned about our own lack of HP and abundance of MP..."

"...I think...we're well...within one-shot range..."

Unlike Steph, who had three long bars' worth of HP and only slightly less than average MP, Sora and Shiro had almost no HP and the longest MP bars of anyone in the party.

*——*Izuna, Til, Jibril, and Emir-Eins, on the other hand, seemed to have a decent balance of both, even if their distributions varied slightly between them.

"I guess we may as well ask, but...Schira Ha, is there a reason behind the difference in our distributions?"

"Mweh-heh...? Not at all. They are, as you say, but a visualization of your *hope*," Schira Ha answered in her usual wicked tone, her head tilted to one side.

*——*Sora and Shiro owned Schira Ha, so she couldn't lie to them.

Her claim was backed by Izuna and Emir-Eins, who both sensed that she was telling the truth, something they communicated to Sora with a nod. Everyone's statuses were evidently a function of the game's inherent mechanics—

* * *

Right... Then I guess we'll have to test out these game mechanics ourselves.

"Jibril, Emir-Eins—I'm assuming you can't use your magic?"

——Seeing as they were only allowed to use hope as their weapon, then it was safe to assume that they could not use their magic... But to Sora's surprise:

"Oh... Actually, Master...it appears that we *can*."

"Report: Sensing presence of functioning quasi-spirit corridor junction nerves. Magic presumed usable."

——*Oh?*

With this news, all eyes fell dubiously on one person.

"Mweh-heh-heh...? Ah, yes. Within this Tower—inside the Devil— you may use magic if you so choose. But I recommend against it, as doing so consumes large amounts of hope."

Their gazes were met by a strange response from Schira Ha.

——*This game is supposed to be fought with hope alone, and yet we can use magic? And...magic consumes our hope...?*

"Jibril...I want you to use as little magic as possible to do something. Say...lighting up your fingertip?"

Jibril promptly held out her hand and concentrated her magic into her pointer finger—but.

............,

"I know I told you to do it...but I'm surprised you can suppress your magic this much."

The tip of her pointer finger was only as bright as a firefly.

Sora was impressed by this, although Jibril seemed confused.

"Oh...? But I intended to use a rite that creates about one hundred times more light than this..."

"Conjecture: Use of magic within the Tower is possible— but its effect is reduced by a factor of more than one hundred...?

Incidental/Report: Irregular Number's MP has been reduced by zero point zero three percent. Current use of magic determined to be the cause."

——Emir-Eins's summation seemed accurate.

Upon closer inspection, Jibril's MP bar had indeed been reduced by the slightest of slivers.

.........Hmmm......

"How about this, Jibril: If you were to, say, shift under these conditions, how much more MP do you think it would use?"

"..............I daresay my best guess would be over a few thousand times more MP."

"Approximation: Magic using three thousand three hundred and thirty-four times more MP would reduce Irregular Number's MP to zero. Conclusion: Use of magic unrealistic."

So while magic was physically possible to use during the game, it was essentially pointless. Sora was thrown into deep thought over this——

............,

".......Hmm, well, I guess we'll figure it out as we go along..."

Nodding to himself as he spoke, he then turned to the party to discuss their strategy for running the Tower dungeon.

"So, Steph. You're gonna be our tank."

"...You're our...meat shield... Thanks, Steph..."

"I'm not sure what a tank is, but *meat shield* certainly doesn't have a safe ring to it!!"

Sora ignored Steph's question about her role and continued:

"Sorry I gotta ask this, but Izuna—you're gonna carry me and Shiro, and Til will carry Steph. Do you guys think you can do that?"

"Yup, you got it, please. Leave it to me, please."

"Lady Steph is light, she is. I always thought she should eat more, I did."

Just as Sora asked, the two petite party members easily hoisted the party's three Immanity heroes onto their backs.

"Jibril and Emir-Eins will be our subs. Get in the bag."

"...Come again, Master?"

"...Confusion:"

——As soon as Sora made this call, the pair was sucked into the floating bag before they could object.

——Per the rules, the party could have only five members active at once. Therefore, two out of their seven members would have to stay in the bag at any given moment. The bag acted as the party's inventory, where their substitutes would wait to be switched out.

According to what Schira Ha had told them back in Elkia, the bag would float behind the party automatically.

This magical bag could also store items. The group took this opportunity to put their backpacks and other things inside when—

"*Report: Space within inventory bag is far more cramped than initially anticipated. Warning: This unit feels intense dissatisfaction about touching Irregular Number. It's too tight in here. Don't touch me. Go away.*"

"*You don't think I'd ever willingly touch a heap of scrap metal, do you? As you are a machine, why not fold into something more compact? ♥*"

"*Rebuttal: Flügel are a magical race and therefore capable of shape-shifting. Recommendation: Maybe turn into a mushroom or something?*"

——*There's gotta be better game mechanics than just stuffing people into bags*, Sora thought while he heard his two friends bickering from within the opened sack.

With that out of the way, Sora moved on to his next and final set of orders to win the game. Which were!!

* * *

"We're gonna have Izuna and Til carry us through the dungeon up to the hundredth floor! Between a Werebeast and a Dwarf, we should be able to avoid any enemies and make it through without a fight!!"

...You expect us to fight every orc, slime, and goblin who comes outta the woodwork ...? Not gonna happen—!!

"——So you're not even going to try playing the game... I suppose that's typical of you...," Steph muttered from atop Til's back after hearing Sora shout out his directions.

"Not even try? Avoiding unnecessary battles is how these games work!"

Sora defended his idea from roughly the same height—atop Izuna's back, with Shiro on his shoulders.

"Or what, Steph? Are you the type who has to kill every monster you see in an RPG? Take a second to think about what you're saying. That would be a literal massacre in this world. I'm actually appalled..."

"There you go again! I don't even know what an *are-pee-gee* is!!"

Sora didn't miss an opportunity to tease Steph—but nevertheless:

"Hope is all we have in this game. We lose it via MP if we attack, and we lose it via HP when we get attacked. We have to keep our hope at all costs, so there's no reason to go out of our way to use it in a fight. Avoiding enemies is our only option."

"I...suppose you're right about that..."

Normally, in these sorts of games, the party gets experience points, money, maybe the chance at a rare item drop by defeating enemies—fighting is how you grow your characters. But with their hope being a set value in this game, it was doubtful there was anything to gain from combat in terms of levels or loot, so there wasn't much reason to fight in the first place.

* * *

——Looks like the UI is on our left wrists, too...
There's something curious about the blank space between my wrist
and my status bars, but...oh well.

"That said, it sounds like we'll be up against bosses on each floor, so we probably won't be able to avoid all the fights."

——There was also the question of whether they could skip the floor bosses the skeleton was so kind in alluding to for them before.

Either way, though avoiding as much confrontation as reasonably possible seemed to be the best course of action in Sora's mind, his directive did not go unquestioned—

"Master...I would like to ask for permission to pose a question about your orders..."

"Evident: Master and Little Sister have critically low HP pools. Advice: Avoid combat."

Two voices could be heard raising their concerns from within the party's inventory.

——They were right: Sora and Shiro both had HP pools so thin that it was well within the realm of possibility they would be taken out of the game in one hit.

Even on Izuna's back, all it would take was one stray shot for it to be *Game Over, You Died.*

While Jibril and Emir-Eins's shared concern was legitimate—

"We need to keep you guys away for an emergency, since you're the only two who can use magic."

...Technically Til—a Dwarf—should've been able to use magic, too, except she was more confident in her ability to accidentally blow up the party than to actually be of any use. Therefore, Jibril and Emir-Eins would have to be tucked away to save their MP pools for a real emergency—

——There's still a lot we don't know about this game.
Sora made this implicitly clear.

"...*Understood. Your wish is my command, Master.*"

"...Consent: *Please be careful, Master.*"

The pair solemnly withheld their concerns, and the party outside of their inventory looked to the far edge of the safe zone.

There sat a door, beyond which undoubtedly extended a vast dungeon.

It was time for them to enter the Tower dungeon—but before that...

"So...Izuna...I think you're gonna have to leave your stuffed toy behind..."

"...We'd like you...to carry us with, both hands...if you can..."

"Uuugh?! I don't wanna, please! Th-this thing's mine, please!"

"As I've made clear, I am no one's *thing*!!"

Izuna clung to her fuzzy toy—the Devil—with great zeal, which left her with only one arm to carry both Sora and Shiro on her back. This gave the siblings pause. Then:

"Mweh-heh-heh... I understand how one could fall to His Evilness's cute allure, but the Devil that you hold in your hands is my own possession."

Going somewhat against the Devil's claim that he was *no one's thing*, Schira Ha bowed her head.

"The fragment of His Evilness that you hold maintains its manifestation through me as its catalyst. Should you move too far away from me, it shall vanish, so you will not be able to take him into the dungeon either way..."

"See? We gotta leave him behind, so give it here—whoa?! I knew you were strong, but holy crap?!"

——Schira Ha and her owners, Sora and Shiro, finally motioned to free the Devil. But *someone* didn't want to give him up just yet.

"Nooo... Uuuugh!"

"...C'mon...Izzy... We'll see him on the...hundredth floor... Okay...?"

Izuna sank her claws into the stone floor, refusing to budge one bit, until the trio eventually managed to convince her to drop her toy.

With that, the siblings climbed onto her back and—

＊　＊　＊

"All right, guys!! Off to the hundredth floor we go!! Let's bust this dungeon as quick as we can!!"

"...Whoo-hoo...!"

"Y-yes, of course!!"

"Yessir indeed!!"

"Hmph... Fine, please!!"

With Sora, Shiro, and Steph on the backs of Til and Izuna, the party rallied themselves before moving forward. Their inventory bag was close behind, floating quickly through the air as they went.

The party rushed through the door at breakneck speed in their quest to beat the Tower dungeon.

————.............

"Schira Ha...tell me, do you truly believe these heroes will make it to me?"

"But of course, Your Evilness. The wisdom you've gifted me tells me so."

The furball and the snake-eyed woman silently watched the party leave the safe zone before exchanging these words.

"They will make it to you... And if Your Evilness so wishes for it, they will go even farther than that—"

Schira Ha didn't just believe this—she knew it, as if she'd already seen it for herself with her serpentine eyes.

Schira Ha held the Devil in her arms and quietly left the Tower......

■■■

——When the party passed through the door, what awaited them was a whole new world of its own. Compared to the safe zone they'd just left, this was...

"Is this supposed to be some sort of big cathedral...? This is the last place you'd expect to find the so-called Devil..."

"…They're kind of…the same…in Fr*m games…"

"…What are you two talking about this time?"

It was a marble palace, adorned in mystical holy markings with a ceiling over twenty meters high. Before them extended an endlessly long hall that was supported by tall, lavishly decorated pillars for as far as the eye could see, with multiple offshoots from the main path in eyeshot as well—but that wasn't all.

A large group of Demonias—skeletons clad in armor—could be seen rushing the party from afar.

——And just like the heroes, above each of the skeletons' heads were red and blue bars. They likely worked the same way: The enemy would be rendered incapacitated should their HP fall to zero.

Without paying much mind to their attacks, Izuna kicked into high gear and followed her party's strategy by slamming her hands into the ground.

——*Ka-boooom!!*

Two small fists slammed loudly against the floor, leaving a crater and creating an echo.

"There! I can hear some stairs, please! This way, please!!"

Through echolocation, Izuna was able to pinpoint the stairs to the next floor within seconds. The path to the stairs was not without traps, but Izuna saw right through each and every one of them using her incredible perception. She did this all while carrying Sora and Shiro piggyback, and following close behind was Til, who did the same for Steph.

"——I knew this going in, but…you guys are so OP as a race…"

"…B-B-Brother…! D-don't drop…meee…!"

"AAAAAAACK! I'm gonna fall!! I DON'T WANNA DIEEEEE!!"

"L-Lady Steph! Please don't scream into my ear!"

——The brilliantly ornate walls and pillars, as well as the high ceiling, were easily scaled by the dynamic duo as they zoomed through the wide halls shouldering their three companions, who clung on for dear life.

No Demonias were capable of catching them—let alone getting a glimpse of them. Those who attempted to chase the group blindly were quickly picked off by Sora and Shiro, who skillfully fired their projectile weapons from Izuna's back.

Less than eighteen minutes passed before the party finally reached the end of the ninth floor and ran up the stairs to the tenth when they came across something new: a door that sat in the middle of a distorted magic circle...

...*Yeah, that just screams, "Welcome... Beyond this door awaits the room of the tenth-floor boss. ♪"*

From the looks of it, I bet we're not gonna be able to skip the boss fight...

Sora, Shiro, and Steph hopped off Izuna's and Til's backs to discuss their next move.

"I'm guessing there's a boss waiting behind that door. One that we won't be able to ignore like the rest of the enemies. In other words, this will be our first battle."

As Sora said this to his party members, each of them clutched their weapons.

"Here's the plan," Sora continued:

"Steph, you're our tank. You're gonna be on the front lines. I want you to get as close to the enemy as you can, and catch as many attacks as you can with your shield. You are going to be our literal shield—our lives are in your hands... We're depending on you."

"————I know. You can count on me."

Steph shook off the doubts she had about this weighty role before giving a firm nod. Sora nodded back.

"Izuna and Til, you two are gonna be our melee DPS. Use your agility to dodge any attacks the enemy throws your way, then deal as much damage as you can from behind Steph's shield. If possible, try to draw aggro away from Steph so she isn't being constantly attacked. Me and Shiro will be the ranged DPS—we'll attack from a distance. You guys got that?"

It was a clear and simple plan, but Sora's eyes invited any questions they may have had.

"…Wh-who's gonna protect you and Queen Shiro, Sir…?"
Til had the same concern that Jibril and Emir-Eins had shared earlier. It was almost as if she asked the question for them once more, as they were in the inventory bag, but with a bold grin—

"…We won't…need it… They won't even…hit us…"
——*Did you guys forget what happened when we fought the Eastern Union? Not even a bloodbroken Izuna could hit us with her hail of bullets.*
The siblings' confidence almost felt arrogant, and elicited a group-wide *gulp.*
But their confidence wasn't as unwarranted as their initial response made it seem—
"Don't worry. If there are multiple enemies, or if the boss uses some kinda attack that can't be dodged, we'll put our backs to Steph's. You two only need to focus on supporting her, and we'll be safe."
Their confidence had its foundation in a contingency for attacks they couldn't handle—it was all part of the plan.
With each party member knowing their role, the group nodded to each other.
Sora then turned to the door that stood between them and the boss once more, and Shiro muttered to him:

"…Brother… This'll be, tough…without a healer…"
——*She's right… There's no way to heal ourselves in this game. This is likely the reason no one's been able to beat it so far.*

"Let's go."
With unusual tension in his voice, Sora said this before touching the magic circle that encompassed the door.
Doing so caused the magic circle to shatter into pieces, and then the door opened with a loud, heavy sound. And then—
《~~~~~~~~~~~~~~~~~~~!!》

* * *

A low sound erupted from the center of the room—so low, in fact, that the Immanity party members couldn't even initially hear it, but they sure could feel it. The sound echoed in their bowels, but what shook them even more was the imposing figure that was the source of the growl.

Standing before them with a massive ax was a Minotaur. At five meters tall, the bovine-headed Goliath growled viciously as it stared them down.

Just like the enemies they'd encountered up until this point, there were two bars above the Minotaur's head—each extra-long, just as one would expect from a boss monster.

Steph couldn't hold back a brief "Eeep!" when she and the rest of the party charged forward.

As soon as they stepped into the boss room, the door behind them roared once more while it closed. The magic circle from before reappeared, this time behind the Minotaur.

——*Looks like I was right! We gotta beat this guy if we wanna go up!*

Sora shouted this to himself on the inside as he cocked his Anti-Matter Rifle, the sound of which acted as a signal for the rest of the party.

Shiro, Izuna, Til, and Steph all followed suit and readied their weapons.

Okay... This guy doesn't look all that quick, but we won't know until we try...

"We need to rush him!! Use as little of your power as you can to beat him as quickly as possible!!"

——Sora shouted these words so loudly that his companions were only just barely able to hear them over the Minotaur bellowing another deep roar. The battle then commenced, with both sides charging toward each other at once, and the party's first real battle began...

■■■

All in all—the battle went smoothly.

In terms of physical strength, the Werebeasts lived up to their reputation as the Ixseeds' strongest race, with Izuna as their representative—especially with her bloodbreak ability active.

Dwarves were always known to be a close second, with their dynamic visual acuity and brute strength; Til, too, did her people justice by adeptly wielding her weapon.

Appearances didn't betray the Minotaur boss, as its sluggish attacks didn't even come close to connecting to the party's two speedsters.

The pair invited attacks that they skillfully dodged by using the walls and ceilings for footing.

Then there was Steph; her Great Shield was more powerful than anyone could've imagined.

Only slivers of damage from the Minotaur's mighty great ax managed to chip through her shield.

Far behind Steph were the siblings—the boss launched throwing axes at Sora and Shiro, but they skillfully dodged any that came their way.

This was how the battle quickly approached its end...

"We almost have him!!" Steph called out to the party.

The massive Demonia was under a constant barrage of blows between Izuna's Kitty Gloves, Til's Great Hammer, and the siblings' bullets.

The long HP bar above its head slowly depleted to its last bit when it happened.

————.........

"Oh...? What's this...?" said Steph.

The Minotaur suddenly fell to one knee and, without making a sound, was engulfed in light before disappearing.

"Whew... That was pretty good for our first fight... It sure ate up a lot of resources, though..."

Steph was caught off guard by the sudden finish while Sora looked at each party member's HP-MP bars and reviewed the battle.

——*This was our party's first battle. Up against a strong enemy, the only damage we took was chip damage through Steph's shield. We still have over 90 percent of our MP left as well. In normal circumstances, this would easily be considered a flawless victory.*

But…the problem is, this is only the tenth floor. You don't need to be a galaxy-brain gamer to know that the Minotaur will be the weakest boss we're gonna face. And not just the bosses—the mobs we're gonna try avoiding will get stronger and stronger, too… Losing roughly 10 percent of our MP on the tenth floor of a hundred-floor dungeon is not great…

Shiro, Til, and Izuna all shared Sora's concern, but the fifth hero had other worries on her mind.

"U-um, hello?! You're acting like this is over, but the boss still had some HP left!! Wh-what if he pops out and attacks us again?!"

What if he's only hiding?

The vigilant Steph looked frantically around the room for a potentially hidden enemy, but Sora filled her in:

"Oh…you didn't notice? The Demonias we defeated all disappeared the same way."

"——Come again?"

"You saw how me and Shiro were picking some off on the way here, right? Izuna and Til beat some, too."

"Oh, yes…I did find it a bit strange, given that your orders were to ignore any enemies before the boss."

"I mean…you didn't think we were gonna go up against the boss without knowing how the system works, did you…?"

Steph cocked her head in befuddlement. Sora winced and explained what the rest of the party had already noticed.

"First, whenever we defeat an enemy, we recover some MP. This goes for the boss and the random mobs we defeated on our way here."

"——Wait, really…?"

The entire party nodded, which caused Steph to blush with embarrassment, but Sora continued.

"Yup, and since this was the first time any of us took any damage, it looks like our HP recovers a bit, too. Take a look at yours."

There were next to no ways for the party to heal their HP in this game.

While they could get some back this way, there was one little problem...

"Here's the thing, though: The MP it takes to defeat an enemy outweighs the amount of HP we get back."

——On the way to the boss, the party—save for Steph—defeated a handful of mobs, mainly skeletons and slimes, but...

Even when they distributed the attacks between the four of them, the MP they received upon a single victory just wasn't worth it. It was a net loss between the four, who were using their MP to make attacks. Though they received a bit more after defeating the boss, it was still a net loss, with them each losing nearly a tenth of their MP pool.

"It looks like I was right about there being little to gain from fights."

——Though there was still the question of *why* they recovered HP and MP in the first place...

"But...we have some bigger problems to deal with. Three, to be exact."

Sora said this, then held out his hand and extended up the first of three fingers.

"One, the attacks in this game deliver no impact physics."

Were the attacks limited to only Sora's and Shiro's bullets, this could be chalked up to the toughness of the Demonias; but neither the random mobs nor the boss budged an inch when taking a hit from Izuna's Kitty Gloves, which had all the force of a truck.

"I mean...seeing as we're using our hope to fight...I'm guessing our HP bars must be some *hope barrier*, and any attacks we or the enemy make are against each other's barriers. How else do you think you stopped that giant Minotaur's ax like that?"

"_____"

Now that you mention it, the boss monster's big ax should have sent me flying... Why did I think I could receive an attack like that without dying in the first place...?

The blood drained from Steph's face once she finally came to this realization, but she was actually glad she'd gone in oblivious.

——Regardless, these settings would likely remain in place because of the Ten Covenants.

This may have been a battle game, but harming one another was still physically impossible.

So this much Sora was able to predict beforehand. The problem was that this aspect applied to the enemies as well...

"This means that we can't stop our enemies from attacking unless we fully defeat them."

The enemies wouldn't flinch or budge no matter what kind of attack the party threw at them—the heroes had no stopping power.

This meant that they wouldn't be able to mow down big groups of mobs because they'd run out of MP too quickly.

This would be a problem should they end up in a map where Izuna and Til could get surrounded—

Steph gulped at the thought, but Sora still had two fingers left to raise.

"Which brings us to problem two: The enemies disappear before we KO them."

It was the very thing that Steph had worried about only moments ago, and Sora explained why this was a problem.

"The enemies in the Tower are Demonia staff operating on a lenient four-person-shift, four-day workweek."

"Huh...? Yes, I suppose Genau Ih did mention something along the lines of that..."

Then it should be clear why the enemies disappeared before dying—

"Basically, the staff running the game are protecting their employees from a welfare standpoint."

"Okay...?"

——*And this means...?*

The significance of this was lost on Steph, who Sora set aside for a moment.

"Hey! I know you're listening! What's the deal here, Schira Ha?!"

He called out for someone who wasn't there, leaving Steph and the rest of the party confused for a good ten seconds, until—

"...*H-His Evilness has given the green light...so if you would please, Schira Ha the Wise...*"

"*Mweh-heh... I suppose I should no longer be surprised by your cunningness, O Heroes.*"

Schira Ha must've been outside the Tower, likely with the skeleton in the Joint Chiefs of Staff office.

It must've gone against their company's compliance for someone who wasn't even staff, let alone owned by the participants, to answer them.

But seeing as the little furball allowed it, Schira Ha's voice, in all its wicked elegance, could be heard over a broadcast.

"*Mweh-heh... Yes, what you heroes call HP is, as you say, your hope being depleted... In the case of our staff, we warp them to a work-related injury rehabilitation center just before they run out of hope and give them the time off they require to recuperate outside the Tower.*"

It was well established that the benefits of the Demonia employment system never disappointed. But this spelled something else for the party—

"_____"

Steph, too, gulped upon hearing Schira Ha's explanation, which elicited a wry chuckle from Sora as he returned to his point.

While there was a safety net for the Demonia staff who competed against them in the Tower—

"If our hope, on the other hand, runs out, we lose the game, correct? And since we're the challengers, it's safe to assume Demonia's awesome benefits don't extend to us?"

"..............."

"And we all know what happens when someone runs out of hope and loses in this game."

They would end up the same way as the people who entered this Tower before.

——Losing all hope—or falling into *despair*, which meant:

"So if we run out of MP, then there's no way for us to defeat the enemy, and then it's only a matter of time before our HP is finished. We end up either killing ourselves, or worse, become living husks of who we were...although which of the two outcomes is worse depends on how you think, I guess."

Thus, with losing one's hope being the losing condition of this game, every attack they made drew them closer to their own demise—little by little.

They couldn't move forward without using their own life force to attack, and there was no way to realistically replenish any hope they lost...

"..............."

After hearing Sora colorfully articulate the direness of the straits the party was in, Steph was joined by Shiro, Til, and Izuna in tensing up at the thought of the desperate game they had been thrown into—

"...*Though it pains me to say, Master, perhaps it would be better for you to remain in the party's inventory bag instead of us...*"

A voice came from the bag. The speaker must have been able to tell what was going on.

Jibril made the same suggestion she'd made before, and this time, Sora thought about it for a moment, before—

"Jibril and Emir-Eins...swap in for Til and Izuna."

As Sora muttered this, Til and Izuna were instantly sucked into the bag and replaced by Jibril and Emir-Eins, who came swirling out.

* * *

——Why swap out Til and Izuna and not Sora and Shiro themselves?

Jibril and Emir-Eins wondered this in confusion while the rest of the party was looking at their status bars.

"You two… Why are you missing HP and MP…?" Sora asked them.

"———Oh?"

"…Confirmation: Both this unit and Irregular Number are missing just under two percent of HP and MP. Question: Why…?"

These two had yet to fight, and yet they'd already lost a small amount of their HP and MP.

No one had an answer for Sora or Emir-Eins, and they spent a few moments at a loss—

"…Til and Izuna. Swap in for Jibril and Emir-Eins."

In the same fashion as before, the two tiniest party members came out with a swirl.

Sora then addressed Jibril and Emir-Eins, who he sent back into the bag.

"We can swap out anytime in an instant. I'm gonna save you guys for an emergency, just like we planned."

"…Yes, I understand."

"…Doubt:… Reluctance: …Understood."

While it was true that it was dangerous for Sora and Shiro to be out of the bag, as they were one hit away from death, there was a new, even bigger risk that Sora had just realized.

——Our trump cards in Jibril and Emir-Eins may only have one use each…

"Til…let me ask you one more time. The Dwarf party that supposedly tied at this game did it in a little over a day, right?"

"Um… Yes, that's right. I don't know the details, but they went into the Tower, and thirty hours passed before the Devil disappeared— or so I heard from the chieftain, I did!"

This was the same four-hundred-and-eight-year-old information that Til had shared with the party before they departed Elkia.

With this in mind, Sora's original goal was to clear the Tower in under a day. The party needed to use as little of their hope reserves to pass through the dungeon as fast as they could, otherwise they wouldn't be able to win.

Or so…one would assume. Right…? But—was this really the case?

"…Aaaanyway… Schira Ha!! I gotta ask: Why does my weapon suck so much?!"

This had been on Sora's mind both during the boss fight and during the trip there.

As it would play into how he would allocate the party's resources, Sora barked out his question angrily.

"Despite how menacing it looks, my bullets only hit as hard as a single shot from Shiro's Machine Pistols!! Between a slow firing speed, a seven-bullet cartridge, and a long reload time, my DPS is in the dumps! What gives?!"

——*Lemme guess…'cause it's ThE sHaPe Of My HoPe.*

Sure, the weapon weighs nothing and has no recoil, so it's actually pretty easy to use despite its large frame. But something about my rifle doing the same damage as Shiro's fully automatic Machine Pistols seems ridiculously unbalanced!

Sora's complaint was met by confusion spoken wickedly over the speakers…

"Mweh-heh… I'm…not quite sure what to say to that. The weapons you possess are the physical manifestations of your own hope, and not something we staff have a hand in designing…"

"…Brother…you're, all talk… Tiny…weak…limp… Your weapon… personifies you…"

"Ahhh, my dear sister… You *are* talking about my weapon, right? Okay, you know what—those are *your* expectations, not mine!! It's not even that tiny!! Or limp for that matter!! WE'RE TALKIN' ABOUT THE GUN, RIGHT?!"

"Um, Stuch. What the hell else could Shiro be talking about, please?"

"Izuna…that's something you don't need to know for another ten years—or, no, maybe even a lifetime. I lament the fact that I've come to understand this aspect of their banter..."

"King Sora! It's like you told me before! It's not the specs of the weapon that matter, but how you use it, it is!!"

"*Indeed, Master. Size and speed pale in comparison to technique in the grand scheme of things.*"

"Affirmative/Conjecture: *Its high accuracy makes it a superior model. Master should be proud.*"

Sora was being teased from all directions—even his friends pocketed in the party's inventory had their minds in the gutter. Sora tore at his hair and reeled back in agony, but he was also plagued by a new question.

——*There's nothing to laugh about; this is way too complex. Of course, Steph's boatload of HP stands out a lot, but it's not just that. Her shield mitigates almost everything that comes her way without costing any MP. It's way too OP.*

Then there's Izuna's Killy Gloves and Til's Great Hammer. Both super powerful, but they eat their MP pools like there's no tomorrow.

Just like how our HP and MP varies, our weapons function differently, and in too many different ways to keep track of.

Our HP and MP are the visualization of our hope, and our weapons are its physical manifestation...

...Hope...

It stems from the soul, which has a distinct definition in this world.

——*But is that really true? If it is, then what causes such significant differences in our weapons?*

"......We don't have time for this. Let's keep going..."

There were so many questions with no answers in sight. Worrying over them wasn't going to get Sora anywhere. He had a game to play.

"We're gonna keep rolling with this strategy. Ignore any mobs we encounter and head straight for the boss. That said, if this dungeon follows the same conventional gaming logic it has so far, then the next ten floors will be different from the first."

The party turned to the door from before, the magic circle that blocked it off having disappeared…

"The stage and mobs are gonna look and act differently than the first level, so stay on your toes."

The party nodded at Sora's warning, and with that, the Immanity members mounted Til and Izuna once more before getting back to the dungeon. Jibril and Emir-Eins followed from within the floating bag.

They went on…but Sora never raised his last finger. His final question was something he himself wasn't sure of, but had been eating away at him in the back of his mind.

That Minotaur boss we just beat… It started acting different when we got it down to around half health…

It was a second phase, something pretty common in these kinds of games. Usually, you'd expect the boss to get stronger, but it was the opposite; the boss had grown weaker. The Minotaur's attacks became more telegraphed after the halfway point, making them easier to dodge than they already were.

——HP and MP were the player's hope levels put into numbers. If the boss grew weaker due to the reason Sora thought he did, and if the same game mechanic applied to the party members…

No…it can't work like that… Or else there's absolutely no way the Dwarves could've ever cleared this game.

Sora shook his head, relieving his mind of this concern and leaving it behind in the boss room as Izuna and Til ran through the door and up the stairs beyond it to the next floor.

——The party had no way of knowing, however, that Sora's worst fear—the very fear he had left behind in the boss room—would come back to bite him only an hour later…

■■■

——Just as Sora had predicted, the eleventh floor revealed an entirely new world. The party left the grand marble castle for a mystical forest. It was hard to believe they were even in a tower, and while there was no distinct path to follow where they emerged, there was a pack of rabid humanoid mandrakes ready to greet them.

Izuna swiftly passed through the horde of mobs with Sora and Shiro on her back, following a path that only she could discern to the next floor.

Not too far behind—and above—were Steph and Til, the latter of the two jumping from tree to tree to keep on the Werebeast's tail.

At this pace, it didn't take long for them to reach the twentieth floor and its boss: a massive Triffid plant creature.

The Triffid used its vines like whips to attack the party while also clouding their vision with pollen, which it spread with each attack. The gimmick didn't amount to much up against Izuna's and Til's visual acuity and high mobility. And despite the high speed of their mount, it was no challenge for Shiro to calculate the trajectory for her Machine Pistol fire, which Sora used as tracers for his own. While the Triffid did manage to connect some attacks here and there, they were met by Steph's shield for little to no effect. Yet another easy fight.

Which brought them to the twenty-first floor. This time, the stage was a complex series of beautiful cavernous limestone tunnels. The first five floors went by easily, bringing the party to floor twenty-six.

" . . . . "
" . . . . "

——The party continued to spelunk their way through the long series of tunnels in search of the stairs to the next floor, but their momentum compared to even only an hour ago had dwindled as they quietly pushed forward.

Sora, swaying atop Izuna's back, reviewed what had happened so far:

——First, there was the battle with the twentieth-floor boss, the Triffid.

The cave terrain they'd been on since the twenty-first floor hindered Izuna's and Til's mobility, forcing the party to fight the groups of goblins and orcs blocking their path, which had cost way more MP than anticipated...

——The active party members had used almost half of their total MP.

"S-Sora...perhaps now would be a good time for a short break...?" Steph suggested, sensing how grim things were getting for her companions.

Steph was right—they'd been on the move for two hours straight since entering the Tower dungeon... She was keeping everyone's physical stamina in mind.

——But Sora and Shiro had spent these two hours on Izuna's back. They'd stuck to safe areas whenever they weren't in battle. Basically, they hadn't moved much more than they'd needed to so far. They were tired—but not in a *physical* sense. A different sort of exhaustion, one Sora was all too familiar with—the worst kind in the context of this game.

...There's no doubting it anymore. This is definitely...

"——?! Shit—I stepped on a trap! I'm sorry, please!!"

Sora's train of thought was abruptly interrupted by a turn of events Izuna's highly acute five senses should've seen coming from a mile away.

There was a flash, and in the next instant—the party found itself transported to a dead end—

"...Crap!! We're right in the middle of a spawn point!!"

They were up against more than fifty orcs, who growled as they each clutched their axes and stared them down. Down the corridor that appeared to be the sole exit was a familiar sight: a magic circle.

——We're gonna have to beat them all if we wanna leave...?!

Sora clicked his tongue at the realization before giving his orders.

"Steph! Get in front of me and Shiro! Izuna and Til, ignore the enemies on Steph and take them out from their flank!!"

His party members nodded. The commands were simple enough, but their execution didn't go so smoothly—

"——?! Whoops. Sorry, please..."
"Eeeep?! Lady Izuna?! Now's not the time for apologies, it's not! Look out behind you!!"
Izuna and Til leaped forward, except their lack of focus made it difficult for them to coordinate with one another. But that wasn't the end of their problems...
"...What...? Did...I...just...?"
——The unimaginable happened: Shiro missed her target.
Sora tried to give his little sister cover fire, but his weapon lacked the speed and power to help effectively.
Without any stopping power to keep the enemy from advancing, the orcs ignored his bullets and pushed forward—

"S-S-S-Sora?! We may be a bit in over our heads heeerrreee!!" Steph screeched.
Sora clicked his tongue loudly under his breath.
It was time for one of their trump cards!!

"Emir-Eins!! Switch with Izuna and mow 'em down!"
In the next instant, Izuna was sucked up into the party's inventory bag, and—
"Acknowledgment: This unit has been deployed. Orders received. Commencing destruction. *Auf wiedersehen.*"
Emir-Eins's maid outfit fluttered as she gently landed on the ground in Izuna's place and bowed. A series of bright lights came surging out from the multiple Drones that floated around her, whiting out the entire cavern.
——.........
——......

——The flash slowly dimmed, revealing the light the enemies shed while they slowly vanished. The party was dumbfounded by the sudden turn of events, but their confusion turned to relief as they slowly processed what had happened. They all sank to the floor.

"Y-you saved us... Hey, Sora! If Emir-Eins is this strong, we should have had her out from—"

The start. But Steph didn't get to finish her sentence.

"Emir-Eins...switch back with Izuna..."

Sora ignored Steph and made the switch, and just like that:

"......I...hate...this......"

——Shiro dropped her Machine Pistols and fell to her knees, wailing. She hid her face in her hands as large teardrops fell down her cheeks.

"——Oh. H-huh...?" said Steph. "Sh-Shiro?! What's the matter?!"

Had she been hit by stray fire or otherwise hurt somehow?

Steph ran over to Shiro, who was white as a sheet—but otherwise unscathed. Her HP was still full as well, which left Steph in even more dismay as her words didn't even reach the weeping Shiro.

It's happening, Sora thought.

His greatest fear about this game came true, and it happened to his sister first. He ran to her, and Shiro finally shared what had her in such despair.

And that was:

"Why... Brother...?! Why won't my boobs grow?!"

"Shiro!! My sister!! Are you really gonna let that be the thing that gets you down?!"

Meanwhile—close by, Izuna was curled up in a ball on the floor...

"...Uuuugghhh... I'm so goddamn hungry, please...!"

"Oh, come on! Now you're just being cute!!"

While these seemed like trifles to Sora, the two youngest party members lamented over problems that caused the utmost despair for them personally.

Tears were pouring down their cheeks like rivers when a voice came from the inventory bag:

"*Already Known:* ...*This unit is useless. This unit betrayed the Spieler six thousand years ago. This unit lied to him. This unit couldn't protect him. This unit failed her master as well... This unit cannot keep her promises...or protect those important to her...*"

"See?! *That's* what despair sounds like—whoaaa, holy crap!! That took a serious turn!! I think I just got whiplash!!"

"*M-Master...what happened...? The scrap metal's MP has been completely drained...*"

———Yeah, I know... *All it took was one fight for Emir-Eins to use up her entire MP.*

It's why he switched Emir-Eins out for Izuna so soon. The problem was, he still didn't know the reason why her MP had bottomed out. Sora was scratching his head from all the stress, when:

"Wh-what's the matter with everyone...? What happened—?"

Steph was deeply confused by the sudden vibe shift, forcing Sora to find the strength to fill her in.

"Nothing's the matter... This is exactly what happened to the tenth-floor boss at around half his HP that caused him to slow down... Dammit, I had a bad feeling about that, and it looks like I was right..."

It's a funny part of playing any RPG—and most other video games, for that matter: The PC can usually move unperturbed no matter how little HP or MP they have. They could be beaten half to death and still be running around and jumping as if they'd just woken up fresh—it's very unrealistic.

That wasn't all... Sora looked at the HP and MP bars above his head and at the bar on his left wrist.

"These HP and MP bars are a visualization of our hope, she said. We lose hope when we attack and get attacked. These two bars are how much *hope* we have left."

So if they ran out of hope, their bars would reach zero.
—*There's a path you have to go down before you reach utter despair, though...*

Although the party was physically okay, the stress was taking its toll. Just like how Shiro and Izuna had succumbed to anxiety and collapsed in tears, there were phases they would go through, and losing a certain amount of hope most likely triggered these phases. Sora doubted Izuna and his sister could even bring themselves to move at this point.

"Then why am I...and you and Til, for that matter, still all right?"

"Do we look all right...? Hmmm... In your case, it's probably 'cause you're a tank—you aren't attacking at all."

Indeed... Steph's MP bar was still completely full.

Even her HP was still over 80 percent—she'd retained most of her hope.

Til and Sora, on the other hand, had about half their MP left, just like Shiro and Izuna.

"...Hm? Oh, heh-heh. I'm used to feeling depressed, I am. I feel like this every day of the week... But I suppose if I had the choice, I would rather be drinking myself to sleep, I would..."

"Same goes for me," said Sora. "Maybe not as much as Til, but I'm pretty used to feeling like this...so I'm kinda just powering through it right now."

Although they could feel the depression setting in, they were coping somehow. Sora kept getting awful flashbacks; if he let his guard down at all, he might succumb to them at any moment.

Steph, holding back her desire to shriek, asked her next question.

"Th-then what are we to do? We haven't even made it to the thirtieth floor yet..."

She was correct...

The party wasn't even a third of the way to the hundredth floor.

* * *

Sora, Shiro, Til, and Izuna were still at full HP and had a little less than half of their MP left. They could probably make it to at least the fiftieth floor if they pushed themselves.

——But that was as far as they could get. This wasn't even taking into account that the mobs would get tougher as they progressed. Not to mention their mental health would deteriorate further as they used more of their hope reserves.

All things considered, a more accurate prediction was that the party was probably going to fully wipe at the thirtieth-floor boss.

Steph must have gleaned this from Sora's silence. She nodded and said:

"Sora…you must have a plan B—right?"

This is Sora we're talking about. The strategic mastermind behind Immanity's strongest gamer pair—Blank. There's no way he would set foot in this dungeon without a contingency or two.

Steph was more than certain that there was a second plan to fall back on, and—

"There is… It's what I'm saving our second *trump card* for…"

"I knew it! Then now is the time to use it! No use in holding back now!"

Steph's expression brightened up as she said this, but it wasn't that simple.

"We can't use it yet! If we do without figuring out the game mechanics first, we're screwed!!" Sora hollered.

"——!!"

Steph froze up from seeing him backed into a corner this much. Unfortunately…he wasn't in a spot where he could tend to her in that moment, for he was busy dealing with the toxic memories that were running through his mind.

He took a deep breath…and steeled his nerves.

* * *

Now's not the time for this. Quit it.
——My friends—and most importantly, my sister—are depending
on me to make a decision. I can't afford to get caught up in my stupid
past right now.
Able to clear his mind of any necessary thoughts for the time
being, Sora approached the problem once more.

...Think, Sora.
That Dwarf party managed to beat this game in a little over a
day. And that was without being able to heal their hope reserves.
This could only mean they cleared it in the most efficient, speediest
method possible. That was what Sora was trying to do—and yet this
was where he ended up.

Sure, Sora's party was probably different from that Dwarf party. They
couldn't bypass all the fights, especially from the twenty-first floor.
Were the Dwarves able to do it using their heightened sensibilities?
No—even if that were the case, they still had the bosses to deal
with. Which meant there was no way for them to avoid losing at
least their MP, which would ultimately lead to them losing hope.
Losing hope meant losing your ability to think and make decisions. Any combat that happened while in this state resulted in even
more unnecessary loss of hope. It triggered a downward spiral.
That said, the Dwarf party had also been on their first run-
through of this game. How did they make it four times farther than
Sora's party...all the way to the top...on their first try?

——It just doesn't add up. There has to be something!!
It's impossible for a party to clear this game as it is—Dwarf or not!!

What if...there was no correlation between the Dwarf party and
the Devil's disappearance? Maybe there was another reason that
the Devil vanished suddenly, and the dungeon was theoretically
impossible?

——No, Sora! Thinking like that will get you nowhere, you eighteen-year-old—er, nineteen-year-old idiot, you!!

Their hope was dwindling, and the slow onset of despair caused them more mental exhaustion.

Sora lifted his head, but then shook it and rejected the premise of impossibility.

It made no sense.

This game—it was made to be winnable; that was a given!

Schira Ha's behavior, the way the Devil acted—it proved this more than anything else!!

It's why I agreed to play a game with such ambiguous rules in the first place—!!

Yeah...there's a way to clear this game, all right. Actually, I'd go as far as to say that the way has already been paved for us! But the question is—how do we beat this game?!

——Why is there such a big difference in how our HP, MP, and weapons work?

——Why do our HP and MP barely recover when we defeat an enemy?

——Why can we use magic in a game where hope is supposed to be our only weapon? Why does it cost MP?!

——Why did Emir-Eins lose her entire MP pool in one fight?!

——Why did she and Jibril lose HP and MP without being in combat?!

The answers have to be somewhere in these details!!

Sora was falling deeper and deeper into thought, which was why...

"——S-Sora?!"

"King Sora?! They're behind you, they are!!"

——There must've been mobs patrolling the cavern, for a group of orcs had spotted Sora and were rushing the party. Sora hadn't realized this until Steph and Til called out for him...

——.........

He turned and faced the aggro coming toward him head-on.

Perhaps because he was lost in such deep thought, where he was thinking a mile a minute, the one orc's sledge looked as if it were moving in slow motion.

But what hit him next was not the impact of the sledge, nor any sense of being damaged, nor despair.

It was two specific sensations that induced a sense of euphoria in him…a mysterious softness. But at the same time, markedly firm.

The sources of the mysterious feeling were his two friends' bodies, which had collided with his as they ran forward to save him. Specifically: Til's belly and Steph's bosom.

And before Sora had time to process any of it—

"——I won't let them get you, Soraaaa!!"

—Steph shouted out, then slammed her Great Shield into the ground while Til collected Sora in her arms and jumped to the far corner of the cavern—and in the next instant…

——Sora witnessed Steph's MP go down for the first time. The group of enemies stopped in their tracks and turned their undivided attention to Steph.

"…Brother…! I'm so…sorry…!"

"S-Sora…I'm sorry, please!!"

Izuna and Shiro had been crying too much to realize quickly enough what was going on.

They leaped toward him and apologized; Sora pulled both in for a hug.

And then:

"What exactly did you just do, Lady Steph?!"

"I-I'm not quite sure myself! M-my left wrist started flashing, and then I saw some writing, but—I—I don't think this is going to last very long!!"

——Sora saw it as well.

He was overcome by a strange calmness. He looked at his own left wrist.

And there, he saw what he needed to see.

He found what he was looking for.

——He knew the exact reason why the blue bar at his wrist—his MP—had slightly replenished just now. And he knew what the blank space between the bars and the base of his left wrist was for.

He also knew what Steph had just done—she had pulled the enemies' aggro...

Everything made sense. Everything...

——*Heh...*

Ha-ha...

"...Ha-ha-ha... AHHH-HA-HA-HA-HAAA!!! *Hope!* Right!! You could call that *hope*, I guess?! I guess it is *hope*, in a way!!! AH-HA-HA-HA!!!"

"...B-Brother...?"

"S-Sir, did you bump your head...?!"

——He'd gone from utter silence to maniacal laughter. The rest of the party wondered if he'd finally lost his sanity, but he ignored their confused stares.

Without an ounce of hesitation or doubt, Sora took up his weapon—his mighty Anti-Matter Rifle. He then lifted the lengthy barrel, pointed it at the enemies beyond Steph's shield, and with every bit of his might, he imagined:

——*Hope is our only weapon in this game...*

——*These weapons are the manifestation of our hope...*

I get why my weapons sucked so much—I'd been using them like normal*!!*

I get why my bullets were so dinky despite the gun looking so cool!!

Sora visualized as clearly as he could what he believed his hope should look like.

With all his might, he pictured what he hoped he had, and then—
it happened. In the blank space between his left wrist and his two
status bars—a string of letters surged into his vision in a brief flash:

Unlocked: Flashbang Shot

The next instant—Sora felt the bullets within his cartridge switch-
ing into something else, which he used as a sign to pull the trigger.

Fire erupted from the vents of the gun as a bullet came rushing
out of its barrel with a loud bang and bright flash. The bullet broke
the sound barrier as it ripped through the space between its ejec-
tion point and its target, striking true. Steph could feel the air of the
passing bullet blow gently by her shield and—

"———?! What was———?!" she screamed, but her words were
muffled by the deafening, blinding explosion.

Before she could even turn to Sora for an answer, she soon realized…

"Huh…? Wh-what just happened…?"

The bright light subsided, and the group of enemies that had been whal-
ing away at her shield had folded into themselves like lifeless puppets.

A dazed Steph stared in confusion, for the enemies were still at
full HP but had collapsed on the ground…

——What just happened?

Steph wasn't the only one with this question, and Sora had the
answer the entire party wanted:

"Ha-ha-ha!! I knew it! Our weapons take on the shape of our hope—
and there's a skill system in place for learning how they work."

The same went for the rest of the party—including Jibril and
Emir-Eins within the floating inventory bag.

Sora knew his friends had no idea what he was talking about, but
he laughed off their dubious stares and continued.

"Til!! Did you hear what kind of Dwarves were in the party that
went when they cleared this shindig?!"

"———Huh? Well, uh, yessir! I did, indeed…?"
I should've checked with her sooner! Maybe then I would've been able to figure this out faster!!

"Lemme guess!! There was a married couple, or two people in a relationship, right?!"
"Uh, hmm… Oh, yeah! Yes indeed! It was the then-chieftain and his six wives, it was! Or so I heard!!"
"Goddamn it, Til!! You mean to tell me he went in with a literal harem for a party?!"
———Sora spat with disdain; this answer went far and above his expectations.
But what mattered was that he was right. He finally figured out how this worked!!

"S-Sora?! The enemies are getting back up!!" Steph screamed.
Sora glanced over at them and grinned.
He knew this was coming. His skill, after all, did nothing more than stun the enemies.
It was only meant to last a moment, and that was about to end—which brought Sora to his next move.

"You wanted a plan B, Steph? Well, here it is! Jibril, switch with Steph!!"
Sora then summoned his second trump card from the party's inventory. Steph was sucked into the bag while Jibril was spat out.
And without a moment's delay, Sora gave his orders.

"I want you to shift us back to the safe zone at the bottom of the Tower!! Can you do it?!"
"But of course. For you, Master, I shall make the impossible possible—!!"
Jibril said this with a brief bow, and in the next instant, the entire party melted into space and disappeared.
———·………

■■■

——Elsewhere…in the head staff office outside the Tower.

A large screen showed the heroes vanishing into thin air.

The footage left the suited skeleton and the rest of the staff in utter disbelief…

"…Hey, Schira Ha! Did they just leave?! Are you sure they will come and face me?!" the evil furball shouted from one corner of the office.

"Yes, they shall. That much is as certain as you are adorable, Your Evilness. But if I may be more precise: They are the only ones capable of ever making it to you."

The wicked lady's snake eyes were brimming with confidence.

"You still think that, even though they ran away before making it to the thirtieth floor…?"

"I do, Your Evilness. I will say it for you as many times as you wish."

Her red lips smiled seductively as she cuddled this fragment of the Devil.

Schira Ha did just as she said—whispering lovingly into his ear for the umpteenth time:

"They are the heroes you have waited an eternity for. They are the only ones who can fully realize your true hopes and desires. The first-ever heroes' party…"

CHAPTER 3
META-FANTASY

THE HEROES ATTACK!

——The preparation room was on the first floor of the Devil's Tower. What had once been an empty room with nothing more than a magic circle in it was...

"Mweh-heh-heh... I have brought the things you asked for, O Heroes."

"Great! Well done! You can leave them there, you can!!"

"...I wonder...," said Genau Ih. "This feels like it is against the rules..."

The suited skeleton helped Schira Ha unload the wagon full of things the heroes had ordered.

Til, with her Great Hammer resting on her shoulder, surveyed the room.

But surveying wasn't all she did...

"Ah, this place looks so dry and boring, it does. Go get us some decorations!!"

"Mweh-heh... Very well. I shall prepare them at once..."

In the center of the room was a large tent that housed a

comfy-looking bed—and even an oven, a table, all the basic cooking utensils, and a bathroom with a simple bath and toilet. It was enough to turn the preparation room into a quite livable space—but there remained changes to be made.

With the bare essentials now available, there was still much to be desired in terms of QOL that Til had asked their Demonia hosts for, but this seemed to be the straw that broke the camel's back—

——*Snap.*

"What do you heroes think you're doing?! You aren't even trying to climb my Tower—"

The Devil finally shared his annoyance at the heroes, who seemed more concerned with setting up their new life in his Tower than with trying to clear it.

Using Schira Ha as his catalyst to appear, the furball made his complaint, but...

"......Now I'm really confused. What are you doing?"

"Can't you tell...?! I'm workin'...out...! Ooof?!"

What he saw when he manifested was Shiro nonchalantly reading a book—no, not that.

It was what was under Shiro that had the Devil so confused—she was sitting on her brother, who was struggling to do a push-up.

"...I probably shouldn't be the one to say this, but I don't think an Immanity doing push-ups will aid you in your quest to defeat me."

——Here was the hero training to defeat the Devil, and the Devil felt bad for dissuading him.

"That's it, King Sora! You finished all thirty-five sets, you did! It's time for a cooldown, it is!!"

Til was leaning against her Great Hammer while Sora was flat on the ground.

"...Heh...heh-heh. You're as silly as you look, my little devilish friend..."

His arms were shaking, and his breath was ragged. A pitiful sight. But, nevertheless, Sora showed a bold grin and shouted his response!

"Yeah, I'm working out, but not to build muscle. It's to build *knowledge!!*"

"Schira Ha... Do you have any idea what this boy is on about?"

——*You don't get it? Heh—I guess that's only natural.*

With an even bigger grin, Sora took it upon himself to enlighten the Devil!

"What is knowledge? The product of a healthy mind. Then what is a healthy mind? The product of good mental health. Then what makes good mental health?! A healthy body, that's what does!!"

"King Sora! Your cooldown is over, it is! Up next: thirty-five sets of squats!!"

Til alerted Sora to the next task in his workout routine.

With Shiro still on his back, Sora began doing squats as he continued explaining his logic!

"More specifically!! It's the adrenaline, dopamine, and testosterone, along with a whole laundry list of other fun hormones, that a healthy body produces naturally that turns into a healthy mind, and in turn, allows you to gain more knowledge!! Basically, by working out my body, I'm working out my mind—and therefore enhancing my knowledge!! Why else would anyone do something as strenuous as this?! Do you read me?!?"

"Schira Ha, make him make sense!!"

Sora's logic was lost on the furball, who scratched his head in frustration while looking around for help.

"And you three!! You're a Flügel, and you're an Ex Machina!! Never mind this canine—why must you stuff your faces incessantly in silence?! You don't even need to eat!!"

The Devil then turned to something even more nonsensical than the exercise routine.

✳ ✳ ✳

"*Munch, munch? Gulp...* Yes...we Flügel do not require food to live, but... *Munch, munch.*"

"Report: This unit can ingest food as well as break it down for nutrition. Taste sensors also present. Report: Yummy."

"......Mmm—wait—mmm, *nom, nom*—please...I'll play with you when—*om, nom, nom*—I finish eating, please..."

The three answered him, gobbling down the laughably large quantity of food that Steph hurriedly prepared for them at a similarly laughably quick rate.

...It shouldn't need to be said, but this was the Devil's Tower.

Which meant that everything in the room and all the space in it were a part of the Devil.

——*What are these fools doing inside me??*

Tears began welling up in the furball's eyes when no one would give him answers—

"Huff...huff... What's the problem...my little devilish friend?"

"That's it, Sir! You're finished with today's workout!! You're glistening with sweat, you are!!"

"That was...a good pump, Brother... Here's some...water..."

Sora accepted a towel and some water from Til and Shiro, along with some words of encouragement, while he caught his breath.

He wiped himself down—

"Let's check something real quick, okay?"

—and while he did so, he addressed the Devil in a matter-of-fact fashion.

"First... This room, the preparation room, is a safe zone where Demonias won't attack us, right?"

This rule was a major premise for what Sora was about to discuss. He continued.

"And there are no rules about a time limit in this game, which means there's nothing preventing us from staying here for an extended period, maybe even setting up a camp or two, right?"

"———I, uh…?"

The furball didn't know what to say, but Sora didn't give him time to reply anyway!

"So while there is a rule that prevents us heroes from leaving the Tower, there's no rule that prevents the Demonia Schira Ha, who is in our possession, from going in and out to fetch things like food and water now, is there?!"

"———————I, er…uh…"

The furball continued to stutter in a stupor, and Sora finished by loudly exclaiming!

"Yup! Us heroes can't leave your Tower! Those are your rules, so I don't want to hear any complaining if we decide to spend the rest of our days here! *Capiche?!*"

…………,

…………………,

"…Sch-Schira Haaa!!! These fools are attempting to make themselves at home inside my Tower!! Inside *me*!! They're not even trying to come and defeat me!!"

"Mweh-heh… You're so cute, Your Evilness, but it is as the heroes say: There is nothing in the rules that prevents them from doing this. In fact, I, too, wish to reside inside you, if I so may."

"You too, Schira Ha?! This must be an oversight with the rules!! What kind of Devil would I be if I became a home for the heroes?!"

The furball cried more as he clung to Schira Ha. Satisfied, Sora headed to the pop-up shower, where he rinsed off his sweat.

———*Obviously, we're not gonna spend our entire lives here. We're only here to recoup our hope, that's all.*

It happened the day before, when Sora figured out what *hope* meant… Or, more specifically, where hope *came from*……

———Yes, it went back to the night before…

"Heh...heh-heh... I see... Much like that heap of scrap metal, I, too, am *utterly disposable*... Oh, Master...how I've failed you... Your inept servant deserves punishment... Specifically, the kind that utilizes my body for your carnal relief..."

"...Jibril's despair is totally within character. She actually seems kind of all right...?"

"...Good thing...she knows Evac... That spell's...super useful..."

——With Jibril's impromptu casting of Evac, the party left the twenty-sixth floor and returned to the preparation room on the first floor.

There, Sora and Shiro stared at the now depressed Jibril.

Sora, meanwhile, was mainly relieved that the spell worked.

Jibril's Evac used the entirety of her MP, as anticipated.

And sure enough, with her MP pool dried up, the spell drew from her HP pool to fill in the gap—Jibril was missing nearly half of her HP as well.

——Either way, Evac was a success, even if it was a close call.

The party made it out by the skin of their teeth, and Sora was relieved—but.

"This...is your big plan B? You just brought us back to the beginning...?"

".........................."

The rest of the party joined Steph in looking to Sora for an answer.

"We may not even be able to get back to the twenty-sixth floor, let alone the hundredth, like this..."

While Steph still had both her HP and her MP reservoirs relatively full, she certainly looked like she was on the edge of despair.

"The thing is, this is exactly how we'll make it there," Sora responded with an intrepid grin. "According to the rules, this is a safe zone. It's our *save point*. We can rest all we want here."

"...So it's the...kind of save point...where we don't get HP or MP back..."

Shiro stared at her dark blue MP bar as she eked out this sentence—but.

"Tsk, tsk, tsk." Sora waved his pointer finger—intrepidly.

"Here's the other thing: I figured out how to *replenish our hope*."

————?!

The entire party stared wide-eyed at their leader, whose intrepidness deepened as he continued.

"I want all eyes on my MP bar!! Notice anything interesting?"

They shifted their gazes up, and after a few seconds—

"............! Your...MP...hasn't, gone down...?"

"Comparison: ...Master's MP...is the same as before arrival at the spawn point...?"

Shiro and Emir-Eins were the first to notice, and what they shared shocked the rest of the group.

The trap the party had set off earlier sent them into a horde of mobs, which they fought their way out of.

Not only that, but Sora even used a mysterious ability toward the end to help get them out—and yet his MP was unscathed!

In other words, the combat earned him enough MP to match what he lost in the battle!

The six other members stared at his MP in awe while they waited for him to tell them the long-awaited reason why.

"Yeah... We gotta play this game using our hope as our *only weapon*—if our HP, MP, and weapons are all visualizations of some vague concept of *hope*, then let me ask this question one more time."

It was the heart of the game and something that didn't make much sense from the very start, and that was:

"What even *is* hope?"

"...Repetition: ...Part of the 'heart' and 'soul'... A general idea."

In this world, there was a concrete definition for *hope*—

It was Sora's third time asking the question, and the third time he received the same answer. It seemed to be common sense in this world.

But with a smirk, Sora declared:

"Nope. If that's this world's concept of it, then *this world is wrong.*" What was considered common sense in this world was utter nonsense, Sora suggested with a big smile.

His claim left the party speechless. Sora began walking back and forth, proselytizing to them in a professor-like fashion—

"*What is hope?* This is something that remains unknown even in my own world. The same goes for the soul, which we have yet to measure in any tangible way—but the mechanism behind hope and its principles are something we understand."

He stopped pacing and turned to the party.

"In other words, *hope* is a highly physical and measurable substance!!"

Sora said this with utmost confidence—could it be...?

That hope, a feeling, an *idea*...

Existed without the soul, and as a measurable substance? Not only that, but Sora even had proof of this?

This was hard to swallow, even for a scientifically advanced being such as Emir-Eins, who stared wide-eyed at Sora as he explained wisdom from another world.

What Sora was getting at clicked for one other member first:

"...Oh..."

Shiro seemed to pick up on things. Sora welcomed her realization with an enthusiastic nod.

So what is hope?

I have the answer for ya right here!!

"Hope is nothing more than *chemicals in your brain*!!"

BZAAAP————!!

Shiro imagined lightning flashing behind her brother as he said this.

*   *   *

——But.

——.........?

The other five members—well, four, because Izuna had fallen asleep already—stood together utterly dumbfounded by what Sora was getting at. But he didn't leave them in a daze for long as he enthusiastically continued!!

"Lemme put it this way!! It's not just *hope*, but your *mental fortitude*, and all your *feelings* that derive from the exact same thing!! It's all an *illusion* caused by chemical physiology in your brain!!"

"...That's...it...! Is that...really all there is...?!"

Shiro seemed to be convinced as she, too, joined in on his fiery passion.

The other four, however, were even more confused now.

Sora needed to continue his explanation before the difference in temperature between their cold stares and the flames in his and his sister's eyes started a hurricane.

"That's right! Serotonin is a good example! Or dopamine, endorphins, adrenaline, oxytocin—take your pick! Any of these pleasure-inducing science-based hormones can induce excitement or tranquility within a person—they are what make happiness tick! What make people wanna get up and go! In other words—these are what we call *hope*!!"

Shiro, his only comrade in the eye of the burgeoning storm, added her two cents!

"...Conversely...an excess or lack of...or the addition of a substance with the opposite effect...makes us depressed and anxious... throwing us into *despair*...!"

Were this the case, the mechanics behind the game would indeed make more sense!

Sora could sense what his sister was thinking and nodded with excitement as he continued!!

——*For instance!!*

* * *

"Our red HP bar is a passive value—our capacity to *handle stress!* It reflects the amount and or combination of chemicals in our brain that keep it healthy! Our blue MP bars are our active values—or our aggression!! It reflects the chemicals that make us proactively work to remove any sources of stress from our lives!"

"...That's why...when we defeat an enemy...the sense of, accomplishment...makes our brains...produce chemicals, that make us happy...and heal us a bit...! You did it...Brother...!"

"Ha-ha-ha!! Right? Right?! I only wish I could've figured it out sooner!"

Shiro's eyes showed a full understanding and a deepened sense of respect for her brother—but meanwhile...

"I-if I may, Master... Perhaps such logic pertains only to your original world..."

Jibril cautiously tried to argue against Sora, but he met her retort with a nod.

——*Yeah, this is all based on our own world's science. It's not even fully understood yet, particularly the significant difference between individuals and how the substances interact with each other at different quantities...*

My world isn't close to quantifying the human mind. We probably can't apply everything I'm talking about to this world, where each being has a concrete soul. Not perfectly, at least...

Yet after a year's worth of experience in this world, Sora could speak with confidence. For his discovery was not without evidence in this world, either—

"B-but that would mean...that the Spirit Theory is true after all, it would!!"

Til suddenly blurted out this comment.

And a smiling Sora urged her to explain herself with a prodding look.

"Um…it was a theory that an Elf came up with a long, long time ago, it was. Basically, feelings and mind power are the results of converting spirits absorbed into the body into two categories: *positive spirits*—a group of spirits that make you feel good—and *negative spirits*—a group of spirits that make you feel bad. Both of which impact your soul, they do… Thinking of these as the passive and active values you mentioned before matches up perfectly with the theory, it does!!"

——*I knew it.*

The logic of this world matching up with his own caused Sora to show a wry grin.

Jibril, however, didn't seem so convinced, and she responded with a scoff.

"…How idiotic. The Elf you're talking about from four thousand years ago was a meat-headed fool who thought *muscles solved everything*. This Elf spent their life honing their body, leaving behind a legacy that consisted solely of silly ramblings."

…An Elf like that actually existed…

Maybe the Elves are more diverse than we thought…

Sora was impressed. This certainly explained why Elf had a few-thousand-years-long grip on this world.

"Y-yes, that's right… This Elf called the physical body *a vessel for the soul*, which is now the established theory, it is. The part about positive and negative spirits, though, was laughed off by contemporaries because the spirits that make these up only account for less than a percent of your entire spirit-body, they do."

Til admitted the theory was not without its flaws—however.

"But! If what King Sora says is true, it falls in line with the theory, it does!!"

For example!!

"You are a magical being, Jibril. And Emir-Eins is a machine, she is. You both live by slowly consuming spirits as energy, you do!! Then why, in the Tower—where we can only use hope to fight—do you think you were losing HP and MP without doing anything?!"

"" _____ !""

The pair was dumbfounded by this realization, and Sora grinned.

The answer is simple... Hope is a type of spirit—and they're called positive spirits!

"That's not all! It would also explain why your magic output inside the Tower is reduced to less than one percent—because the only spirits you have access to are the positive energy spirits! It all adds up, it does!!"

In this game, *hope* was the only weapon they could use.

But for some strange reason, they could also wield magic.

The reason wasn't so strange when *hope* was the *same spirit energy* that they used to cast magic in the first place!!

—— ......,

—— ....,

"Indeed...this doesn't leave much room for retort—nor should it, as it is Master who proclaims this to be true. If the entire world has been incorrect about hope up until now, then so be it. I apologize for my stubbornness."

Jibril, kneeling before Sora to ask for his forgiveness, appeared satisfied with the new definition.

Emir-Eins wasn't convinced yet, though. She muttered a statement that suggested she'd been thrown even deeper into despair...

"...Confliction/Anguish: ...The 'heart' the Preier shared with Ex Machina...was merely a spiritual reaction? Mere physiology? Confusion/Disappointment: ...This unit...doesn't know what to think..."

Her despair, however, was a bigger mystery for Sora than the initial question of hope.

—— She was a machine with a "heart."

That in itself was proof enough that any "heart" was merely a physical compound.

Whatever the principle behind it may be—even if the "heart"

of both Ex Machina and all other Ixseeds was simply ecological programming.

Being so did not preclude said "heart," and the hope it felt from being legitimate.

"…Um, honestly, none of what any of you are saying makes any sense—but…"

Steph was unabashed about her lack of comprehension on the subject at hand, but she did understand one thing, which she dubiously confirmed with a question of her own:

"So the reason for Sora's and Shiro's lack of HP is because they have the mental fortitude of a wet paper bag…?"

"Heh…sounds like you know exactly what we're talking about for once, Steph… And you're exactly right!!"

"…We wouldn't be…recluses if…our mental health was better…"

"And yet the both of you are bursting at the seams with MP. It's quite fishy, I must say…"

"Don't treat us like we're the weird ones with those three fat HP bars of yours."

"…Steph…have you ever…even felt depressed…?"

"I'm stuck with you two, who can dish out mental stressors but can't take them—I suppose the fact that I can put up with that makes me just as weird as you! We're two sides of the same coin!!"

Steph conceded that both types were uniquely strange, and Til asked a question.

"B-but, King Sora—how did you realize all this?"

——Til knew it most likely happened back in the cave when Sora fell into deep thought, got ambushed, and then started laughing just in the nick of time.

Something happened in that brief exchange that led Sora to this conclusion.

He looked into his fellow party members' eyes—Til's included—and with a bold grin, he named sacred things that brought about his divine revelation. And those were!!

"No point in hiding it, eh?! It happened when I was sandwiched between your belly and Steph's jugs!! In that moment, I saw my MP rocket back up to full!!"
Figuring it out from there was super easy!
And the reason for that was!!

"Basically, my *horny thoughts*—and the endorphin rush in my brain—turned into MP!!"

This means we need to spend time rebuilding our MP reserves here in the safe zone by doing things that make us feel good!!
——We can recoup our hope reservoirs and run this dungeon as much as we need to—!!

"...You—you really are the most *despicable* person!!"
"——————Huh? What'd I do?!"
Sora, who'd been basking in the glorious moment ever since it happened, watched Steph cover her breasts and blush as she disparaged him for it.
"Is that really all your sex-addled brain thinks about?!"
"I thought we went over this the other day—but it really is!! In fact, I'd wager that just about any man on the face of the planet would cheer up if you let him cop a feel!"
"Maybe it would for you, Sora!! But not for all men...right?! Say it isn't so!!"
Steph looked to the other members for opinions, but Sora cast that aside for the time being.

"——Anyway, it looks like my instincts were right."
".........Oh? What do you mean, Sir?"
Sora met Til's orichalcum eyes and smiled.

* * *

——Why did Sora bring Til instead of the Dwarf race's strongest member—Veig—let alone Steph, who should've never even been considered?

Though he had no justification when asked this before, he knew that defeat in this game was related to despair.

So it only made sense that the two party members who were the farthest from that state would be the key to winning the game... That was what Sora's gamer senses told him.

With those vague senses of his being validated by reality, Sora felt proud of himself.

Though maybe not as much as Veig, I guess I can be a pretty sensible guy, too, eh...?

"It's not just Steph, Til. I knew you would be a key to winning this, too."

"——Huh?"

"Well, for starters, you sure knew a lot about *Spirit Theory* for it being written off as some Elf weirdo's ramblings lost in history, yeah?"

"——Oh. Oh, no! It's not like that, it's not!!"

Sora grinned roguishly at the Dwarf girl, who scrambled to defend herself.

Just like Steph, Til was another person who lived in a state that was the polar opposite of despair—

"I knew that all of us, even Jibril and Emir-Eins, could rely on you to teach us how to tap into the positive spirits around us effectively. Actually, you're probably the only one in the world who *can* do it."

"......What makes you say that, Sir...?"

"What? I mean, that should be obvious. It's your *eyes*."

Til's orichalcum eyes were timid and yet always aflame with red-hot passion.

——She was trying to overcome her uncle Veig, a once-in-ten-lifetimes genius.

All while understanding her own ineptitude. Her arms were called garbage. But she stood on top of that pile of garbage. Alone. With her hammer, she forged and would continue to forge for as long as she needed to. It could all be seen in her eyes.

She used every conceivable tool available to her—even studying obscure Elf magic theory on spirit-based mental care—to eventually achieve her dream.

In other words, a Dwarf girl who should've spent her life in utter despair—

—went more than fifty long years trudging through the despair without ever succumbing to it.

"You know better than anyone else in the world how to deal with despair, Til."

"_____"

The extent of Sora's trust and the depth of his respect could be heard in his tone as he said this.

Til's pale-blue eyes widened. She looked down and thought:

So... All that failure...all the disappointment...is about to amount to something...?

You gotta be kiddin' me... Please, say it ain't so.

'Cause this—this isn't something you ever wanna get used to, it isn't—!!

"Heh————heh-heh-heh!! You're right about that, you are!!"

Til lifted her gaze, and puffed out her small chest as much as she could...

"All this talk about losing and recovering hope never made any sense to me, it didn't—but if getting back up when you feel down in the dumps is the name of the game, I've been playing it for fifty years, I have! And I'm not gonna lose to anyone, I'm not! I'm a pro!"

Til exclaimed, loud and proud, almost as if she was copying Sora—

"I'm a pretty strict teacher, I am. Don't go thinking I'll go easy on you just 'cause you're my li'l bro!!"

Til grinned with fierce tenacity as she said this.

"Um…you know, you always ignore us when we point this out, but what is with the whole brother-sister thing—?"

"So you better eat up and get a good night's sleep!! And we'll need booze, we will!! But wait—we only brought the bare essentials, didn't we?! What are we gonna do about beds?!"

——As per usual, Til brushed aside Sora's remark and continued her spiel.

She remembered that the party had ventured into the Tower with the plan to speed-run it, and they'd brought as little as they could afford with them.

Til's confidence evaporated and her eyes filled with tears upon this sudden realization. Sora responded with a sigh.

"Oh, yeah… You don't gotta worry about that— Hellooo, Schira Haaa?!" he shouted, and once more, a few seconds passed before the elegant voice spoke over the intercom.

"Mweh-heh…? Is there something you need…?"

"Yup. I want you to get everything Til asks for, and bring it here, chop-chop. Thanks. ♪"

"Mweh-heh…? My apologies, but I am not one of the selected heroes, so I am unable to—"

Schira Ha, a literal possession of the hero's party, didn't have the option to say *no*; but since she herself wasn't a hero, she was forbidden by the rules from entering the dungeon—or was she?

"O RLY? Would that mean you broke the rules when you showed up to the preparation room after we *Aschente*'d and all that? I guess since you broke the rules, that means this game is over—"

"I've just now registered Schira Ha the Wise as a temporary member of our staff!!"

"I will be right there!! What is it that you would like me to bring?!"

Forgetting their evil laughs, the skeleton and Schira Ha rushed to get everything in order.

With that, Til began her stringent lessons in recovering hope——

■■■

As Til stated, she was a strict teacher in every sense of the word.

"The secret to getting back up when you're down is very simple, but impossibly difficult to actually do, it is!! And that includes: sleeping well, exercising well, eating well, and laughing a whole lot! That's all there is to it, there is!!"

——It truly was a simple concept.

Til had spent half a century realizing that true technique lay in mastering the basics.

First, in order to sleep well, she had Schira Ha and the Demonia staff prepare them a nice tent and set of beds.

This included a bathroom with a shower and a hot bath, as well as a toilet.

Within a few hours, the barren preparation room turned into a nice place to sleep, which was what they did the first night.

Next on the agenda was *exercise*—

"King Sora, Queen Shiro—you two are wildly out of shape, you are!!"

The following morning—Til, waving her Great Hammer around like a baton, announced this to the duo.

"You can't produce positive spirits without putting your body through enough physical stress, you can't! You also need to keep yourselves limber!! Forget spirits—you can't get air or nutrition properly distributed throughout a tense body, you can't! So you guys need to move!!"

She handed Sora a strength-training regimen that would push him about a half-step past his limits.

Shiro, who didn't have muscles to build in the first place, would be working on her flexibility.

With Emir-Eins's help to scan their bodies, Til was able to create perfectly tailored workout plans for both gamer siblings.

Up next was *eating well*—

"...D-do you really want me to cook this much food...?" Steph asked.

"That's right! By the way, this is a full day's worth of ingredients, it is!!"

Schira Ha and the gentlemanly skeleton brought a large quantity of cooking utensils to the Tower, but even more impressive were the several wagonloads of ingredients they delivered via multiple trips. Speaking on behalf of the group as they gazed upon the mountain of food in awe was...

"...I-I'm goddamn starving, but...I don't think I can eat that much, please..."

——Sure, eating well may have been important, but all the food had Izuna worried about overeating.

"Oh, yeah. Most of this food is for Jibril and Emir-Eins, it is!"

"...Pardon? You do realize that I am a Flügel, yes?"

"Report: Ex Machinas do not require ingestion of food to produce energy. Demand: Reveal your intentions."

But Til, in an unusual move for her, hit them with a sharp look.

"The two of you are constantly consuming *hope*—positive spirits—just to stay alive, you are!"

Though they did create positive spirits on their own, *hope* was consumed more quickly than they made it.

Which meant that any effort they put into creating more spirits would be outpaced by their consumption.

That was why:

"Positive spirits are produced in *all living beings*—which means you can absorb them directly by eating, you can!! You two are going to stuff your faces with food to absorb their positive spirits, you are!! We don't know how much food it's gonna take, so you're gonna keep eating until your HP and MP start regenerating! I want you to eat, eat, eat! All day long!!"

"＿＿＿＿＿"

The group was at a loss for words after hearing about the severe regimen, except Til wasn't finished yet!

"Oh, but don't eat so much that it becomes a pain, obviously. That would defeat the purpose, it would!! Enjoying what you eat is the whole point—and it's what makes your positive spirits, or MP, heal! Lady Steph! I'll need you to cook a wide variety of meals so things don't get monotonous, I will!!"

"Ah…I'm starting to understand why I don't have a training regimen planned out for me—"

"That's right, Lady Steph!! You'll probably be so busy cooking all day that it should be a workout for you, it should! It's two birds with one stone, it is!! Now, you better hop to it! Jibril and Emir-Eins are losing hope by the second, they are!! Let's go, go, go!!"

Each of the members could accept the various regimens, but when it came to the last one, *laughing a whole lot…*

After a good workout, some nice stretching, and a delicious meal—the team had finished the bulk of their training regimen.

The sun in the red sky peered through the window at the group, which was ordered to take a break they could spend as they wished, whether by playing games or reading a book.

They looked a little happier than they had the day before as they went to bed that night.

————·………

The next morning, the party emerged from their tents after a good night's sleep.

It was hard to remember what they'd been so depressed about only a day or two before…

Til's training regimen had an effect more tremendous than they could've ever imagined.

With that, Sora and the group faced the entrance to the dungeon, ready for their second attempt.

But it was Til, the strict teacher, who stopped them in their tracks.

"No matter how much you rest, you can only recover physically in a single day, you can!! In order to rest our minds, we must ease our tension and stress, we must!!"

The party looked at the status bars on their wrists and above each other's heads.

——It was true; their HP and MP were not yet completely full...

"Hmmm...I guess it's pretty hard to tell whether you're tired..."

"...Can we...have these bars...outside of this game, too...?"

Having convinced her party members to stay, Til nodded before continuing.

"First of all, King Sora's muscles should still be sore from yesterday, they should. We need another day of light exercise and stretching, and after that, we'll do nothing for the rest of the day, we will!!"

The party wanted a little more info on what exactly that meant, but Til shook her head.

"I can't be giving you *orders* 'cause there's no fun in that, there's not. I want you guys to think about how you'll spend your day off, I do. What makes you feel relaxed? What makes you feel fulfilled?"

Their strict teacher spoke in a gentle tone.

It was like a good-cop bad-cop routine, and Sora obliged her with an answer.

"A good handful of Steph's, Jibril's, or Emir-Eins's milkers would prolly fix me right—guh?!"

The euphoria Sora had felt only two days earlier seemed to linger in his mind, but his sister cut him off with an elbow to the stomach.

"...Brother...you wanna...cuddle with Izuna and...play games... and have your ears cleaned...and rest your head...on Jibril's and Emir-Eins's thighs...right?"

"Yeah, you got it! I'm just happy if I'm together with my lovely little sister, whoo-hoo! ♪"

——*Sorry, Brother... I know you wanted a little sister with a larger chest...!!*

Sora had replied at breakneck speed under his sister's gaze, which was fiendish enough to end a small mammal's life.

——Thus, Shiro also asked for her brother to clean her ears.

And perhaps jealous of her, Jibril and Emir-Eins, too, timidly asked for the same treatment, all three of them laying their heads on his lap while he did the cleaning, one at a time.

Afterward, they ate a delicious meal before snuggling up together and playing video games for the rest of the night.

The party ended up sleeping as a group...with the exception of Steph, who opted to sleep on her own in the corner.

■ ■ ■

...Another day passed—it was the morning of the fourth day since entering the Tower dungeon.

"Whew...my body hasn't felt this light in...forever...?"

——*In fact, this may be the first time in my life I've felt so great.*

Sora thought this as the sunlight from outside shone in on his face—something that would normally annoy him, but it actually felt good for once.

Ah...another morning, another day I get to wake up in a bed full of diverse nonhuman babes. So warm...so beautiful... If this ain't heaven, then I don't wanna go there.

It was a good morning, to say the least. And so the day began—

"Mmm, you guys did a good job these past three days enduring my training, you did!!"

The party was lined up next to Sora—their previous stress was now completely gone from their faces. To top it all off, Til thoroughly checked each of their HP and MP bars before giving them a happy thumbs-up.

With their strict teacher finally giving the go-ahead—

"Okay, it's been three days. Who wants to beat a dungeon?!"

"""""""""We do!!""""""""""

—the entire group was raring and ready to go, with all six members joining Sora in raising their fists in the air.

Jibril and Emir-Eins went back into the bag, and with a forceful *hup*, Izuna shouldered the siblings, and Til picked up Steph.

The two squatted down and prepared to kick off the ground at full power, when—

"Hold up. We're changing our strategy. I want you two to forget how we ran this the first time."

—Sora asked the two runners to stop.

They looked up at him in confusion, along with Steph and Shiro, and he shared the new plan.

"We're still gonna stay mounted on you two and avoid any unnecessary conflicts the best we can—that much is the same, but...this time we're gonna explore each floor entirely before we progress."

"Oh...? And why would we do that?"

"Entirely? There were corners of the dungeon where monsters were grouped up, there were?"

"Our MP won't last long against every damn one of 'em, please?"

Sora was hit with a series of fair questions, but he answered with a smile.

"You don't gotta worry about that. We can always come back to the starting room if things get sticky. Right, Jibril? I want you to always have Evac...er, shift ready to cast."

"Yes, Master. As you wish."

A polite bow could be felt from outside the inventory bag. However—

"But...Brother...can we afford...to do extra fights...if it means going slower...?"

"Yeah, things have changed since we entered. I'm thinking fighting might not be as wasteful as we initially believed."

Shiro tilted her head in confusion, and Sora held up three fingers.

"First, I want you guys to try and focus on unlocking your skills during fights."

"...Skills...?"

"Yeah, like the one Steph used to pull hate, or like how I stunned the enemy with an attack."

——This was the other mechanic that Sora figured out along with the definition of *hope*.

This was a game where the party members had only their *hope* to fight with.

The game system had their *hope* take on the shape of weapons that they could use to fight with—

"Watching Steph's skill unlock after she showed a strong desire to protect us all, I figured that we can unlock our skills by having a strong awareness for how our hope-based weapons are meant to be used. I already proved this concept by doing the same: focusing on what my hope would look like, which unlocked my skill for me."

Under the status bars on each of their left wrists was a blank space.

Steph's UI showed the following text: You'll have to get through me first!

And for Sora: Flashbang Shot

——Sora unlocked this skill by being conscious of his own hope, meaning *this ability emulated him.*

The rest of the party looked at him with asking eyes, but he ignored them.

He still had two remaining fingers' worth of reasons that needed explanations.

"Number two, you guys should figure out on your own soon enough, and number three—let's make it a surprise for later. ♪"

Sora said this with a teasing look, but then his face took on a more lighthearted expression.

"Y'know, I'm thinking the reason we got MP back by defeating monsters is because this is *fun.*"

It was something the party forgot along the way...

"——This is a game, after all..."

Games were meant to be fun; it was the basic of the basics.

And the party must've agreed, because they ran into the dungeon with smiles on their faces—

"That's all that really matters!! So we should have fun with it!!"

■■■

Only twenty minutes passed before the party's second expedition into the Tower dungeon revealed the answer to Sora's second reason, though it was sooner than even Sora expected.

"And there it is…I mean, it wouldn't be much of a dungeon if it didn't have these… I knew they would be here."

——It was something that caught Sora's attention during their first trip into the dungeon.

Every now and then, there were mobs that noticed the party but refrained from attacking them.

It was a group of skeletons—they were blocking the path, and it wasn't one that led to the stairs.

Though the party didn't have the leisure to investigate during their first run, Sora had an idea of what those mobs were there for.

And it was the biggest reason he wanted to investigate each floor in its entirety.

——Well, it was, but…

"Uh…Schira Ha?"

"*Mweh-heh… Yes, O Heroes? Is something the matter?*"

"I just wanted to double-check that our eyes aren't lying to us… Is this a treasure chest?"

The roads these enemies were blocking had to lead to something… but what?

The party soon learned after defeating one of the groups of mobs that—assuming the box wasn't an illusion—were there to protect treasure chests…

"*Mweh-heh… Your eyes are quite all right, for that is indeed a treasure chest.*"

"Okay…and lemme guess… There's items, like weapons and armor, in there that will help us…?"

"*My apologies, but the only weapon you heroes may use is your own* hope. *Inside the treasure chest, however, there are other pieces of equipment and tools that you may use. Mweh-heh...*

Mm-hmm... Is that right...?

"Then do you mind answering a question that's been on my mind for many, many years?"

Sora gave an exaggerated nod, then took a deep breath before shouting his question back at her.

"Who the hell's leaving these treasure chests here?! And inside the Devil, for cryin' out loud!! With gear that just screams: *Here, use this to deck the literal Devil, tee-hee!!* Why don't you guys keep your shit in an armory like normal people?! Huh?!"

This video game trope always bothered Sora—but:

"Mweh-heh... Inside the chests you find is the lingering hope of heroes who have fallen to the Devil."

"Lingering *hope...?*"

"Yes. The heroes who perished before they could reach the Devil entrusted their manifested hope to those who would attempt to defeat him in the future. In other words, these hopes are an inheritance— a donation *to other heroes. Such treasures are subject to protection from the Ten Covenants; our staff cannot collect them since that would be considered theft. Mweh-heh..."*

——Is that right? Huh...

Much to Sora's surprise, Schira Ha's answer actually made sense.

——It's true... Treasure chests are always hidden in mazes or paths with only one exit.

So these treasures must be left over from heroes who ran away or hid until they ran out of either their HP or their MP. And yet they still wanted to pass on what little hope they had left to the next heroes— that seems to be the story here.

The staff can't collect or move the treasure, so they have mobs guard the chests to make things more difficult for the heroes...

That explanation doesn't work for all RPGs, but it makes sense here!

*　*　*

"...It doesn't smell like a damn trap, please..."

Just to be sure, the party had Izuna check the treasure chest before opening it.

She gave her okay, and nervously, Sora opened the chest—

"It looks like...some kind of outfit? Maybe it's armor?"

He looked at the treasure—an amorphous object that glowed faintly—with confusion.

While the shape wasn't distinct, there was something about the light that made it clear that it was meant to be worn—

"...*Hypothesis: Remnants of someone else's hope. May take shape upon being equipped...?*"

Emir-Eins interjected from within the bag, prodding Sora to think for a few moments—

"Hmm... Welp, let's have Steph try it on."

"Huh? Why me? Seeing as I have the most HP, wouldn't it be better for you or Shiro to wear it?"

"Nope. We don't know if this even gives any defense."

There was no way of knowing whether Sora and Shiro would die in one hit even with the armor on.

"Since you're the one who takes the most damage, we need you to test out how effective the armor is before deciding whether me and Shiro can wear it. It's just safer..."

"Ah, I suppose that's true."

With a nod, Steph took the dim light that was thought to be armor from Sora's hands.

She then wrapped it around herself—and just as Emir-Eins had predicted...

The amorphous faint light began to take on a distinct form, covering Steph's body.

——The party watched, and...

"**——Wh-wh-wh-what kind of armor is this?!**" Steph screeched.

"I-it looks like the legendary armor used by a powerful female Dwarf warrior, it does!!" Til answered, her eyes lighting up.

Oh, that's legendary armor, all right...in the sense that you don't see it much nowadays.

It protected little to nothing and covered only spots that needed to be covered for a different reason...

It was none other than legendary—bikini armor!!

"Legend has it that the armor protects its wearer from all attacks, it does!!"

"Protects what?! My dignity?! It's not even protecting what little of that I have left!! This isn't armor; I think my regular clothes offer more benefit!!"

"Don't worry, Steph!! Protection and coverage have zero correlation when it comes to ladies' armor—it's common sense!!"

"Maybe in *your* world it is!!" Steph screamed back at Sora as she ran away from him; he was trying to take pictures of her with his smartphone.

"...Same goes...for men, too... The strongest characters...are always...practically buck naked..."

——Which begged the question of what kind of armor Sora would be wearing.

Shiro's comment appeared to pique the interest of the party members in the bag. Sora, meanwhile, shook his head.

"Calm down, O sister of mine... That logic only applies to a handful of games, where player skill is not represented by armor. Taking off any more than I'm already wearing won't make me roll any farther, and I don't have any invincibility frames to extend."

"I don't know what you're trying to frame, but could we at least stay on topic about whether or not I should wear whatever this is?!"

It was true that the so-called armor only covered...well, almost nothing...

Thus, Steph's concerns were warranted—however.

* * *

"I don't think you gotta worry about that anymore, 'cause there's a good chance we're about to find out," Sora muttered.

Steph turned to where Sora was looking and saw eight skeletons running down the hallway they'd just passed...

There were four with spears and armor and four with bows. They covered the only way out of the hall.

Steph took up her shield and joined Izuna and Til, both of whom had realized long before that something was coming.

"Steph! Catch their attacks with your shield! Once we know how powerful the armor is, we'll strike back!!"

Shiro, Izuna, and Til all responded with an "Okay!" but—

"Argh! I suppose I'm already wearing this thing, so I may as well roll with the punches!!" Steph shouted as she convinced herself to move forward.

She jutted her shield toward the charging enemy, who took the attack as an opportunity to focus fire on her—but...

——......,

"——Huh? Th-they're attacking me, right?"

Steph let slip her surprise at the situation.

While the attacks did hit her shield, the chip damage that went through was nearly nonexistent—

"...Whoa... Does her armor...give a fifty percent damage... reduction...?"

"Between her shield and the armor, she's taking next to no damage, she is!!"

"St-Stuch, you're freakin' invincible, please!!"

The entire party was in utter shock, including Sora.

"Wow... Who woulda thunk it...? Bikini armor...actually works...?"

"You're the one who said it would!! Why are you acting like it might not have worked?!"

But! In any case!!

* * *

"Never mind what this armor looks like! I can use it to defend you all!!"

Never mind what this armor looks like!

Steph said this more for herself than anything else before touching her left wrist!

"——You'll have to get through me first—!!"

Without waiting for her party members to join the fray, Steph activated her skill and focused all aggro on herself.

She called out to the party, holding her shield as she ran forward with the mobs all focusing on her.

"We can get out of here without wasting MP! I'll push the enemies out of the way, and once there's an opening, we can flee!"

It was a good idea, something rare for Steph.

Maybe she wanted to justify the armor she was wearing by making it useful for the party.

The group of skeletons continued to whale away at her shield—until all of a sudden:

——————*Shatter...*

"——? ......??? ....! AAAAAAAAAHHHH?!"

The bikini armor that (barely) covered her body had *shattered into pieces and disappeared into thin air.*

Steph needed about five seconds to process what the sound was before she screamed at the top of her lungs, triggering Sora, Shiro, Izuna, and Til to go in and kill the skeletons ganging up on her.

And while they came to her rescue—

"...I see...the armor...broke because it was hope...left behind by previous heroes...!"

"It doesn't reduce the damage, but the lost heroes' hope instead takes a portion of the damage until whatever hope left over runs out, it does—"

"And when it does run out, it breaks!! Hot damn, what an incredible system!!"

"It's a *terrible* system!! Where are my old clothes?!"

—Shiro and Til analyzed the armor, and Sora made an impassioned conclusion.

Steph was more preoccupied with looking for her clothes that had disappeared. She was searching frantically when two voices could be heard from the inventory:

"*Report: Previous clothes are assumed to have been swapped with the armor upon being equipped and automatically deposited within inventory.*"

"Yes. *Little Dora's outfit appeared inside this bag when she put on the armor.*"

"Oh! Perfect!! P-please, lend it here—"

With tears in her eyes upon hearing the news, Steph pleaded for her old clothes—when:

"Jibril! Emir-Eins! Are you sure that was really Steph's outfit?! I want you to be really, really sure!!"

"———What?"

Sora's sudden question caught Steph completely off guard. She stared blankly.

——A few moments passed.

"———*Oh, I understand... What's this?* ♥ *I can't seem to find Little Dora's clothes anymore.* ♪"

"*Restriction: Temporarily unable to identify Object X... Wherever did it go?*"

"Y-you two——Soraaaaaa?!!!"

"Never fear, Steph!! We'll make sure nothing hits you!!"

"...We got...your back...Steph... Izuna and...Til do...too...!"

"That's not what I'm worried about!! I don't think my old clothes offered any protection anyway!! It doesn't matter—somebody give them to me this instant!! For the sake of my dignity!! Hand them over!!!"

Steph continued to bear the brunt of the attacks like a true tank, all while suffering harassment from the two siblings behind her, who refused to give her back her clothes.

* * *

"Steph...those who lose their cool are the first to die on the battlefield. You must calm yourself."

Sora took on a calmer and more collected tone as he said this.

"Nobody can see you from the front so long as you have your Great Shield. There's nothing to be embarrassed about, am I wrong?"

"I'm more worried about my behind! I can hear you and your sister snapping photos with your cameras!! What can you see—? No, it doesn't matter—just stop taking pictures!!"

————.........

————......

Steph's plea was ignored.

Sora and Shiro skillfully picked off the enemies while also capturing shots of Steph's bare bottom.

They joined Izuna and Til in clearing out the enemies and eventually securing their way out of the closed-off path.

"Okay... We're going to search the entire dungeon, just like we planned."

Atop Izuna's back, Sora looked behind him to make sure the coast was clear, and he addressed the party.

"The lost heroes' *hope*—if there's armor that absorbs damage, there might also be equipment that amplifies MP to our attacks, maybe even allows us to attack without using MP."

These items might end up being necessary for the bosses on the higher floors.

The party agreed with Sora, who nodded before continuing.

"Any armor we find, we'll make sure to give to Steph. I feel bad that she has to stay naked for so long."

"...If you truly felt bad, you'd give me back my clothes! And I still think that you and Shiro should be the ones who wear the armor!!" Steph shouted, looking utterly resentful.

Til's back was covering the front of Steph's body while the Great Shield covered her rear.

＊ ＊ ＊

——They were able to test the armor, which absorbed damage from a few dozen attacks.

While Steph agreed to test it, she insisted that it was the siblings who should rightfully wear it.

But shaking his head heavily, Sora responded...

"Sorry, Steph, but that's gonna be a *no*... We don't know how much durability any given set of armor has, and if it leaves the wearer naked when it breaks, we can't have Shiro or Izuna wearing it... Though maybe Til might, if she's okay with it...?"

"Why does *she* have the right to be okay with it and not me?! And what about you, Sora?!"

"Uh...Steph? Where exactly is the demand to see a naked me?"

Sora brushed off Steph's assertion like it was nothing, but...

"...? There's...plenty of demand...for that..."

"*Obvious: There is only demand. Warning: Master should equip the armor for his protection. Strongly recommended.*"

"*Pardon me for saying this, but I would like to call into question how you believe there is no demand for such a sight, Master. Geh-heh-heh.* ♥"

Sora cringed at the idea his sister and their two companions in the bag had in mind—

"Uhhhh... Oh! Right!! We can't let a guy get naked in front of Shiro and Izuna!!"

"......Fine... Til and I will wear any armor we find..."

Sora used every brain cell available to think up a new excuse, which was accepted by a defeated Steph and met with a loud *Tch* by the other three......

■■■

——A little under two hours had passed since entering the Tower dungeon for the second time.

The party was standing before the boss room door, a point that they'd reached in just over ten minutes on their first attempt.

"Welp…I guess this is what happens when you check every corner of every floor?"

Compared to the first day, when the party reached this spot with full HP and MP bars, each member had currently used about 20 percent of their MP on average.

It was a good chunk of MP, but the sacrifice did not go unrewarded.

The party found multiple chests, each with valuable gear along the way.

Just as they had predicted, they found an item that improved their attack power by 20 percent in the form of an armband.

There was also a ring that reduced MP cost by nearly 50 percent. That said…

"We don't know when these items will break like the armor from before… I'd rather save them for the higher floors if we can, ideally the last boss, even."

These items could be particularly effective when paired with Jibril and Emir-Eins's abilities.

If they could halve the cost of Jibril's shifting, it could help to get her back on her feet afterward—

Sora mumbled to himself, and Steph interjected with dubious eyes.

"Then why am I the only one forced to wear my armor…?"

"What's that, Steph? You'd rather fight naked?"

"…It's time…you admit…you have, a voyeur fetish…Steph…"

"Give!! Me!! Back!! My!! Clothes!! I can't believe you made me run around the dungeon buck naked until we found the next set of armor!!"

"Oh, how strange! I could have sworn it was right here. ♪"

It took an hour after finding the first set of armor to find the second.

During which Steph was forced to strut her stuff throughout the dungeon.

When they eventually did find a new set of armor, it still covered barely any of her skin, though not quite as little as the bikini armor. Sora and the others kept refusing to return her original outfit, so Steph eventually gave up.

"Um, I don't disagree with saving the equipment, I don't—but we should probably use it on the boss, shouldn't we...? If it's the same boss as last time, we're probably going to lose around ten percent more of our MP, we are."

——That would leave them with 70 percent...which was when their mental health started to show signs of deterioration.

If that did end up happening, they could just warp back to the beginning like it was planned.

Til knew this but timidly made her suggestion nevertheless, which was met by a grin from Sora.

"Well, if my best guess is right, we might not even have to worry about that—"

"Whatareyou—?!"

"K-King Sora?!"

Sora finished his sentence by leisurely walking into the boss room. The rest of the party scrambled after him, but——...

————,

"...? Where's the giant cow guy, please?"

The Minotaur from the first day was absent.

The party stared at the stairs to the next floor, which were left unsealed like when they'd first cleared this floor.

"...Bosses in this game...don't respawn...?"

"I guess you could consider it a part of the game, in a way. ♪"

Sora seemed to know that the boss wouldn't be there, leaving his sister to tilt her head in question.

This was his surprise that he'd talked about before they left the safe zone—

"And that, ladies and girls, is my *third reason*. We'll press on with the same strat, searching every corner of every floor along the way!"

Though not without their questions, the party agreed to Sora's strategy. With Steph on Til's back, and Sora and Shiro on Izuna's—

"Our goal for today is to beat the boss on the thirtieth floor. We'll head home after that."

"Not having to beat this boss indeed makes this easier…but will we even be able to make it to the twenty-sixth floor at the rate we're going?"

Steph spoke for the party in questioning the goal Sora had set.

He happily waved her comment away.

"Oh, we'll make it, all right. Til, Izuna—we'll be relying on you guys to take us there. ♪"

With that, the two makeshift mounts made a break for the next floor.

■■■

And then, after the third hour had passed…

"——We really made it to floor thirty…"

"Things are going way smoother than our first attempt, they are…?"

"Even though we're running around like hell, please. Maybe 'cause there's no damn boss to fight, please?"

——The party fully cleared every floor in search of treasure and to unlock new skills.

Despite taking the enemies in combat, the team was able to pass the twenty-sixth floor, where they were forced to give up pretty easily.

And thus, having cleared the twenty-ninth floor—the party stood before the stairs that would lead them to the thirtieth floor, where a boss was assumed to be awaiting their arrival. It wasn't just Steph, but Til and Izuna, too, were confused by how smoothly things were going.

Sora forced himself to smile as he told them why this was happening.

"It's 'cause we're winning this time... We're recovering MP by beating the enemy."

"...? But...I thought that happened the first day, too?" said Steph.

"Yeah...it did, but things are different this time around, aren't they...?"

Unlike their first day in the dungeon, the party knew that they could recover their MP.

They also had a more realistic goal for themselves this time around—defeat the thirtieth-floor boss.

Not only that, but they had in their possession various treasure and skills... Now they knew that defeating enemies wasn't so pointless.

In other words—they were *enjoying the game*...

And of course, they were recovering more *hope* than when they went in blindly.

Though the rate they gained it at was still an overall loss—

"But I don't think we can beat this next boss like this. Shouldn't we return to the safe zone for the day?"

Steph looked anxious—it wasn't just her; the entire party was beginning to show signs of fatigue.

The MP bars above Til's and Izuna's heads were at a little over 50 percent each, and Sora's and Shiro's were already under 40 percent...

——On the way to the thirtieth floor, Shiro unlocked two skills...

And Sora obtained four more.

They both tested their new skills to learn their effects, and doing so naturally consumed MP.

As such, Shiro looked down at her flat chest with empty eyes.

She opened and closed her hands, motioning to grab something that just wasn't there—and a tear ran down her cheek.

Sora, on the other hand, tried his best to make it seem like nothing was wrong, when he, too, was very clearly distracted by something.

——Neither of them were in any shape to fight a boss, let alone a regular monster. And it could spell the end for them should Izuna and Til end up losing more than half of their MP pools midfight.

We should turn back now, no matter which way you slice it, Steph thought—however.

"No...we can still fight... Til thought of a way to restore our MP. It's our secret weapon."

"That's the first I've heard of this... If such a method exists, then why haven't we used it yet...?" Steph asked.

Sora shook his head heavily, and the rest of the party nodded.

Evidently, Steph was the only one who *didn't* know about this so-called secret plan.

"Because it *takes time*...and we need somewhere safe to do it..."

"That's right! When we enter the boss floor, there's always a room where there aren't any mobs before the boss, there is! We can use that room to recover King Sora's and Queen Shiro's MP before we fight the boss, we can!"

——*Even if that is the case, it still stands that Til and Izuna might lose more than half of their current MP.*

Steph wasn't entirely convinced that this was the right thing to do that day, even after hearing Sora and Til's idea—but.

"We'll be fine, we will! Just as long as we have enough MP to use our skills—"

"Mm-hmm! Sora and Shiro can lock down any boss and kick their asses, please!"

Til and Izuna seemed sure of the party's ability to win.

The silence from the bag suggested that the two inventory-bound members agreed as well.

With that, the group walked through the door and up the stairs to the thirtieth floor.

"Fine! I'll just have to believe in us, too, then!!"
Steph, too, nodded firmly before steeling her nerves and running up the stairs—

——Something she would soon regret.

"See?! Sometimes I'm right, too!! I'm not happy about it, though!!"
"I didn't think the battle would start the moment we entered the thirtieth floor! Normally, they'd work just like the tenth and twentieth floors! You know, with a similar format!! What kinda shitty game is this?!"
"...*Hic*... I hate...boobs... They're just big...lumps of fat... Brother...tell me you'll love me...even if I don't have any..."
"Waaaagh?! My sister!! I'd be lying if I agreed with the first half of what you said, but the second half I can say with extreme confidence! Except now's really not the time for that; couldja just stand on your own, please?!"
The party didn't have an opportunity to use Sora and Til's secret plan, because the first step they took onto the thirtieth floor triggered a shower of rocks thrown by the golem boss awaiting them.
The party was forced to take refuge in the only safe space they had: behind Steph, who was screaming, and her shield. Sora was likewise screaming as Shiro clung to him and wailed from her insufficient MP...

——The golem boss launched fistfuls of rocks at the party like a giant shotgun. These rocks fanned out, pelting everything from the floor to the walls, where they smashed into pieces—the violent AoE kept on coming at a rapid clip, left arm after right.
Though Sora and Shiro were safe behind Steph's shield, it wasn't an attack a human could dodge...

And on top of this:

"——?! K-King Sora!! This boss is hard as rock, he is!!"

"Our attacks don't hurt him, please!! What the hell are we gonna do, please?!"

——Just like the party could acquire equipment along the way, it seemed that their Demonia enemies, too, had access to special armor!

This Rock Golem was wearing a big shell, not unlike the armor the skeleton soldiers had worn.

The problem was—this shell seemed to reduce the damage the golem took by nearly 70 percent.

While Til and Izuna just barely managed to dodge the hail of rocks being slung around, any attacks they landed did little to no damage.

And to make things worse—!!

"Gahhh! My armor just broke!! At least let me have my shame, will you?!"

After taking an onslaught of attacks through her shield—Steph's armor finally broke.

She didn't have time to lament over an exposed heinie, however—with every fistful of rocks, her HP was depleting noticeably!!

It wasn't just the number of rocks; every shard packed a punch!!

Should any of the rocks even scrape against Sora or Shiro, they would most definitely perish!

The same went for Til and Izuna... How many hits could both of them take?!

——*This battle... It's...*

"Sora!! This is impossible! We need to retreat, now!!"

Steph finished Sora's thought for him—this battle wasn't one they could win...

Shiro could barely move, and that was the least of their problems. Sora gritted his teeth.

We came into this under the pretense that we could heal before the fight. We should've quit as soon as we realized we couldn't!!

I don't have the brain power for this right now; we need to—

—use Jibril to escape.
Before Sora could shout this, he heard two voices.

"King Sora! Now! We need to deploy our secret plan now, we do! Here!!"
"I'll distract 'em, please! Hurry up and heal your damn MP, please!!"
The two party members were yelling over the rocks smashing against the walls. Sora gasped in a daze.

——*It's gonna take time. That's why we need a safe spot to execute our plan...*
And she wants me to do it now? In a fight? Against that? But...why...?

I was the one who made our goal today to beat this boss.
But there's no reason for us to stick to this goal if it puts us at risk...
*We should just leave and come back when we have more MP—*Sora thought.
"This guy's got nothing on you two with enough MP, he doesn't—!"
"You'll lock the boss down and kick their asses—I know you can, please!!"
The voices he heard calling fiercely for him were from two gamers, having fun.

——*Run away? Us...? What was I thinking...?*
Maybe if there was no way to win, but we still have a fighting chance.
——*And things are* just startin' *to get good!!*

Hearing the two call out to them opened Sora's and Shiro's eyes, and they each let out a wry chuckle of embarrassment.
Look at us. Who cares if we lost around 60 percent of our MP...?

——*Getting out of a bind like this is what makes gaming fun—and we almost gave up!!*

* * *

"Jibril! Emir-Eins! Switch with me, Shiro, and Steph!!"

"What?! Sora, what are you—?!"

Steph shrieked in confusion at Sora's orders, but was sucked into the bag before she could finish.

And Sora had more orders for the two party members fresh out of the bag—!!

"Make sure you two don't attack!! I'm pretty sure you guys will lose hope *just from moving too much, so focus on unlocking skills for now, and support Izuna and Til!!"*

"With pleasure: This unit will analyze enemy attack patterns, give commands, and provide support during Master's absence. I got this."

"You needn't worry about me. Enjoy your time together in the bag. ♪"

The two bowed—and then they used their OP abilities to elegantly waltz through the barrage of stone, dodging all the projectiles with the minimum movement necessary.

Til nodded briefly before calling out to Steph, who'd been sucked into the bag.

"Lady Steph!! Sora and Shiro are in your hands, they are!!"

"What's that supposed to mean?!"

Steph, however, didn't receive an answer to that question......

■■■

——Which brought them to the inventory bag...

"Does somebody want to fill me in on what all this talk about a secret plan is supposed to be?! Is everyone going to be all right without me, the tank, in this fight?! And are we even allowed to have three substitutes in the bag at once?!"

"A maximum of five members can be active at once. The key word being *maximum*. There shouldn't be a problem with us three being in here."

"Okay?! I'd appreciate it if you answered my other questions, too!! And it sure is cramped in here!! I'm pretty sure this bag isn't built for three people— Wait, I'm naked!! I'm naked, and we're sandwiched toge— A-are those…my clothes?! I knew they were in here! I need to get chang——it's too cramped in here to do that!!"

"…Pipe down…Steph…and stop smooshing me…with your over-sized boobs…"

The inside of their inventory bag was so cramped, there wasn't much space to move.

Steph flailed around frantically at the sudden turn of events while Shiro started getting pissed off from being crushed by her breasts. Meanwhile, Sora pondered—

——*Now that I think about it, this is our first time in the bag.*

Jibril and Emir-Eins have been in here the entire time…smooshed together like this…

I'm surprised they didn't bicker more.

Though he found himself moved by their improving relationship, he had more important things to worry about. He decided to oblige Steph's two other questions with answers.

"Steph, how do you think that Dwarf party cleared this game?"

"——What?"

It was a mystery Sora had uncovered back on the party's first day in the dungeon.

According to Til, the entire Dwarf party that beat this game were in a polygamous marriage…

It was an actual harem party—!!

So the question remained: How did they clear this game?

This much should be obvious; Sora shared the long-awaited answer in the most exaggerated way—!!

"Methinks they got into the bag and did *you-know-what* to fill up their status bars!!"

"_____"

...Steph was absolutely dumbfounded by the truth of the matter—but!!

"...While the enemy...throws his rocks...we need you to...get ours off..."
"Oh, Steph! How bold! How courageous of you! You are a true hero!!"
"That sounds absolutely barbaric!! And watch your language, Shiro! You're only twelve years old!!"
Shiro and Sora's approach was relentless, causing Steph to scream at the two of them.
But Sora didn't have time for it—he continued!!
"I was thinking this would happen after we were in a safe spot, you know, during a break—like before or after a boss—but we don't have that leisure anymore!! We have to do it here and now!! You follow?!"
"...I wish I didn't, but—wait, you're not asking me to...?"

——*That Dwarf party long ago did that thing boys and girls do and...got back their HP and MP, I guess?*
And Sora wants me to do that with him in the middle of a fight? Do it here and now...?
Do it...? Do what exactly?
By it, do you mean...it—?
"Um, wait...! So when Til said you were in my hands, she meant literally—?"
As much as she wanted to hightail it out of the situation, there was nowhere for the rosy-red-cheeked Steph to run inside the bag.
She couldn't even get dressed. They were so close, the siblings could probably feel her heartbeat through her bare skin.
Steph turned to Sora, who was practically breathing onto her face, and asked:
"This is...all a big joke, right? I mean—"
"This is as serious as a heart attack, Steph—we've got no time to lose."
Steph knew a joking Sora when she saw it, and this wasn't the case. He looked back at her with utmost intensity.

Her heart was beating like an alarm; she could barely think straight—

—I...I...I can't!! *There are stages in a relationship that we need to go through before we get to this point... At...at least give me some time to process all this!! A-and what are we going to do about Shiro?! She's right there!!*

..............,

......Hold on... Didn't Shiro say she was okay with it...?
I mean, she couldn't participate even if she wanted to...given her age—
No. Calm yourself, Stephanie Dola!! Using this emergency as an excuse would be dishonest to Shiro!! E-especially considering that she would be watching... I wish it were at least just me and Sora...
Her thoughts were running a mile a minute.

Though confused, she was subconsciously convincing herself to accept this turn of events.

Also likely subconsciously...she was staring at Sora's lips as his face approached with utmost seriousness.

Steph was quivering, but she could accept her fate. She closed her eyes and waited.

Sora, with the intensity of a thousand burning suns, looked straight at her...and said:

"We need you to **hurry and spoil us rotten by patting our heads and complimenting us and stuff!!**"

......,

————,

————————Hmmm?

"......Could you repeat that, please...? Surely, that's not what you just said?"

"Listen to me, Steph! We need you to compliment us!! Pat us on the heads, maybe rub our bellies!!! Do whatever you can to make us feel better and recover MP, while keeping it PG!! Why, what the hell were you thinkin'?!"

——*Give me back that fleeting feeling of innocence...*

Also, I'd rather die than ever admit that this was somewhat of a letdown!!

Her nerves went from boiling hot to freezing cold, but now Steph was calm and ready.

Perhaps due to the intense change in mental temperature, she managed to push past the headache to eke out her next words.

"Absolutely not. ♥ Actually—now I'm confused why you're being so tame in a situation like this!" she screamed, tears forming in her eyes unbeknownst to her.

This time, the answer she wanted came from outside the bag.

It was Til—still fighting the Rock Golem, she cried out:

"I said you two should just do the deed, I did!! But King Sora insisted on keeping it PG!! He knows it will work because of how much MP he got back the first day, he does!! You're the only one who can do this, Lady Steph!! Both King Sora and I know it, we do!!"

——*Or would you rather go all the way?*

Til didn't need to say this last part for Steph to understand, which had Steph reeling.

Sora buried himself in her lap, and Shiro in her bosom—

"C'mon! Our friends are fighting for their lives out there! You need to mother it up!!"

"...Steph...hurry... You gotta be...an efficient mommy..."

Steph finally understood what she had to do.

——*Ohhh? I see what's going on here.*

Now I know why they refused to tell me about the secret plan.

It's because they knew I would never agree to this!!

"You two sadists are using the situation against me to make me dote on you!! Would forced doting actually have any effect?! Would it really help your mental health?!"

——*Forcing someone to spoil you rotten... Isn't a part of being spoiled the fact that someone else does it for you...?*

"Steph, what aren't you getting about this? You're not going to spoil us—we're *letting* you spoil us!!"

"How is that any different?!"

"...It's completely...different... We're the ones...with power...here...!"

"We're making you pat our heads like a good little boy and girl—of our own volition!!"

"...We're making...the decision...and that's what counts!"

"I'll ask this one more time... Is that really going to do anything for your mental health?!"

"You bet it will! All it takes for the body to produce oxytocin is a single touch!! It doesn't matter what we think about it!! And if you make it sexy—while keeping it PG, of course—that'll trigger a lot of other hormones in me!! We'll definitely recover our MP!!"

"...Steph...don't make us...repeat ourselves... Hurry..."

Urging Steph to get a move on, Shiro shifted her eyes—*outside...*

——At their friends, who were fighting outside the bag.

Steph scratched her head furiously before steeling her nerves—she was ready.

She put her hands on both of the siblings' heads and began rubbing them, just as she'd been asked to.

"Uh...there, there, you two— I'm, uh, not quite sure in what way, per se, but...you're both such good children... Just don't ask for specifics, okay? My good little girl and boy...?"

——Steph didn't really know what she should do to spoil them.

Try as she might, she didn't have any words of praise for the two.

So she focused more on rubbing their heads.

"...Mommy...how...can I make my boobs...as big as yours?"

"Oooh...Mommy...I'm so tired..."

"Stop calling me Mommy!! I—I won't do this if you're going to tease me!!"

Hearing Sora's and Shiro's words—Sora's in particular—gave Steph goose bumps, causing her to yell at the two.

"We're spoiling ourselves with you the best we can!! You'd better take this seriously, Steph!! Compliment us more, FFS!!"

"...And be...more specific... You need...to pretend to be...our mommy..."

"I can't do this!!!"

Despite having steeled her nerves only moments earlier, she fell apart quite easily.

Steph motioned to throw in the towel—when...

"Little Dora? Are you dissatisfied even though Master chose you over me—?"

"Proposal: Still possible to switch roles. Certainty: This unit can meet Master's and Little Sister's needs."

"Stuch! I dunno what the hell's going on in there, but you gotta do it, please!!"

"If you guys really can't figure this out—then we'll hafta retreat, we will!!"

——It wasn't just Sora and Shiro who were pleading to her, but those fighting outside.

Steph could hear in their voices that Izuna and Til were also struggling to keep up with the enemy.

"_____"

Inside the cramped inventory bag, Steph looked up and quietly closed her eyes...

——We're in a battle to save the world.

It's my duty to protect everyone. To defeat the Devil. Winning this game will ultimately save the world...

I need to protect everyone. I can protect them—my friends fighting outside the bag, too, and the world! And all those who wish to live in it——!

"...Oh, children... Come here, you two sillies..."

——And thus, with the weight of the world on her shoulders,

Steph took on her role in the most natural of ways. Her tone was compassionate beyond compare.

She pulled Sora and Shiro in close, and they both looked up at her, wide-eyed in confusion—and then.

Steph let go of her pride and dignity to oblige them in a way that they wished her to—nay, in a way that went far beyond their wildest dreams.

She poured into them all the *love* she had to offer...

——With that, Steph awakened to her new role: the party's main healer.

No—the siblings bore witness to the sudden emergence of this world's Mother Teresa......

——They were in the bag for all of thirty minutes...

"Report: This unit acquired the skill Analyze. Praise me, Master?"

"Master...I apologize for interrupting you during your time of rest, and having yet to unlock a skill of my own makes it even more difficult for me to say this...but I believe I am approaching my limit in terms of saving enough MP to warp us back..."

"King Sora, Queen Shiro!! This is getting pretty tough, it is!! Do you still need more time...?"

"I-I'm not finished yet, please...!"

The room didn't even look the same after the many rocks the golem had thrown, but the team managed to dodge the nonstop barrage—no.

Though the four members' physical abilities far surpassed that of the Immanities', dodging all the attacks proved to be impossible. This, combined with the use of newly unlocked skills, left the active members with nearing critical levels of HP and MP.

Signs of weakness could be heard in their voices as they called for help.

* * *

Their calls, however, didn't go unanswered.

Though it wasn't quite the answer they were expecting:

"Everyone except me and Shiro, into the bag."

———*Huh?*

The members of the party who got sucked into the bag were equally confused.

The moment Sora emerged, he unleashed a Flashbang Shot, whiting out the room.

In the bag itself:

"It's r-really cramped in here! I thought it was bad with three people, but five is going overboard!!"

"L-Lady Steph...your two giant— They're killing me, they are... I can't...breathe..."

"Ow?! Who the hell stepped on my tail, please?!"

The rest of the party was stuck trying to figure out how to fit themselves in the tight space, but their bickering turned to utter shock when the bright light quelled.

Their shock was not at the Rock Golem lying facedown on the ground, but toward their two friends who fought it—or what was above their heads.

"Lady Steph, what did you do to them to get them back that much MP?!"

They had been in the bag for only thirty minutes...

Though it was by no means a short amount of time for the four members fighting the Rock Golem on the outside, it was an unimaginably short amount of time to recover the amount of MP the siblings had.

Til and the rest of the party stared at Steph, who they were pressed up against—but.

"I will never tell you! And I'm never doing it again!!"

Red in the face, Steph shook her head and refused to answer.

But above her embarrassed face were her own HP and MP bars, which had also regenerated.

Not only that, but even her skin condition seemed to improve, for whatever reason...leaving the party with one question.

——*Whatever they did, it was PG. So what exactly did Sora, Shiro, and Steph do to get this much MP back? Why is she acting like this? What did they do in this bag...?*

It wasn't just Til; Jibril and Emir-Eins stared questioningly at Steph.

But she shook her head once more.

"Enough about that! Are we really going to let those two fight the boss alone?!"

"———*!!*"

The party remembered the severity of the situation they were in, albeit belatedly.

They looked outside the bag—Sora's Flashbang Shot didn't seem to last as long against the boss.

The two Immanities were far too weak to face off against the Rock Golem, which was already starting to get back up.

The girls in the bag were just about to cry out in horror, when:

"C'mon, guys...we can't let you have all the fun."

"...Now...it's our...turn... ♪"

——Only thirty minutes ago, the siblings were depressed and emaciated. But it was as if none of that had ever happened.

The Rock Golem was several times larger than the two, but it didn't matter.

They were their usual selves again—savage, fierce grins and all.

Immanity's most powerful gamers—Blank.

"You said it yourselves: This guy's got nothing on me and Shiro when we have all our MP."

"...It's time...to lock down...the boss...and kick his ass."

*   *   *

——Til and Izuna were right about what they said about us. So now it's time to put on a show!

《~~~~~~~~~~~!!》
With a low bellow—the Rock Golem swung its mighty arms, flinging rocks violently through the air.

Mere humans such as Sora and Shiro couldn't possibly dodge this attack.

It should've thrown the two into despair. But it didn't.

The siblings calmly reached for their left wrists, each using the buttons on the menus under their status bars.

They held up their *hope-based* weapons—and Shiro was the first to speak:

"...Ricochet Shot... Hollow-Point Shot..."

Undodgeable rocks? Yeah, okay.
But who says you have to dodge 'em?

《~~~~~~~~~~~?!》
The Rock Golem had thrown one of its massive hails of stones toward the siblings with its right arm—but.

Not a single one found its target; neither Sora nor Shiro took even a single step.

Then came the left arm's attack, which had the same result. The Rock Golem spoke in the Demonia tongue—probably something to the effect of *"How can this be?"*

Shiro's two skills...

The first, Ricochet Shot, made her bullets bounce from target to target. The second, Hollow-Point Shot, allowed her to clear this game's biggest hurdle: It added a knockback effect to her bullets.

——The Rock Golem had no way of knowing that these two skills stacked.

Nor did it realize that Shiro *didn't need a skill* to land eight bullets from her twin Machine Pistols.

The magical bullets struck the stones in midair, sending them off course and away from the siblings.

Some of the bullets even found their way to the Rock Golem's left arm, preventing its next attack with the knockback effect...

The Rock Golem definitely didn't know any of this.

And even if it did, it would neither understand nor accept the power of these incredible bullets.

Sora knew what Shiro was capable of, and he didn't bat an eye when the Rock Golem tried to continue attacking out of confusion.

He knew that the result would be the same this time, too.

Therefore, without fear, or much emotion at all, he got down low and aimed his gun's massive barrel—and thought.

About his own weapon, his own *hope*...and what that should look like:

——*Yeah... This game turns our hope into weapons.*

I thought each of our weapons looked and functioned way differently by nature, but that ain't the case. The rules are the rules—our weapons are just the shape of our hope.

——*Firing my weapon will deal* a certain amount of damage...

It all depends on how much damage you believe you'll deal—how much MP you use!

This was why Emir-Eins used up all her MP in one OP attack.

The same probably goes for Jibril—so. If that's the case...

How much damage will I actually do...?

——*Sure, my weapon may be weak... It makes sense, 'cause I'm* weak!!

I'm not strong like Emir-Eins or Izuna or Til, that's for sure!!

And I'm not a genius like Shiro, either! I'm just an ordinary, weak dude!!

So why the hell was I given a high-caliber Anti-Matter Rifle?!
The strength of my weapon probably lies in the bullet I use—

—the payload of its bullets is where my damage hides!!!

"——Projectile Shot!!"
Clunk! Feeling the weight of his gun shift as the bullet in his chamber changed—Sora pulled the trigger!
It left his barrel with a beam of light, only to split into multiple pieces before hitting its target.
These pieces were explosives that destroyed the outer shell that protected the Rock Golem.
The skill was a *debuff* that lowered the target's defense!!

With this debuff active, Shiro's bullets began dealing their original damage.
That said, this wasn't over yet.
In fact, the siblings were just getting started!
With a fierce grin, Sora shouted again before pulling the trigger!!

"There's more where that came from! Flashbang Shot!! And how about this?! Napalm Shot!! Venom Shot!!"
The same loud flash from before stunned the enemy and threw it off-balance, knocking the golem to the floor.
This was followed by a bullet that left its target engulfed in flames, then one that covered it in toxic venom.
These were DoT—damage-over-time—effects that slowly applied damage.

"And for the finisher!! Detonation Shot! Eat this!!"
Sora's fifth shot used the most MP yet—except it fired a tube that attached to the Rock Golem, instead of dealing damage.

——Thus, the enemy was on the ground, unable to do anything.

Its shell had been ripped off, its defenses were lowered, and it was on fire and covered in poison.

All the poor golem could do was flail around while it tried to regain its bearings, when:

"Heh, ha-ha—HAAA-HA-HA-HA!! That's right! Have I ever tried to fight a battle head-on?! Why did we think I could use a weapon based on pure brawn?! I'm Sora, the pathetic nineteen-year-old virgin!!"

That's right—my weapon. The shape of my hope. My true nature!!

——Is to be a debuffer! To incapacitate my enemies by getting in their way!!

"First, we stopped you in your tracks! Then, we defanged you!! Now that you can't move, we're beating you while you're down!! And the best way to end these things is to make you *end them yourself*!!!"

"...Brother...you're so, cheap...! You're...the coolest... ♥"

Sora was shouting at the top of his lungs—it was clear he was enjoying himself.

And just as the siblings said, they continued to pelt the immobilized giant with bullets.

"Not so tough now, eh?! Where'd Mr. Big Scary Rock Guy go?! Go on, get up! We'll just hit you with another Flashbang Shot and Hollow-Point Shots when you do! Ah-ha-ha-haaa!!"

"...Heh...heh-heh... You're just...another trash mob... ♥ Look at you...on the ground... How's it...feel...to be a...trash mob...? We love...to see it. ♥"

Incessant gunfire followed.

The Rock Golem that Til and Izuna could barely damage saw its HP get whittled down to almost nothing—

"Wh-whoa... Sora and Shiro are gonna freakin' do it, please!!"

"Whew! I knew it, I did! I knew this guy would be a cinch for those two!!"

"Re-recognition: Master is incredible. This unit's favorability of Master has risen more... Blush."

"Oh, I knew you could do it, my lord...! That was incredible!"

"...I think Sora and Shiro might be the real devils here..."

From within the bag came four voices of praise and one of utter shock...

——When your HP and MP—your hope—run out, despair gets the best of you—it slows you down.

Sora didn't even need to stun the Rock Golem anymore; it had stopped moving.

Everyone thought this meant victory for Sora and Shiro...until it happened.

As soon as the Rock Golem's HP fell below 20 percent—

Its MP—which was around 30 percent—*shot down to zero.*

However:

"Whoo-wee! Another one down... He was tough even without the armor, eh?"

"...I hate bosses...where the gimmick is their HP and defense... It's just...tedious..."

Either the siblings weren't worried about it, or they didn't realize, because they turned away from the Rock Golem—

"M-Master?! The enemy seems to be attempting something—!"

"S-switch with me, Sora!! Use me in the fight!!"

Sora and Shiro heard Jibril and Steph panicking in unison.

It wasn't clear what the golem was trying to do.

But despite how many attacks it'd made during the battle, it still had 30 percent of its MP left, which it used all at once.

The scale of whatever attack was about to come had the entire party screaming, but:

* * *

"Ya hear that, Shiro? They think some big finale, self-destruct kind of attack is about to come. You better tell 'em."

"...Mm. Let's just...say...they shouldn't...doubt Blank... ♥"

The siblings spoke with smiles plastered across their faces—and *boom.*

The Rock Golem was engulfed in a bright light—and then *self-destructed.*

———,

————,

"...........*Did it just...?*"

That's right—it *self-destructed...*

At least, that was what it looked like to Steph when a small explosion occurred and depleted the remainder of the Rock Golem's HP in one go.

But that wasn't how things looked to the higher-ranking races in the bag.

The Rock Golem had tried taking the siblings down with it, but just before that happened...

The tube that Sora had attached to the golem during the fight began to light up.

The party realized that all the MP that had gone into the self-destruction turned into an attack that affected only the Rock Golem itself.

It was Sora's fifth skill—Detonation Shot...

Detonation Shot *turned the target's MP against it...*

The skill itself didn't deal any damage on impact and took a lot of MP—but.

Depending on how much MP the target used to attack, the damage that Detonation Shot did to its target increased accordingly—a quintessential Sora move.

*   *   *

"And I even told them the enemy would finish himself off for us."

"…You guys…need to listen to people…more… ♪"

With only a sliver of HP left, the Rock Golem was enveloped in the light that signified its defeat.

The siblings turned around, stuck out their tongues, and gave each other a high five.

"And with that…we've cleared today's goal of beating the thirtieth-floor boss."

"…Let's…go…home…"

The siblings said this—accomplishing the goal they'd set for themselves.

They really did beat the Rock Golem without the help of their tank, and their impressive feat didn't go unnoticed.

——Outside the Tower, the game's overseers watched the fight come to an end on a big screen.

They were the Joint Chiefs of Staff of the Devil's Army, and they all gulped in unison.

Sure…the party was still only on the thirtieth floor.

That was less than 30 percent of the entire dungeon.

But…the thirtieth-floor boss, the Rock Golem, was supposed to be one of the dungeon's biggest challenges.

Even the Dwarf party from four hundred and eight years ago couldn't beat this boss without losing some members…

There were still many Demonias who awaited them…

This, of course, included Demonias far stronger than the Rock Golem they'd just defeated.

And that Rock Golem, the leader of its tribe, could barely even move…

——It called into question something vital:

What could anyone in the Tower do to stop these two heroes...?

The Joint Chiefs of Staff knew every one of their personnel, and yet they couldn't envision any of them winning against the hero's party.

Even worse...

"...They can't possibly...defeat the Devil, can they...?"

——*What if they could defeat the Devil...?*

It was a highly disrespectful idea to toy with, but Genau Ih spoke for his staff when he let these words slip—however.

"Gah-ha-ha-ha!! Finally!! Heroes worthy of battle with me!! Excellent!! You deserve praise, Schira Ha!! These are, as you say, the heroes I've long awaited!!"

"Indeed!! Mweh-heh...Your Evilness, everything shall go as you wish."

The Devil—that is, the fragment of him in Schira Ha's arms—cackled.

It was an arrogant and fearless laugh, but it put the staff at ease. Embarrassed, they realized:

——*This is the Devil. Our creator. The one who shall destroy every-thing and yet leave us with an eternal fantasy.*

Yes—there is no being capable of defeating Him...!!

"...Yeah... Let's go home... Might as well just die... So, what, my only talent is ruining all the fun for others with debuffs...? Who gave this hopeless virgin who brings others down permission to live...?"

"...Dying... I could get...behind that... I mean...my boobs aren't gonna...grow either way... I've known it, from the start..."

The siblings had put on a show like Til and Izuna had asked for—and now they had less than 10 percent of their MP left and were wrestling with true despair.

"Oh no!! W-we should switch, we should!! E-everyone, get out of the bag!!"

"Sora! Shiro! I'll cry my damn eyes out if you guys die, please!!"

"*Urgent: Formulating emergency protocol.* Designation: *Would Master like a good handful of these milkers, as mentioned previously?*"

"*King Sora!! What were you going to do if your Detonator Shot didn't finish the boss off all the way?! You don't have enough MP right now to finish off the last twenty percent now, you don't!!*"

"*...I put on a show...despite having a flat chest... Just let me...die... okay...?*"

"*I'm really sorry, guys. I was born without a plan and still can't make one. At least let me plan my suicide.*"

"*J-Jibril!! Please shift us back to the start, this instant!!*"

"*B-but of course!! Master, please find the will to live for just a moment longer!!*"

The party rushed out of the bag upon their slow realization of Sora's and Shiro's mental states—

...Uh...maybe our staff can deal with the problem before the heroes reach the Devil?

It might end up solving itself, if we're lucky...

The Demonia staff had such high expectations for the siblings during that battle, but they watched those expectations plummet with a smile.

"...Schira Ha...are you certain they'll be able to make it to me?"

The Devil shot Schira Ha a questioning look.

"Mweh-heh...heh-heh-heh......... Y-yes...?"

She averted her eyes and responded with a quavering voice......

——It was ten floors a day from there.

Every time the party entered the dungeon, they explored each corner of the next ten floors, defeated its boss, then went home.

They spent two days working on their mental health, then returned on the third day, where they speed-ran the dungeon until the point where they'd previously left off.

Then they were back in for ten more floors and a boss battle before going home.

It was a long process, yet they stayed the course; slowly but surely, the party advanced through the Tower dungeon.

With every tenth floor, the terrain changed—first, they were on a beautiful beach, and then, a glittering desert.

And with each new stage came new mobs and a new boss, all stronger than the previous ones.

Each hero unlocked more skills and obtained more gear from treasure chests.

Some of the armor they found—primarily armor that Steph was forced to wear—they used during the boss fights, only to end up getting destroyed, leaving Steph a naked mess. The other powerful armor, though, they held on to—

Before long, thirteen days had passed since their initial entrance into the Tower dungeon.

On their fifth trip, the party headed to the fiftieth floor—

"Ha-ha-ha! There they are!! I've been waiting for this!!"

"Sora?! Wh-what do you think you're doing?!"

——It was a harsh volcano stage full of molten magma.

The cliff that jutted out of the lava flow was connected by a series of suspension bridges, which acted as a maze. At any given moment, they could easily fall into the magma, where they assumed the heat would eat through their HP for an instant game-over...and thus...death—however.

When the volcano stage's enemies came to attack, Sora screamed with joy.

Steph, who clung to Til for dear life, screamed at him in horror...

"Why did you attack the enemies?! They didn't even notice us yet!!"

"Why, you ask? Because I'm happy we've finally made it to the stage with some mobs I've been waiting for—these *beautiful Demonia babes*!!"

The mobs that Sora aggroed were none other than flying Demonias with two wings instead of arms.

Harpies—and *without a stitch on them!*

That explained why Sora was so happy when he answered Steph.

Oh yeah... There's been humanoid Demonias—but they were all monsters.

These babes are demons—a higher-ranking species. I knew we'd come across them at some point, but I thought it would take longer!

This earlier-than-expected encounter meant it was time for Sora to use a new skill!!

The second he saw the harpies on the fifty-first floor, he deployed this skill in rapid succession.

——He used...his Projectile Shot.

This skill ripped the armor off skeletons and the Rock Golem from earlier floors—lowering their defenses!

Which meant it should have a similar effect against the clothes of the beautiful harpies!!

As such, the enraged group of harpies came flying toward the party—while skillfully keeping their most private parts hidden—screeching the entire time.

"Jibril! Are they speaking a Demonia language?! Can you tell what they're saying?!" Sora yelled, and the answer came from within the bag:

"*It roughly translates to:* You do realize this is flat-out sexual harassment, right?! This might be a game, but that doesn't mean we won't sue you!! *Or something along those lines.* ♪"

It was what he thought they were saying, although a bit more modern than he'd expected.

"Then tell them to shut up!! 'Cause we're playing by the same rules that leave you naked when your armor breaks!! If they wanna sue someone, they need to sue their boss who made this game!!"

"The only one who ever ends up naked on our side is me, though!!"

"Sora! Sora! Can we kill these damn birds, please?!"

"It's getting difficult to dodge them on such uneven ground, it is!!"

Sora instantly answered his fellow heroes with the calculated risk-based decision expected of an IGL—all while ignoring Steph's question!

"Nope!! They're too embarrassed to fly straight—we'll use our speed to outrun 'em! They shouldn't be a threat as long as they focus on Steph's shield, so let's keep searching the floor!! The eye candy should keep my MP pool healthy!! Steph might even lose her armor again!! Emir-Eins, I want you to record everything within sight and send it to my smartphone later!! Can you do that for me?!"

"*Report: Recording already in progress. Capturing images with maximum zoom, picture quality, and frame rate.*"

"...Brother...I wonder if...I can knock just the...arms they're using, to cover their chests...with my Hollow-Point Shot...?"

"Your genius never ceases to amaze me, Shiro!! Do it!!"

"Hello, harpies?! I will join you if you sue these two in a court of law!!"

——As they navigated a stage where one wrong step could lead to a fiery death...

Sora and Shiro never stopped enjoying themselves, for the most part.

Until...

——They made it to the fifty-ninth floor with ease, where they stood before the boss door, which sat at the end of a very long hall.

However, two powerful-looking suits of armor were standing on either side of the door, guarding it.

And although they saw the party members, the Living Armor didn't charge the party aimlessly.

The party had been stuck in this spot, thinking about their next move, for almost twenty minutes...

"So...what are we going to do? Those two enemies look powerful."

"*Affirmative: As per this unit's Analyze skill, each monster is*" *ninety-one percent as strong as the Minotaur boss from the tenth floor.*"

"Then perhaps we should forgo fighting the boss today? Seeing as a certain someone wasted their MP playing around? What have you been contemplating for twenty minutes anyway...?"

Steph shot Sora and Shiro a doubtful look upon hearing Emir-Eins's analysis.

——It was unclear how powerful this upcoming boss would be, but the party had only about 60 percent of their MP at this point.

It was difficult to imagine they would have the strength necessary to fight the next boss after clearing out these two enemies, each of whom was as strong as the first boss.

Which left the party with two choices:

Beat the two sets of Living Armor today and go home, or—

"...Just so you know, I will *not* help you recover MP this time, either."

——Steph refused to assist the siblings who'd just been dicking around with naked harpies and nagas.

Which really left the party with only one choice—but Sora and Shiro ignored Steph and kept their eyes on the enemy—

"That's fine... We're just waiting for *those two* to leave."

"Come again...?"

Evidently, there was a third option, which the party was already taking, unbeknownst to Steph.

"Did you forget how great this country's work environment is?"

Some monsters that the party didn't defeat—and sometimes didn't even engage with—disappeared and reappeared.

Sora looked to his sister, and they both nodded.

"...Almost there... In ten...nine...eight..."

"Awesome. Get ready to go, guys. Ready, aaand—RUN!!"

The two began running straight for the two sets of Living Armor, and the other three members scrambled to follow.

So we are *going to fight?!*
——Steph held up her shield and prepared for battle—but.

"…Two…one…zeeero… ♪"
As soon as Shiro had finished her countdown, the two mobs suddenly vanished.

————————*Huh?*

"All right! Time for the boss, guys! Get ready to fight!!"
"Wait, what?! What just happened?!"
Steph spoke for the rest of the party by sharing her confusion.
"That should be obvious! They're changing shifts!!"
Sora answered her while he sprinted down the hallway past the spot where the Living Armor was—
"It's what we heard before we started! This game is being run on four shifts to keep it running twenty-four seven!! This is a shift change!!"
——Passing by the spot where the Living Armor left exactly on time for their work schedule, the party arrived at the boss room doors. They watched as the magic seal disappeared from the door, and—
"There are a few seconds of lag when the staff changes—we can skip the boss this way, too!!"
Two new sets of Living Armor respawned, but didn't start moving yet…

"Wait, so—the reason the bosses we defeated don't respawn is…"
Til was finally up to speed on the boss situation, and Sora nodded with a grin.
Just as Schira Ha had said before, when the staff's HP reached zero, they were sent to a facility outside the Tower where they rehabilitated their work-related injuries and were given some time off.
——Whenever the Demonia staff were about to run out of HP, they were teleported out of the dungeon…which meant!

"The staff that need treatment are given month-long breaks for their mental health. And there's no replacements for the unique monsters such as the bosses! This place really does have the best benefits. ♪"

All the bosses the party had defeated thus far...

The half-cow, half-man Minotaur; the giant plant creature Triffid; the boulder-slinging Rock Golem...and the rest of the monsters...

The party imagined them all being on vacation, taking the time they needed to recover—

"Wow... What an incredible place to work...!"

Steph was moved by the realization she'd finally made as the party leaped through the door, and when they saw the two-headed Cerberus woman who awaited them in the sixtieth-floor boss room—

"Got another babe in my sights!! Preparing my Projectile Shot!! ...Crap!! Looks like bosses can't be stripped in one hit!! Then you're just gonna hafta eat a lot more of these!! I've got this, guys!!"

"...Til...Izzy...! Give, us cover until we...can strip the boss..."

"You want us to save our MP until she has less defense, you do!! Got it!!"

"*Correction: Course of action also maximizes time of boss nudity and video length captured by this unit.*"

"Oh, that's the plan?! You sure are a hopeless little brother, you are! Roger that!!"

The party—Steph's coworkers—engaged in fierce sexual harassment against one of the Devil's beautiful henchwomen, and Steph thought:

——*I'd rather work for the Devil's Army...*

She watched as the poor Cerberus woman's clothes were ripped away. A tear ran down her cheek as she held up her shield...

■■■

The party defeated the Cerberus woman without trouble.

They returned home with Evac and got a nice night's worth of sleep, bringing them to the next morning.

The light of the morning sun shone in on the preparation room—and just like every morning they spent there, the party ate the food that Schira Ha and the skeleton brought into the kitchen for Steph to busily prepare. With Til's expertise no longer needed, she was allowed to drink some ale while tending to her hammer. Shiro worked on her stretches and Sora, his exercise regimen.

After two weeks, the party had grown accustomed to their daily routine.

And the furball—or Devil—said once more...

"...C'mon, guys. Why do you keep coming back here...?"

He had the same question for the party every time he saw them, and they always gave him the same answer.

"Really? We've been over this: Is the head of state seriously going to neglect his own nation's laws? You guys are the ones with an eight-hour workday and four-day workweek here. You do know that eight hours is the *max* and not the *minimum*, right? I'll report you to the Department of Labor if I have to."

"And what party of heroes goes through the Department of Labor to fight the Devil?! And you fools are only working every third day!! That's not even four days a week!! Me and my staff have been waiting for you for fourteen days straight, I'll have you know!!"

Even the rattling skeleton who was nodding to the Devil's statement appeared to be very tired—

"...We're just...gonna...chill."

"You guys should take some more time off. We're not going anywhere while we rest."

The siblings responded with a distinct lack of interest in the question in the first place.

"That's not the issue here!! I don't know what happened in there, but I do know your party has a method of healing MP inside the bag, right?! You could use that to progress much faster than this!! And I've grown tired of even pointing it out, but you really must do something about this blasted pooch!! You're gonna make me cry!!"

"I'm not lettin' you go today, please. You smell damn nice, please. You're sleeping with me tonight, please."

This was Izuna's routine—gnawing and nipping at the Devil whenever he came to complain about them.

Tears were welling up in the Devil's eyes. The entire party looked to Steph.

——It remained a mystery to everyone—save for Sora and Shiro— what exactly Steph had done inside the bag to heal MP.

They looked to Steph with pleading eyes, hoping against hope for an answer: *Are you ever going to tell us?*

"…I will *never* tell you what I did, and I'm *never* going to do it again."

"——There you go. She's not gonna let us do it that way, so we need to get some R and R."

Steph flat out rejected the group's interrogation, leaving them pouting in disappointment.

And then:

"R-right. Very well, then. It doesn't matter in the long run, for I am immortal and almighty, and your efforts are futile!!"

The furball menaced the party like he always did, but the party had figured it out a long time ago:

This furball's just bored and wants something to do…

"I suppose if you heroes are given the time, you will eventually reach me. Then so be it: Time I shall give you!!"

The Devil, oblivious to his own boredom, flashed a big smile.

"It doesn't matter how many years I must wait—use the single life you are allotted to try and defeat the Devil, O Heroes! Gah-ha-ha-ha— Hey, pooch. I'm trying to make an exit!!"

"Hell no…please…! We're sleeping in the same damn bed tonight, please!! Mnghhh!!"

Izuna fought to keep her toy, who vanished with a *poof* whenever the skeleton and Schira Ha eventually left.

The preparation room soon filled with Izuna's wails.

Then Steph gave herself a little pep talk:

"He is right! With enough time, we should be able to win this game!"

——The Demonias the party faced were growing stronger and stronger.

It was getting to the point where if they weren't careful, some of the regular mobs could pose a threat.

For Sora and Shiro, it would take only a single mistake for the game to come crashing to an end—this much hadn't changed.

But what did change...

——Sora and Shiro, who were untouchable by the thirtieth floor, had each gained another skill.

Til unlocked three, Izuna two, and Steph one more skill.

Any equipment they found along the way remained largely untouched. The party always had Emir-Eins's burst damage and—most important—Jibril's ability to shift the party back to the first floor, which she could do during a fight...

It was the party's backup plan, should a boss battle take a wrong turn.

They could run the dungeon as much as they needed, healing HP and MP when they needed...

"It's true... At this point, nothing about this game can make us lose," said Steph.

"We just need to get to the hundredth floor and fight the Devil to win this, we do!!"

The rest of the party seemed to agree with Steph's optimistic take, with the exception of one person. It was Sora, who was heading to the shower along with his sister—he remained silent, not even nodding.

He was thinking about questions that had been on his mind the entire time...

*   *   *

——These were questions commonly held by people who played RPGs where the objective was to defeat a nebulous Devil character...

For example: Why does the Devil want to destroy the world?

Or: Why do the player characters recover HP and MP by sleeping in an inn?

Why are there treasure chests in dungeons? Et cetera, et cetera...

Why do the enemies' bodies disappear?

Why don't the bosses respawn...?

All questions Sora had gained over a lifetime of gaming...

And this world had reasonable answers for most of them.

——But...if that was the case.

Then, just as the Devil had said so plainly only a moment before, with a wicked smile; something he said with *hope* and *desire*—and *another emotion*—in his eyes.

A standard line, and something that always had Sora confused when the enemy said it in games—

——It was his biggest question—and if like the others, it had a simple answer...

"Then...this might not be so easy...," Sora whispered to himself with a grim expression......

■■■

In the Republic of Elkia—in the parliament president's office sat Chlammy, who was diligently coping with her nausea to get through another stack of documents...when suddenly:

She came across a lone sheet of paper—which stated that it had been two weeks since the Commonwealth challenged the Devil.

She then turned to her friend sitting next to her, Fiel, and asked a question out of the blue...

"...Fi. Why do you think the Devil waged war against *Elkia alone* this time?"

∗   ∗   ∗

——Whenever the Devil revived, he challenged the *entire world* to war.

During the Great War, after the Covenants were established—and when he revived four hundred and fifteen years ago, this was how it always happened.

But why was it different this time...? Chlammy asked Fiel this, but—

"The Intelligence Department believes *Schira Ha the Wise convinced the Devil to do so.* They claim that Demonia is on the same side as the Front... Though that doesn't make much sense to meee..."

Fiel had the same question, to which she received only lackluster answers.

Even more confusing was that Schira Ha had resigned from the Devil's Army Joint Chiefs of Staff...

——Many questions about the game that was being played and the situation behind it went unanswered, leaving Fiel in deep thought.

But once more, out of nowhere.

A new question arose in Chlammy's mind.

...It was hard to tell whether this came from her own thoughts, or if they were part of Sora's memories, but she asked it anyway.

"...Fi... What *is* the Devil?"

"...Hm? It is a Phantasma that is trying to destroy the world, yesss?"

Fiel looked confused by Chlammy's question.

She had told Chlammy this over and over. It was written in every document they had on the subject matter...

But Chlammy was never satisfied with it.

And although she wasn't satisfied, she didn't quite know how to express what exactly she took issue with, so she usually kept her doubts to herself.

This time, however, she tried to work out with Fiel what had her so confused...

238 NO GAME NO LIFE Volume 12

"It's not that... I'm asking why the Devil exists."

Fiel looked even more confused, and Chlammy tried to pick her words more carefully.

"First...there's something so unnatural about the Devil's game, isn't there?"

——The Devil gave you everything of his if you won his game.

He had the power to create and steal life—he had his own race, and their own Race Piece.

He waged all of this against nothing more than the *despair* of those who challenged him. Not only that, but—

"There isn't a single agent plenipoitentiary who would ever bet their Race Piece in a game like this."

——When Immanity split into two factions, and the republic came into existence, Sora and Shiro were no longer the Immanity agent plenipotentiary—they were just the Kingdom of Elkia.

Jibril, Emir-Eins, Nýi Tilvilg, Izuna Hatsuse, and Stephanie Dola—all of them were...

"What does the Devil have to *gain* from winning this game? Why would he wager his own life and creations, the Demonia race— against anyone who was willing to accept his challenge...?"

"——Ah, are you referring to the conspiracy behind this game?"

This was something that Fiel thought when she first learned the rules.

She now understood where Chlammy was coming from. Red light shone in on the office from the setting sun as Fiel gave her friend a thin grin.

Fiel knew there was something more to the game, but—

"No, that's not what I'm talking about. I think it is something *more fundamental*..."

"...?"

——*No, not that.* Chlammy shook her head at Fiel.

She thought even more about how to convey this strange feeling she had about the game...

"The Devil did the same during the Great War: Challenged any hero willing to face him—though it wasn't framed as a game back then. He was supposed to be a nightmare that would bring the world to its end, and yet he went out of his way to have heroes fight him? It's almost as if—"

————,

...*As if...*

Chlammy stopped herself there. She figured out where this strange feeling came from.

It was clear to her that her doubt stemmed from Sora's memories...

————In Sora's memories were countless questions posed toward an imaginary Devil...

A being who tried to destroy the world, and always had a convenient way for heroes to defeat him.

He had so many questions—and criticisms—about the idea of an *ultimate evil*.

But his biggest question was:

"...Why does the Devil act as if *he wants someone to defeat him*?"

"————————Because..."

————The Devil said he wanted to destroy the world, and yet always left a path for others to prevent him from doing that—he contradicted his very own existence.

It was as if he was a mere plot device. Something that *needed* to be there.

To give the illusion of a *good story*—and if this was the case.

"Who shared the same fantasy of a Devil that brings about world destruction...?"

".........................."

Though Fiel didn't have an answer to this question, Sora's memories led Chlammy to a certain explanation...

——In Sora's world, the concept of a Devil—of a big, bad enemy—existed only in fiction.
It was an obstacle for players to overcome—nothing more, nothing less.
But in Disboard...the Devil actually existed.
He was real, but only as a convenient plot device for heroes to overcome—an *ultimate evil*.

——If the Devil...a Phantasma...was born from the world's imagination...and if the theory floating around in Sora's memories was correct...

"Then this is just...too cruel..."
So cruel that the nauseating documents that piled up on her desk seemed almost innocent.
It was a wickedly hideous theory—one Chlammy prayed was incorrect.
This much she hoped with disgust as she looked off into the distance, toward Garad Golm...

■■■

——It was day nineteen of the heroes' party's time in the Tower dungeon.
On their seventh trip up the Tower, they ventured into the seventy-first floor, which—like each ten-floor set prior—took on new terrain.
This stage was something out of a certain toxic valley that stole life in the most brutal fashion. The party waded through the disgusting mire...

...until they reached the boss on the eightieth floor—a very high-ranking Demonia.
The party barely managed to defeat the beautiful arachne—barely...

* * *

"Damn... I know we can go back and recover, but you never get used to this *despair*..."

The party needed to make liberal use of their stronger skills to stand a chance against more powerful enemies—

Doing so required a lot of MP; everyone had around 20 percent left after the boss fight. Sora was mentally and physically exhausted—but Steph responded to his remark with visible skepticism...

"You sure looked happy earlier when you stripped the poor arachne woman naked, and you never even gave her the chance to cover her exposed breasts with any of her eight hands... You deserve what you get."

"*Negative: No inefficiencies in Master's operation. Every action taken was a well-calculated, strategic decision.*"

"*Also, Little Dora?* Post-battle clarity *is a healthy part of Immanity male physiology. ♪*"

——Steph still had her doubts about her inventory-bound companions' evaluations, but she agreed, for the most part, with Sora.

This time, Shiro, Til, and even Steph had used the lion's share of their MP pools, leaving them visibly exhausted.

While it was true that they could go home and recoup—it didn't change the fact that they felt this depressed whenever they approached utter *despair*.

And they knew it would happen again, too.

Though their mental fatigue was plain as day—

"B-but! We only have the ninetieth-floor boss left! Twenty more floors and one more boss until floor one hundred—the Devil! And then we clear the game!! We're almost finished. ♪"

Despite her low HP and MP, Steph shook her head and forced a smile as she hit the party with some positivity—however.

"——We'll see about that..."

".........Oh?"

——*Crap… I'm letting my lack of MP get the best of me…*

Sora had accidentally shot Steph down.

The party looked at him. They wanted to know the meaning behind what he'd said, and he got frustrated with himself for his slip of the tongue.

He then turned to the open door and asked:

"You guys wanna do just one more floor this time…?"

"Huh? But look at everyone, and look at you! There's no way we can stomach any more today."

"Yeah, I know. We'll shift outta here as soon as we get a look. Jibril and Emir-Eins, I want you two out of the bag on standby."

Sora spoke with no enthusiasm as he began to lug himself up the stairs.

Jibril and Emir-Eins warped out of the bag, and together, the six confused party members followed Sora.

——*Even if we leave now, we'll find out what's up here in a few days after a break. So why not get a peek and take the time to process it while we recover?*

Sora wanted to forget about the words he'd just let slip. He turned around and looked at his party members.

Every ten floors, the terrain changed drastically…

——Their adventure started in a holy castle befitting a holy king.

Next was a forest paradise. This was followed by a limestone cavern that oozed with nature's mystique.

After that was a glimmering cove with deep blue water and a desert dotted with treasure-like oases…

Each stage was defined by its stunning beauty.

But this all changed from the fifty-first floor on.

First was a volcano that had them staring death in the face, and then ruins that were tucked into thick fog and darkness.

And finally, a gloomy, toxic, swampy valley with miasma floating through the air…

Which meant it was about time for—

* * *

"...I think...the Devil's *true nature* is gonna manifest in the last two stages...," Sora muttered to himself as he dragged his legs through the door.

And just as he suspected...

He and the rest of the party had the same reaction to what awaited them on the eighty-first floor.

"——————Wh-what is this...place...?"

The group was at a loss for words, struggling to contain a scream.

This—was the *answer* that Sora had predicted.

If there was an answer as to why the Devil was an all-too-convenient trope—then it would be this.

Sora finally knew his suspicions were correct, and he proceeded to show a troubled, strained grin before thinking...

——*FML...I guess I was right......*

⏻ ROLE-PLAYING END

...A long, long time ago, a mass of earth was flung through the heavens during a battle between the gods.

A powerful, earth-shattering attack sent the land hurtling into the heavens by coincidence.

It gradually broke apart—a calamity of shards plummeting toward the ground before vanishing...

This calamity was mere happenstance...and yet.

——It remained in the memories of all intelligent life as *the calamity that floated through the heavens.*

And after an eternity of being immortalized in memory, it eventually gained a core and became a Phantasma...

——It wasn't clear who gave it this name, but at some point in time, the Phantasma became known as Avant Heim.

And while the mass of land continued to float through the heavens, raining down hell on earth...

It was nothing more than an apparatus that replicated a past event. A system.

*   *   *

It had no goal or intent to harm—it didn't even have an identity. Someone feared it. Someone dreamed of its return. And someone—desired it. And so it existed. The calamity was born again—as a *monster*...

Why did the monster rain destruction on the earth below? ——Because...that's what monsters *do*.

——Because it was a monster. It was doing what it was born to do, as a phantasm. No one wondered why clouds rained, and no clouds would answer them should they ever be asked. This monster was like a cloud—one that rained destruction on all it passed over.

——————.............

"——?! Th-there it is...! The light!! Heh-heh-heh. So you gonna tell me what's up, Av'n'? I wanna know why you're ignoring me!!" said a one-horned Flügel hunched over on the ground.

She was wearing a helmet and had a pickax in her hands—Azril, struggling for breath...

"Nyaaa! It was hard to dig to your core while I have the strength of an Immanity, Av'n'!! And I'm stuck here wonderin' why no one wanted to lend me a hand!! You'd think it'd help to open up a little hole in space or something!! It was my first time even touching a pickax! Why should the leader of the Flügel be the one doing all the digging?!"

The young woman shared her discontent—from beneath her previous lord's throne.

It was the deepest part of the Phantasma Avant Heim...in other words—

"....................."
It sluggishly turned to Azril without saying a word. But the hollow boy—what *looked* like a boy—soon stared elsewhere.

More than half of its body was covered in bluish-white crystals, and whatever it was, it was clearly not human.

Like Azril, it had a single horn, a sign that the two shared their power with one another. The vaguely humanoid figure had one eye closed, as if it was dreaming...

This—was where Avant Heim's core resided...

"Hrm... Is that still on your mind? So much that you'd ignore me?!" Only a month ago—Avant Heim had stopped responding when she called.

So three days ago, I decided to come see his core. Try and ignore me, face-to-face.

Azril had started digging three days earlier and had finally reached Avant Heim's core.

But evidently, he ignored her once they were face-to-face.

——I think I'm gonna cry!

Tears were welling up in Azril's eyes when—

"...On your mind...? Who? The Phantasma—?"

The young boy looked back emotionlessly at Azril and tilted his head in confusion.

——Oh... Looks like Av'n' can't tell.

Azril didn't share only her power with Avant Heim—but their subconsciousness as well.

That's how she knew why he was reminiscing about something that had happened so long ago.

And she understood what that eye of his was watching so dreamily—more so than Avant Heim did.

Av'n's gaze was fixed on a tall tower in the center of Garad Golm...

The Domain of Despair. The Hope-Consuming Beast. The Phantom of Destruction—the Devil.

Av'n' lacked the self-awareness—if he had any at all—to vocalize why he was looking over there.

Azril, on the other hand, could put his subconscious feelings into words:

——The Devil is a Phantasma, just like me.
Something born without reason or purpose.
An existence without meaning or will.
A calamity. A monster. Just a system—

Just...
A Phantasma... A dream someone saw...

That's what he should be. How it should work, but...the Devil had *something*.
A role, a goal, and a meaning to his existence—things Av'n' had once been *given* but had lost.
Most of all, the Devil wanted something, and he worked to get it.
He had a clear sense of *self*...

The Devil has everything I lack. Everything.
We're both Phantasmas—we should be the same...but why are we so different?
In other words, Av'n' was...

"...Oh-ho, nya? So you're jealous? Of *him*...?"
Azril said it for him.
"...Jealous...of him...? A fellow Phantasma—?"
It only confused Av'n', who lacked the self-awareness to really understand it all. Azril chuckled wryly to herself.

Maybe a year ago, I would've felt jealous with Av'n'.
But not anymore. Her little sister worked for two masters who were far too weak for comfort.
Azril, just like those two masters, spent a little less than a year crawling along on the ground like an ant.

And like an ant, she had a tiny brain…

Despite its size, it was her own to use, and she would use it—and she continued:

"But, Av'n'…I doubt he's *anything* like how you imagine."

——*At least, not yet…*

With her tiny brain, Azril thought of the Devil.

Knowing that this was unlike her, and that she was the last one who should ever say this—

Failing to stifle a sad smile, she'd muttered those words to Avant Heim…

"……………………"

Unable to process what he was being told, Av'n' looked to Azril with confusion—perhaps his first-ever show of emotion…

"But now's not the time for that! We're super-duper busy!!"

Azril kept her thoughts to herself and changed the subject.

"We have our own game to do! If you keep ignoring me, I'm gonna set up a railcar through this tunnel and ram you with it every day until you respond, you hear?! Nya?"

——*I'mma hold it against you for making me dig this darned tunnel.* ♥

Azril said this with a grin reminiscent of how she, the First Number, used to grin during the Great War.

——Avant Heim, the Phantasma…

Its core—the young boy—was largely void of all emotion and a concept of self, but nevertheless…

"…I-I'll…try to do better… Azril………I'm…sorry?"

——He didn't need emotions to tell that it was better for him to apologize and avoid confrontation.

Although it was clear the boy was not actually sorry at all, Azril snorted and then nodded to him before turning to leave.

* * *

The boy spoke once more before she left, though.

Avant Heim was gazing off into the distance, where the Devil was—but then he looked farther up.

Above Garad Golm, and above the tower that jutted toward the heavens.

At something that made him weep whenever he saw it—the bloodred moon.

"Azril...is the moon falling...?"

——He realized that the moon was *following him.*

"Didja finally notice?! That's why we're so busy!! Honestly— whatever happens, things ain't lookin' good for us!! So I wantcha to get a move on! Hop to it!!"

With that, Avant Heim's consciousness went to Azril's from his core.

There he could feel her irritation before returning to his own consciousness...

——The eighty-first floor of the Tower...

What Sora and the rest of the party saw when they reached the top of the stairs was a new stage, just like they'd expected.

Shiro, Steph, Til, and Izuna—and even Jibril and Emir-Eins— were at a loss for words.

The landscape that unfolded before them was nothing short of indescribable—a sight that defied description, a spectacle beyond imagination...

——It was the aftermath of a battle...

The corpses of various races that must've fought each other piled up into mountains and filled the rivers—rivers dyed red with blood.

All life—even microbes maybe—was dead in this hellscape. It was a never-ending vista of death, but left unrotten.

Even more horrifying than this, however, was that—aside from the lingering embers of finished battle—there was no motion, and nothing made any sounds. There was only endless silence in the world of death.

——But this wasn't what left the party speechless.

What stole the words from the Flügel and Ex Machina who'd rained terror down on the world during the Great War long ago.

What caused them to fall silent and avert their gazes.

Was an invisible something that enveloped the deathscape.

Though intangible, even the Immanity of the group could sense its presence—an invisible *something*.

"——Wh-what is this…? What is this?!"

Steph was half panicked when she cried out, but no one there could answer her.

There were no words for what it was. They could neither perceive nor understand *it*.

One member of the party gazed toward what the others averted their eyes from—Sora.

——With a grim look in his eyes, he opened his mouth to answer Steph…

"Steph…you know how I told you what *hope* really is?"

——Hope…a chemical reaction in your brain.

In this world, the mechanism was referred to as positive spirits, but nevertheless, it was a highly measurable substance.

A physical, physiological reaction that happened in the body—in other words, an illusion.

So—

"So…what do you think *despair* is?"

When Sora asked her this, Steph turned to see what he was staring at.

"——Th-this is...what you think despair looks like—?!" she yelled, before quickly turning her gaze away and facing Sora.

——*Something* was looming over the world of death...
Something that completely and utterly rejected any form of comprehension...
It was a nebulous feeling and, thus, could not be described in words.
Instinct was what made its presence clear. The party members could feel the overbearing presence of *something*—
If a word had to be assigned to it...it was—

—hatred.
Or lament. Or anger.
Or maybe resentment? Regret? Contempt, disgust, hostility, fear—no, none of these.
All this world's evil—feelings of evil—was compressed into this spectacle. What lingered over it was something they could only sense, something their fight-or-flight instincts screamed to escape from.
It must be—*true despair*. That definition made the most sense.
The party gasped, but Sora shook his head sluggishly and rejected the idea:

"Nope, not quite. This is the same thing we've seen on every floor—it's the Tower."
The beautiful house of worship. The lush forest. The volcano, the miasma-filled valley.
"In other words, it's all a part of the Devil...the Phantom of Destruction, the Hope-Consuming Beast."
And if the Devil was a beast that consumed hope, then—

"This is also just—*hope*."
"...Brother...what are...you saying...?"

The concept of ultimate evil, so evil that even Jibril and Emir-Eins hesitated to look directly at it.

Why would that ever be considered hope?

Sora's dark eyes were void of any light as he looked forward.

Shiro gazed into them, questioning his sanity. The party was starting to sense fear in those eyes when he apathetically continued:

"*Despair* is what happens to you when you run out of hope... It isn't the opposite of hope. If hope is a positive, then despair is zero... not a negative. There's *no such feeling* as despair. It's just what happens when there's no hope... Despair has no shape."

Then what was this essence wriggling before them?

"...You hate someone. They disgust you, annoy you. You detest and abhor them. You're jealous, envious. They're so unlikable and gross, so disgusting and intolerable. You want to hurt them, make them suffer, break them, tear them up, destroy them, get rid of them, kill them—no, death isn't even enough; you want them to live forever in pain—"

It was all these ideas, and more:

"You want *everyone* to die, you want the world to be destroyed... These are all just emotions you feel, what you wish for. It's chemistry in your brain. A physiological reaction. There's no right or wrong, good or evil behind it. It's—"

In essence—

"—just *hope*...hope that the Hope-Consuming Beast consumed."

Namely:

"The end of the world—an envisioned phenomenon that will never happen—a collective fantasy called hope..."

——This was the true essence of the Devil.

——Sora's words left the party in a deep silence.

What were those dark eyes of his looking at?

Even the Flügel and Ex Machina knew little about Phantasma, let alone the sudden mutation that was the Devil.

It personified the fantasy of a phenomenon that had yet to happen, something inexplicable.

"...M-Master...what do you mean by...a phenomenon that will never happen...?"
Jibril came forward, apologizing for her inability to comprehend the incomprehensible.

Sora finally averted his eyes, and with a self-deprecating grin, he replied, "Ah, yeah...that part perfectly describes exactly what the Devil is."

——Throughout the ages, all across Sora's original world—or no? The same went for this world, and for each of the races, too.

It's strange, really. All people—

—*want to think of themselves as good, clean people...*
I hate them. I want what they have. I want to steal it and hurt them and kill them... This is all *hope.*

Evil hope—so evil that it's viewed as bad to ever feel that way, which is why:

——People always want to blame others...
They want to blame other people for their own base emotions. It's someone else's fault for making them feel that way—or yes...

"The devil made me do it...right?"

——Nobody ever wants to own their evil thoughts. Nobody wants to be evil.

They think they are good, pure, innocent, and righteous.

But they can't reject the feelings they have deep down. Which is why it's always someone else's fault.

They're the bad ones for making me feel this way. I'm in the right.

Ah, I hope something bad happens to them. I hope someone kills them. Ah...

"They call it karma, or whatever, and hope that something bad happens to others, just because it should."

"*And they don't even feel guilty about it. They just hope for it within the confines of their own minds...*"

*   *   *

"_____"

——Sora didn't say this out of ill will or animosity...

It was almost as if he was talking about himself—the party was speechless.

Therefore, Sora apathetically continued...

"So. The Great War. People died as often as the wind blew—creating hellscapes like this stage here. It was an era full of hatred. Ask anyone, and I'm sure they've thought at some point or another—*I wish everybody I hated would just die. I wish someone would destroy everything except for me.* But...what if everyone wished that?"

It would create the exact scene that they saw before them—and the vortex of *hope* that swirled around them.

Thus, this collective fantasy, this hope took shape—a phantasm of the world's destruction, a monster that killed everyone and everything.

——This must have been how the Devil—the *ultimate evil*—was born...

"_____"

...The party was at even more of a loss, however:

"The brain works in a pretty convenient way, y'know?"

Sora wasn't finished.

"They can blame their own evil thoughts and hatred on a nebulous ultimate evil—but this isn't really constructive, is it? Because evil is still evil. So they're forced to accept and recognize its existence as something that needs to be done away with. An *ultimate evil* that needs to be defeated."

——Which is why...

"The Devil is *a Phantasma that includes its own defeat...*"

Which was why the Devil sought out heroes to defeat him.

"The Devil consumed the evil hopes the world had of killing

everyone, and he tried to destroy the world, but the world then hated him and killed him for it—he was a convenient stage for the world to place and quell its evil..."

That was why the Devil created a *theoretically winnable game.*

And why the Devil asked for nothing from the heroes who challenged him.

The heroes inherit everything the Devil had if they destroy his core at the top of his Tower.

————Destroy his core... Everything he *had...* It was in *past tense...*

"If we defeat the Devil at the top of this dungeon—the game is set up on the assumption that his core will break and, well..."

There's only one thing that will happen then...

"What the Devil wants from all this is...for someone to kill him... That's it..."

————...........

"——I...see... Then the Devil is not a mutant, but the same as the other Phantasmas—"

"Hypothesis: The Devil has never acted proactively. The Devil is a passive system that represents all living beings' evil desires for each other's demise... This explains the as-yet-undiscovered reasoning for his sudden deviation from other Phantasmas."

Jibril and Emir-Eins seemed to accept Sora's suggestion—but conversely...

"And you're okay with that...? What are you saying? Is this some sort of joke?"

This very notion was even more wicked than the hellish sight of the piles upon piles of corpses sprawled across the abandoned battlefield before them, or even the vortex of hatred-for-others that they could instinctually feel swirling around them.

"So everyone can hate each other?! And wish for each other to die?! And then it all gets forced onto the Devil, who has to be killed for this?!" Steph shouted with trembling, clenched fists.

And then—

"So he was born for everyone to hate and kill?! **That's just...too cruel!!**" she yelled.

Shiro and Til looked down at their feet.

Izuna was holding back tears.

——That cute little furball.

The one who was so excited for the heroes to come and fight him.

That big smile on his face was his way of saying...

————*"Please, kill me"...?*

——*It can't be.*

I won't stand for it!! So what if he's the Devil...?

This world created him, so it's the world that should suffer————

".......There's a way around this... Right, Sora...?"

Just as the very ideas that were at fault were rearing their ugly heads, Steph stopped herself.

She wasn't going to let these thoughts into her mind. She shook her head and turned to Sora.

Looking into his eyes, which contained only darkness, she asked him:

"You agreed to participate in this game because you knew there as a way to defeat the Devil, yes?!"

——*This is Sora. The man who says games are already won before they start. The man who, in the name of the Commonwealth, chose the incredible disadvantage of not letting anyone die!! He would never play a game that necessitates a sacrifice—!!*

* * *

Steph's gaze was imploring him—as were Shiro's, Til's, and Izuna's.

But within Sora's eyes that were darker than darkness, there was nothing to be seen. He looked away...

And then he held out his smartphone—and replied:

"...No, Steph. There's no way to do that... None."

———— ,

"...We're the heroes, and the Devil is our enemy... If the Domain of Despair spreads, it'll end the world. The heroes need to defeat the Devil—this is the plot of the game we have to play..."

——————— ,

Sora turned around after giving an answer no one would have ever expected from him.

He then ordered Jibril to shift the party out of there, leaving the eighty-first floor hellscape behind——

——Meanwhile...outside the Tower...

Atop a hill on the outskirts of Garad Golm.

Within the fierce blizzard that showed no signs of ceasing, a suited skeleton was kneeling as if in prayer.

"Ah... I remain safe, thanks to the Devil's revival and your great power, Emperor."

The skeleton, who called himself Genau Ih, rattled as he spoke.

"Both the Commonwealth's intervention and my seizure of the Devil's Army Joint Chiefs of Staff have gone according to your plan—and while I had my doubts, the party may well defeat the Devil, as you so predicted. Everything is going smoothly."

From atop the otherwise nondescript hill, the skeleton bowed low as he gave his report.

*   *   *

Ah, yes—even if the heroes have indeed come within reach of victory over the Devil...

And although highly unpredictable—should they so choose to accept his sacrifice...

Or more realistically, if they refuse to do so—and they lose the game...

Or perhaps—they find some other unforeseen method to win...

The fact that they have already entered the Tower means—it is too late.

Whatever they do is futile and in line with the plan. It will not impact the results...

——The skeleton looked pleased, but then he suddenly picked up the slightest amount of displeasure aimed at him.

"——?! Ah, ah... Please, forgive me! I ask your forgiveness for sundering your eyes with this abhorrent vessel!!" Genau Ih shouted in a panic as he did away with his skeletal body.

Then Genau Ih knelt once more, this time in his...or *her* true form before looking up to the heavens and begging for forgiveness—

——The girl, with a single horn growing from her forehead not unlike a one-horned rabbit, and eyes as red as the moon above her head, spoke once more...

"——Demonia's Race Piece is as good as within the palm of your miraculous hand...my lord."

Her body shook as soon as these words left her mouth.

She did so, of course, not because of the blistering snow that pelted her.

You shine your crimson light on those trapped on this planet with the utmost mercy. From a place higher and more supremely noble than any god's.

Your glorious essence sits atop the heavens and crowns the crimson moon.

Should your true voice ever grace my ears, I would do away with them, for you need not address this humble servant—
—O Creator. My lord.

"Ah... It is all for you...the Moon God. ♪"

The Moon God, Xenathus——
For as long as history existed, his forever goal of descending to the wretched planet below was beginning to look plausible.

——The young woman before him was of Ixseed Rank Thirteen: Lunamana.
And she was overjoyed, quivering with ecstasy...

⏻ AFTERWORD

A paradigm shift flips the world, and its established playbooks, on its head. This isn't something that can be done by swinging a sword or through thoughts and beliefs, however.

The premise is what must be flipped first, through a technological breakthrough.

…I can't quite remember who said this, but I, the author who established this series' Ten Covenants, felt these words deep in my bones for the first time in the summer of 2022—during a "meeting" with my editor, O…

"I'm really sorry, but…I don't think I can get the new volume in by the end of the year…"

2022 marked *No Game No Life*'s tenth year in publication.

It was a celebratory year, but by the time it was over…things weren't looking good for my manuscript. I really did feel terrible about this when I had to share the truth with my editor, but to my surprise…

"It's all right. If we think of things in terms of the fiscal year, it's 2022 until February 2023! I know you are having a difficult time with your health while you write your series. Let's get it finished without going overboard!"

O said this…with *an alluring smile and a gentle tone.*

"Th-thank you…! I'll make sure it's done and ready to be published by February, then!!"

"Okay. I know I can trust you, Yuu Kamiya. Let's both do our best."

I cried at how kind those words were. Words said with a bright expression.

——What do you think?

We stayed respectful of each other, recognized where we both had shortcomings, and joined hands in mutual forgiveness.

Was it not the most logical and magnanimously peaceful meeting you've ever seen…?!

Usually, these things go more like:

"So, uh, where's the manuscript…?" *(Said with irritation.)*

"I told you this deadline was way too short. I'm writing as fast as I can." *(Said with irritation.)*

"Then where is it? It's way past the deadline." *(Said with irritation.)*

"Writing would be easy if these things wrote themselves on a basic schedule." *(Said with irritation.)*

These sorts of exchanges are usually made with irritated and sarcastic banter—however!!

That day…we were in the middle of a technological paradigm shift…one that both revolutionized our meeting and made it peaceful!

——That's right…

——We had our meeting via VR! More specifically, we both donned cute avatars to hold a meeting in virtual reality!! Voice changer and everything!!

Thus, creating the revolutionary environment for a peaceful meeting…!

Yes, sometimes your writers may take a long time to send in their manuscripts… But if they look and sound like a cute girl with fluffy cat ears, maybe it'll be easier to deal with them?

Sure, your publisher is bugging you to finish your manuscript that you're working as hard as you can to finish… But what if it's a maid with giant tits and a cute voice on the other end of your call?

It only makes it hurt more!!

——No matter how good things may look, the truth is the truth: Cuteness and beauty are justice, and humans are easy to convince!

In other words, even if those avatars are actually middle-aged men! So long as they look and sound cute or beautiful, then they will allow most injustices to slip!

Were we to personify the word "cute" with an animal—cats are the perfect example!!

That's right… We humans can overcome any battle. They just need to be sexy women inside a VR chat room…!!

——Which brings us back to my afterword.

Hello, this is Yuu Kamiya. I come to you after an emergency meeting with my editor during their time off to tell you that I realized in a matter of milliseconds that humanity is still far from world peace, and I anxiously await the day we can all move to a virtual world.

As I stated above, this is the tenth year *No Game No Life* has been in publication.

I have only my many editors, the sales team and art team and everyone who works with them, my family, and most of all…

My readers, who are willing to put up with my slow, slow writing pace.

There are so many people who support me, and it is thanks to them that I've made it this far.

…As usual, I'm writing all this amid my health issues.

It took another year, something that brings me great pain, but it did eventually happen.

Thanks to all your support, I managed to finish this twelfth volume without any hospitalizations.

I already have the plot for Volume 13 ready, and some bare bones writing out of the way, so fingers crossed I can get it to you without too long of a wait this time.

——I'll say it again: Thank you to everyone who's stayed with me these ten years. I hope you'll be willing to stick it out for the rest of the series.

With that, let's meet again in Volume 13! See you there.

"The Domain of Despair is still in effect even under the Ten Covenants. We need to beat the Devil; it's gotta happen. But *no one* can beat *that thing*. Absolutely no one."

"So listen——no matter what happens, don't lose hope."

*"...BROTHER...WAIT...FOR ME...
I WANNA...DIE, TOO..."*
*"NO! I REFUSE TO BELIEVE
THIS SHIT, PLEASE!!"*

The moon will fall——

A game where aspirations clash will bring about the end of the world 6,000 years in the making along with a new start——but whose hands pull the strings, and what kind of stage will they make?

Nobles: Welcome to Disboard.

No Game No Life, Volume 13

OUT BY SUMMER, HOPEFULLY...

THE APPARATUS OF RUIN

THE HOPE-CONSUMING BEAST

THE DEVIL

THE BLACK NIGHTMARE

THE PHANTOM OF RESURRECTION

WHY DO I DESTROY?
I'LL ASK YOU THIS —
WHY DO YOU LIVE?

The one forced to shoulder the world's evils and then be killed—— The beast who dreams of world destruction, a hope that will never come true.

"I was born to be killed—— what's wrong with that? All things that live die—— you, too, were born to be killed."